VARIANT SERIES

BOOK ONE

Revival

JENA LEIGH

To Mimi,
Without your endless love and support,
this never would have been possible !!!
Thank you for everything!

All my love (& then some!),

Jennifer

ISBN: 1481090801
ISBN-13: 978-1481090803

DEDICATION

To Carrie.
For her endless encouragement and her unfailing
ability to distinguish apples from pears.

You're the best, ma'am.

ACKNOWLEDGMENTS

First and foremost, my family. Without your constant encouragement these last few years, none of this would have been possible. Thank you for caring for me in hard times and for giving me the courage to follow my dreams. I love you all. Special thanks to my parents; to Mimi; and to my Aunt Donna and Uncle Charlie for giving me such an amazing place to call home. To Jinnie, for cheering me on and reading those early drafts. And to Carrie, for believing in me from the start; and for the countless e-mails, phone calls, and plot points settled over Japanese take-out. Thank you for loving these characters as much as I do and for helping me get their story onto the page.

ONE

"Alex? What in the world are you *doing* in there?"

Alex Parker's elbow collided with the dressing room wall, resulting in a loud *thunk* and a spike of pain that radiated through her forearm. She let out a grunt.

A deceptively lightweight, three-quarter sleeve, eggplant sweater—the very latest in spring fashion according to her best friend Cassie—was currently holding her captive. The fabric had wrapped itself around her neck and shoulders in some strange, cloth imitation of an Amazonian anaconda. The more Alex struggled to pull it off, the tighter its hold became.

She craned her neck from side to side, hoping to wiggle her head free from the material. No such luck.

This was why Alex didn't do shopping.

This. Right here.

Alex stopped struggling and let out a sigh of defeat.

"Cassie?" She turned toward the curtain. At least, she *thought* she was facing the curtain. The world around her was being filtered through midnight-colored cashmere.

"Yes?"

"... Help?"

Curtain hooks scraped across a dingy metal rod as Cassie pulled aside the canvas partition and slipped inside the tiny dressing room.

"What in the..." Cassie mumbled. "How did you even...?"

Alex could feel a gentle tugging at the fabric and tried to hold still as Cassie worked the material loose.

"Scratch that," said Cassie, pulling the sweater off of Alex with one final yank. Her expression was wry. "I don't want to know."

A wayward lock of hair fell into Alex's line of sight and she blew it out of the way. Sweeping her noncompliant curls back up and into a ponytail, she tugged her muted gray tank top back into place.

With a sigh, Cassie tossed her the man-eating sweater. "So much for bringing a little *color* back into your wardrobe." She frowned at the purple material as Alex worked it back onto the hanger. "I understand your desire to be invisible, Lexie, but a little color never hurt anyone."

Cassie's original suggestion had been a pink and white RVCA dress that cost a fortune and barely made it past Alex's hips. The sweater had been a compromise.

It's not that Alex particularly *liked* the dark colored shirts and jeans that had overtaken her closet in the last few months. They just seemed safer. Less likely to attract attention.

"Have I earned my lunch yet?" Alex asked, daring to sound hopeful.

Four months ago, a day of surf, sun and shopping at the boardwalk with her best friend would have sounded like the perfect way to spend the first day of spring break. Now it was just another cruel reminder of how much things had changed.

"Alright," said Cassie. "Enough outlet shopping for one morning. When the clothes start fighting back, it's definitely time for a lunch break."

Relieved, Alex reached for her messenger bag and made her escape from the dressing room.

"Pizza?" Cassie asked, working her way toward the register. Alex trailed a few steps behind her, eyeing a lime-green bikini hanging on one of the mannequins. Her hand traced the three-inch scar that marred her right side.

If only.

"I was thinking seafood." Alex tore her gaze away from the tiny swatches of fabric. "What do you think? In the mood for lunch at The Mainsail?"

Cassie's march to the checkout had come to an abrupt halt. She now stood stock-still in the middle of the aisle, staring openly at a guy perusing the men's section on the opposite side of the store.

"Hello, *gorgeous!*" Cassie said under her breath. She snagged Alex by the arm and spun her around so that they were facing each other. "Lexie my love, I think I've found your rebound man."

Alex fought back the urge to roll her eyes. The grimace, however, wasn't about to be contained.

This made the third rebound man Cassie had picked out for her today and it was only lunchtime.

"I don't need a rebound man, Cass."

"It's been four months!"

"And?"

"And you need to get back in the game! A little bit of romance is *exactly* what you need to get you out of this ridiculous funk that you've been in."

"I'm not in a funk!"

Okay, so she'd been single for a while now and things hadn't exactly been going her way in the love department. Or, for that matter, in any department.

That didn't mean she was depressed.

"I'm not exactly prime dating material right now, Cassie," she continued. "Or have you forgotten about my little affliction?"

Little affliction was putting it kindly. Alex usually referred to it as her one-way ticket to life in a traveling freak show.

Cassie huffed. "Would you at least *look* at the fine specimen of masculinity I've picked out for you before you start in on all the reasons why it won't work?"

Resigned, Alex glanced over her shoulder at the guy in question.

And, okay, wow.

There was no questioning Cassie's taste.

He was tall, with tousled dirty blonde hair, a couple days worth of stubble, and the most beautiful hazel eyes Alex had ever seen. The gray military-style jacket, dark jeans and motorcycle boots were a bit unwarranted given the 80-degree weather on the beach today, but the look definitely worked for him.

It obviously worked for Cassie, who couldn't stop stealing glances at him from over her shoulder.

He was certainly interesting. And maybe Cassie was right. Maybe *interesting* was what she needed right now.

Seeming to sense that he was being observed, he glanced up from the t-shirt he'd been inspecting, fixed his gaze directly on Alex… and smirked.

"Ack, crap!" Alex whipped back around to face Cassie before he could see the blush creeping into her cheeks. Nothing like getting caught staring to start the blood pumping.

Alex took a deep breath and worked to calm her nerves. She could feel a charge building in the air around her and knew that she needed to relax before it built into something more *destructive*.

"Well that was embarrassing," Alex mumbled.

Cassie didn't respond. Her attention was fixed on something behind Alex, near the front of the store—something that had caused her eyes to narrow and had twisted the corners of her mouth into an angry scowl.

Before she could locate the source of her friend's aggravation, a heavy hand came to rest on Alex's shoulder.

"Lexie," said a familiar voice.

Alex couldn't help it... She jumped.

The tingle of static electricity that had begun seeping into the air of the shop a moment earlier rose quickly to a crescendo.

No stopping it now. Alex cringed.

Two computers at the register kiosk shorted out with a fizzle and a pop. Alex listened to the salesperson cursing behind her as he attempted to resurrect the fried machines.

Perfect.

Alex turned around.

Her ex-boyfriend, Connor, was staring down at her with an apologetic expression. His gaze traveled between the register and Alex.

He, of all people, knew better than to sneak up on her like that.

She risked a glance toward the guy in the military jacket just as the bell attached to the shop's front door chimed. Her mystery man was already making his way out and onto the boardwalk.

Great. Well, so much for that.

Could this morning get any worse?

Connor's hand still gripped her shoulder. The heat radiating from his palm had her remembering a time when his touch hadn't been quite so unwelcome.

"Connor." Alex did her best to mimic Cassie's scowl. "Where's Jessica?"

He winced and had the good sense to look abashed.

As if the mere mention of her arch-nemesis was enough to summon the creature out of the darkness from whence it came, the long-legged, bleached-blonde bombshell sashayed through the front door of the shop. Her bright green eyes locked on the two of them.

Alex wished she were somewhere else. Anywhere else.

"We need to talk," Connor said to her quietly.

She held tight to her anger and ignored the charge that was once again building in the air. Nothing left to fry... Except maybe the cell phone Connor carried in his pocket. The thought of it going nuclear while still trapped in his shorts almost made her smile.

Almost.

Alex sighed. Connor was a jerk. But even he didn't deserve that. She took another deep breath to calm herself and the static in the air began to dissipate.

"Please, Lexie..."

Those big brown eyes of his were *not* going to suck her in again. He was a jerk. And he certainly didn't deserve her pity.

Even if he *did* somewhat resemble a kicked puppy.

He took hold of both her shoulders then, and she was loathe to discover that his grip was still as warm and reassuring as it had been back when they were still together.

"What do you want?" asked Cassie, her voice dripping with venom on Alex's behalf.

Still unsure of what to say to him, Alex stole a moment to look him over while Cassie had him distracted.

He definitely hadn't waited until spring break to get to work on that tan. And judging from the wet sheen of his jet-black hair, he'd just come from the shore. He'd spent the morning surfing with Jeff and Tyler, no doubt. She tried not to picture the rock hard abs and perfectly toned shoulder muscles lurking beneath Connor's black t-shirt.

She tried. And she failed miserably.

What *was* it about exes? Why were they always twice as attractive after a break-up?

Meanwhile, after her run in with the wrap-sweater-of-doom, Alex's frizzy curls and flushed expression probably had her looking like she'd just finished the Boston marathon on a humid day.

How was that fair?

"Please, Alex," he was saying. "I've got to talk to you. Just five minutes... Please."

Alex could feel her resolve cracking around the edges. What was *wrong* with her?

Before she could figure out the reason behind the traitorous emotions, Jessica's shrill voice cut the air like a knife.

"Connor! There you are!"

Connor dropped his hands from Alex's shoulders.

That did it. The inexplicable urge to forgive him evaporated as quickly as it had appeared. Her determination suddenly restored, she gave a nod in the direction of the irate girl stalking toward them.

"If you want someone to talk to, I'd try your girlfriend," she said.

"But, Lexie—"

"Sorry, Connor." Cassie dropped her would-be purchases onto a nearby display and grabbed Alex by the wrist. "You lost that right when you made the exceptionally bad decision to cheat on my girl here. So you can take whatever it was you wanted to say to her and shove it up your ass. She's not interested."

Alex turned on her heel and followed Cassie out of the store. As they emerged into the bright sunshine of the boardwalk, Alex let out a breath she hadn't realized she'd been holding.

"Ugh!" Cassie led the way down the promenade at a steady clip, her blonde hair whipping around in the breeze. "The *nerve* of that guy!"

Alex sucked in a deep breath of the warm salty air, grateful to be walking out onto the pier and away from any more electronic equipment. The last thing she needed right now was to accidentally barbecue another computer.

She sighed. So much for a peaceful start to their vacation.

Two

It hadn't always been like this.

Alex hadn't *always* possessed the freakish ability to fry a television set from twenty paces. She had been normal once. Just like Cassie. Just like Connor.

Four months ago she had been relatively popular, making straight A's, and had her sights set on an Ivy League college. Alex had also been the envy of every girl in their junior class—she'd been dating senior-class hottie, Connor Talbot.

Her life had been picture perfect.

And then one day, out of nowhere, Connor went and broke her heart... and everything had changed.

Alex had since realized that most major, life-altering changes came in one of two varieties.

The *first* was the kind of change that you saw coming.

Take Alex's beat-up Jeep Wrangler, for example.

It had taken two summer jobs and months of saving, but three weeks after her sixteenth birthday, Alex had finally pulled together enough cash to afford a new car.

Well... New-*ish*, anyway.

"Dear God," Connor had said. "You're not *serious* about buying this thing, are you, babe? This is a joke, right? You're joking."

"I've got to hand it to you, Alex," Cassie had said. "That is one Grade-A, top-of-the-line, *heap* you've picked out for yourself."

"It's a bucket of rust, Lee-Lee," her Aunt Cil had

argued with a sigh. "Surely we can find you something more suitable than *that*."

It had taken Alex less than thirty seconds to fall in love with that Jeep. And in less than a heartbeat, her boyfriend, her aunt, *and* her best friend had all ruled it out.

Undeterred, Alex began listing what she saw as the Jeep's selling points, ticking them off on her fingers as she went.

It was jet black (if you overlooked the reddish-brown accents of the slowly oxidizing framework), it had air conditioning (a *must* if you didn't want to die of heat stroke during the dog-days of a Florida summer), there was a soft-top that could easily be rolled up on sunny days (it was basically the convertible that she and Cassie had always wanted—only, you know... not), and it got excellent gas mileage for a Jeep its age (which is to say, she'd be able to afford the gas—provided she never had to drive it anywhere that was farther than ten miles away).

It was perfect.

And besides that, it was the only car on the lot that was even remotely in her price-range.

"Are you offering to help pay for a better car, Aunt Cil?" Alex had asked.

She and her aunt had been over this. Aunt Cil wanted Alex to *earn* her first car and pay for it with her own money—and Alex would never have dreamed of asking her aunt for the cash, anyway.

"...No."

"Then the rust bucket it is!" Smiling, Alex had turned toward the nearest salesman—a smallish man who smelled vaguely of onions and was wearing a rather unfortunate toupee—and started the negotiations.

The instant Leo down at Vinny's Auto World dropped that jangling set of keys into her outstretched palm, Alex had known her life would never be the same again.

But that had been the point.

That change was one that she'd worked very hard, over the course of many months, to achieve.

The second variety of life-altering changes, she'd learned, were the ones that struck you like a bolt from the blue, usually turning your life upside-down in the process.

Only twice in sixteen years had Alex experienced that sort of upheaval.

The first had happened when she was four.

The second had taken place exactly four months, three weeks and one day ago.

It happened on a Tuesday.

Alex and Cassie had been stuck in the computer lab since school let out, working on a PowerPoint presentation for their economics class. The computer science teacher, Mr. Hanson, had gone home an hour earlier, leaving them alone in the lab to finish their report.

At least they *were* alone… until the door opened and a couple of students came stumbling though.

Alex had been standing by the printer, copies of their PowerPoint slides still warm in her hands, when she noticed them—a rather familiar looking couple, six feet away and frenching the life out of each other. His arms were wrapped tightly around her waist and her mouth seemed to have been permanently adhered to his.

A full five seconds passed before her brain managed to process what it was she was seeing.

Jessica and Conner had slipped into the computer lab, assuming it was empty, and were well on their way into a serious make-out session.

"Oh. My. God," Cassie managed.

Suddenly realizing they weren't alone, Connor broke off the embrace and pushed Jessica to arms length. His face flushed bright red as a look of panic flickered in his expression.

Jessica, on the other hand, appeared smug.

"I can explain!" said Connor.

Alex couldn't find her voice to speak, but she didn't have to. Her best friend did it for her.

"You lousy, cheating, *jerk!*" Cassie spat, leaping to her feet and shoving the rolly chair under the desk with a little too much force. "How *could* you? And with *Jessica Huffman*? Could you have picked anyone skankier?"

"Who are you calling a *skank*?" Jessica shot back.

Cassie and Jessica's argument faded into the background as Connor finally turned to face her. As their eyes met, something inside of Alex snapped.

At first, she assumed that the unfamiliar sensation coursing through her was simply the *shock* that came from seeing her philandering boyfriend in the arms of another girl—but that assumption didn't last long.

As the feeling intensified, the air around them grew thick with the smell of ozone and the tingle of static electricity.

Before Alex could make sense of what was happening, a bolt of electricity arced from an electrical socket on the far side of the room and slammed into the nearest computer. One by one the computers shorted out, the surge of electricity working its way toward them in a wave of blinding light and shattering glass.

Cassie jumped out of the way and pressed herself against a window as the surge passed by.

Alex could see the wave getting closer, could hear the strange whirring noise coming from the printer in front of her, but her feet were frozen in place. Her mind screamed at her muscles to move, but all she could manage was a surprised gasp as the wave of destruction reached the computers across the aisle.

"Lexie, lookout!"

Connor slammed into her as the printer Alex had been standing in front of exploded into flames. The next thing she felt was the jagged corner of a waist-high filing cabinet tearing through her right side.

She cried out in shock and in pain and only barely registered the impact when she and Connor landed in a heap on the linoleum floor.

Outside in the parking lot, half a dozen car alarms wailed to life. All Alex could hear, though, was the ringing in her ears.

When she opened her eyes she found Connor kneeling next to her, staring blankly at her stomach.

"Are you okay?" asked Alex.

Connor looked up. "Am *I* okay?" He seemed surprised by her question. Alex struggled to sit up, but Connor held her still. "Lexie, stop! Don't try and move."

"But I need to check on Cass," she protested.

Cassie was hurrying toward her, grabbing a discarded sweatshirt along the way. "Don't move, Alex," she said.

Confused, Alex looked down to see what it was about her stomach that had so captured everyone's attention.

Shaking fingers traveled to her waistline. A steady flow of blood was pouring from a gash across her abdomen, turning her white cotton shirt a muddy shade of crimson.

Cassie knelt beside her and pressed the sweatshirt hard against Alex's side.

Her memory went a little hazy after that.

According to Cassie, it took Connor less than a minute to put out the flames of the printer and the smoldering computers thanks to a nearby fire extinguisher. The paramedics Cassie called arrived minutes later and whisked Alex off to the hospital for a blood transfusion and eighteen stitches.

Since she wasn't family, Cassie hadn't been allowed to ride in the ambulance. Instead she'd been stuck at the school with Connor and Jessica, explaining to Principal Snyder what had happened. Despite Jessica's attempts to implicate Alex, the accident was eventually ruled to be the result of a freak power surge.

Officially, that was the story.

Unofficially, Jessica wasted no time in telling half the school about Alex's "bizarre psychotic episode" wherein she had tried her best to *murder* Jessica and Connor, in true Carrie-at-the-prom fashion. Jessica creatively edited the details so as to make the tale more believable, but in the end, Alex had still been branded a freak.

With Connor's testimony supporting the claims, Alex's social standing went up in flames faster than the Hindenburg. She'd gone from social elite to social pariah before she could even be discharged from the hospital.

It didn't help that she'd been trapped at home for the next two weeks while she recovered from her injury. Without Alex there to defend herself, the rumor mill ran wild.

Alex's Aunt Cil had spent the entire two weeks glued to her side, insisting that Alex stay off her feet so that she could heal. She'd always been something of a worrywart when it came to Alex's well-being. It was a maternal and over-protective side of her personality that stood in contrast to her normally carefree nature.

Cecilia Cross—or Aunt Cil, as Alex called her—was about as free-spirited as they came. As a professional artist, Cil had earned quite a name for herself in their small, seaside community; her tiled sculptures and handmade porcelain pottery often fetched a pretty penny in the busier galleries down on the boardwalk.

And, like most artists, Cil had that quality about her that occasionally left you wondering if she was really there *with* you, or if she'd slipped into some other world entirely. There were times when they'd be in the midst of a conversation and Alex would start to suspect that, in her mind, her aunt had already disappeared into the small workshop that stood behind their blue, two-story Victorian home, in order to plan out her next creative project.

Before becoming Alex's guardian, Cil had embraced a much more bohemian lifestyle. At 27, she'd long since decided to put off starting a family of her own and, instead, had thrown herself into her artwork. The "white picket fence, 3.2 kids and a dog" mentality that her older sister had so readily embraced had been a foreign concept to her.

Then, shortly after Alex turned four, wet roads and a drunk driver had taken the life of Cil's sister and brother-in-law, leaving young Alex with a single living relative— her Aunt Cecilia.

That had been 12 years ago.

"Ground control to Major Tom...? Alex!"

Cassie's voice snapped Alex from her reverie.

They'd made it to the end of the pier and now stood leaning against the wooden railing, staring out over the water.

"Sorry," said Alex, not wanting to admit where her thoughts had just been.

But then, that was the great thing about having Cassie for a best friend. She didn't have to.

After the rumors started flying, Cassie was the only one of Alex's so-called friends who stuck around, proving herself to be—quite literally—loyal to a fault. She refused to betray their friendship, even though standing by her friend meant that Cassie would share in Alex's new persona-non-grata social status.

"It's alright," said Cassie. "How about crab legs at The Mainsail? You can pretend it's Connor's legs you're breaking. And then there's that nutcracker they give you for the claws... It'll be therapeutic."

Alex smiled in spite of herself.

As they made their way back to the shoreline, Cassie started outlining their plans for the afternoon: lunch at The Mainsail, tanning on the shore, a little more shopping…

Alex was only half-listening. Up ahead, leaning against the railing, stood the military jacket clad mystery guy from the shop, staring intently in their direction. The luminous hazel eyes Alex had been so taken in by seemed darker now, a strange intensity burning behind them.

An uneasy feeling stirred in the pit of her stomach.

"So what do you think?" asked Cassie.

"Huh?" Alex snapped back to attention. "What do I think about what?"

"About renting a bunch of movies and having pizza for dinner," she said. "You have *got* to keep your head out of the clouds, girl. The whole point of today was to get your mind off of things! And, okay, I realize the Connor incident was a setback, but that little toad is *not* going to ruin our day."

"I'm sorry… It's just that guy—" Alex came up short. Mr. Military Jacket was no longer leaning against the railing up ahead. In fact, he'd disappeared from the pier entirely.

"What guy?" Cassie looked around, her voice hopeful. "Yay, guy!"

Alex stopped in her tracks and turned to see if maybe he'd slipped past them while her attention had been fixed on Cassie. The other end of the pier was completely deserted.

"What the crap?" Alex mumbled.

They were still a good 150 yards from shore and there was *no way* he'd crossed the entire pier and made it to the boardwalk in less than ten seconds. So where had he disappeared to?

"What the what?" Cassie arched one perfectly shaped eyebrow in confusion. "Alex, what is it?"

"That guy from the store—"

"The hot one?" Cassie chimed.

"Yeah." Alex wandered to the railing and peered over the edge. Surely he didn't dive off the pier... The tide was too low. It would be suicide.

A seagull gazed dolefully up at her, but there was no sign of Mr. Military Jacket. He'd vanished.

"He was standing right there a second ago, I swear!"

Cassie glanced around. "Well he's gone now. Shame, too. He's exactly the sort of distraction you need this afternoon."

THREE

Babysitting.

Declan O'Connell had been reduced to *babysitting*.

This was so humiliating. He was going to have to have a talk with Grayson when he got home. Surely his punishment for last month's misunderstanding should be nearing an end.

It wasn't his fault they needed a new roof in the atrium. That had been entirely Nathaniel's doing. Declan had merely supplied a little motivation. It was the Golden Boy that did the glass breaking.

So how was it that the Golden Boy kept picking up all the choice jobs, while Declan was stuck trailing around after high schoolers?

He leaned heavily against the brick wall of the alley and watched as his target disappeared into a restaurant across the street, only to reappear a few moments later on the wraparound patio, trailing after a hostess. They settled in at a table overlooking the water.

At least with this vantage point he wouldn't have to follow them into the restaurant.

She'd spotted him twice already. Not that he was particularly trying to hide from her at this point. It made things easier when the target didn't know he was there, sure, but there wasn't any hard and fast rule about it.

Declan had been shadowing the pair for nearly an hour before he'd realized that something was off.

Usually, his job involved protecting innocent humans from the monsters that walked amongst them unnoticed. From the things that went bump in the night. Things a whole lot like him, just without the charm … or a functioning moral compass.

Judging from the haze of static electricity that followed the girl around like a rain cloud, however, there was something very different about this mark.

Playing a hunch, he'd broken his cover and followed the two girls into a clothing shop. Ten minutes later the store's registers were toast and his suspicions had been confirmed.

He wondered if the girl knew what she was.

Better yet, he wondered if Grayson had known when he'd given Declan the assignment and just hadn't said anything.

"I want you to keep an eye on the girl, Declan."

"No other specifics?"

"Just keep her away from bookstores, if you can."

Bookstores.

Thanks, Grayson. That helps.

Apparently whoever said, "no harm ever came from reading a book" hadn't met this girl.

Grayson's orders were usually pretty detailed. The fact that these weren't could mean a couple of things. Either Grayson didn't *know* the specifics of the danger the girl was facing, or he *did*, but for whatever reason, he felt Declan didn't need to know.

It was the second possibility that worried him.

He didn't think that Grayson would ever intentionally send him out on an assignment at a disadvantage—but if Grayson felt like he couldn't trust Declan with the details, then Declan wanted to know why.

The cell phone tucked in his jacket pocket began to vibrate. He fished it out and checked the screen.

The caller ID read "GRAYSON."

Declan narrowed his eyes at the shuddering phone. Weird. Grayson never called anyone while they were in the field. He knew better.

Returning his gaze to the restaurant patio, Declan answered the call. "Miss me already?"

"I want an update on the girl."

Declan considered telling him what he'd learned about her, and then thought the better of it. That could wait. "She's spending the day shopping with a friend."

"Shopping?"

"Clothes shopping. No bookstores in sight. Not so far, anyway."

"Hmm."

"You going to tell me why this girl is so special you're calling me for updates? My next check-in's not for another two hours."

"Just do your job, Declan. Keep her safe."

The line went dead.

If Declan had been suspicious before, now he was outright convinced that something was up.

What was so important about this girl?

"You need to work on being a bitch."

"I... what?" Alex nearly choked on her latte. "What's that supposed to mean?"

"You're too nice!" Cassie punctuated the sentence by slamming her styrofoam cup onto the counter.

They'd spent another two hours after their lunch at The Mainsail shopping before Alex could convince Cassie that it was time for another break. She was praying that the caffeine fix wouldn't leave Cassie too wired to consider making their way to the beach.

Alex wasn't sure she was up for another round of shopping at the hands of the fashionista she claimed as her best friend. She was fairly certain that neither her tired feet nor her aunt's borrowed MasterCard would survive the massacre intact.

For the moment, anyway, Cassie seemed content to sit there in the window of Bayside Brews watching the tourists wander the boardwalk. She had her digital camera sitting on the counter in front of her and was occasionally snapping off pictures of the men who passed by wearing ridiculous Hawaiian shirts.

Alex wasn't sure what her friend planned on doing with all those images and, to be honest, she was a little scared to ask.

Like Alex's Aunt Cil, Cassie was constantly creating. But while her aunt preferred to stick with more traditional mediums, such as oil painting and working with ceramics, Cassie's creations tended to be of a much more *modern* bent.

Alex rarely got their meaning.

Physical works of art like those created by her aunt and her best friend didn't *move* her by their beauty, so much as *perplex* her by their overly subjective nature.

Now *words*, on the other hand… Those she understood.

The countless stacks of books piled high in every corner of her bedroom attested to that, as did the half a dozen leather-bound journals she'd filled to the brim with her thoughts and stories.

Plot, characterization, metaphor. Those she understood. Half-naked sculptures of a man sporting a giant cube where his head ought to be? Um. Not so much.

"Niceness—*especially* for someone in your position—is no good," continued Cassie. "It turns you into a doormat."

"When did being nice become a bad thing?" asked Alex.

"The second Connor and Jessica ripped out your heart and danced a jig on it, that's when. Back in the shop, you should have been tearing Connor a new one, not giving serious consideration to *talking* to the jerk."

"But I—"

"And don't even try to tell me you weren't considering it, because I saw the look in your eye, Lex. You were about two seconds away from hearing him out. That's the only time in my life I've ever been grateful to see Jessica Huffman walk into a room," Cassie shook her head. "After the whole computer lab thing you completely lost your backbone! Not that you had much of one to begin with."

"Hey!"

"I'm only telling you this because you're my friend and I love you. And because I know that somewhere, deep down, there's an Alex that has some *moxie* just waiting to break through."

Alex swirled the coffee around in the bottom of her cup. Suddenly it wasn't all that appetizing.

"Oh, honey," said Cassie, snatching up her camera. "Who let you out of the house in *that*?"

It wasn't what Cassie had said that bothered her, exactly. It was the fact that she might have a point.

Sticking up for herself had never really been Alex's strong suit. Generally, she avoided conflict like the plague. Before the computer lab incident, that had never really been an issue. But now...

Well, these days, conflict seemed to be all she was capable of attracting.

"Speaking of the she-devil." Cassie directed a withering glare out the window. "There goes Jessica and her merry band of bootlickers. God-forbid any of them let an original thought enter their pretty little heads. The world as we know it would probably unravel."

"Jessica's world would, anyway."

Emily, Marcie, and Veronica—Jessica's perpetual, syco-phantic shadows—trailed obediently behind their leader as they bypassed the coffee shop in favor of the frozen yogurt place next door.

As she passed by the window, Veronica caught sight of Alex sitting at the counter. Biting her bottom lip, Vee averted her gaze and hastened to catch up with her friends.

Alex sighed.

Talk about not having a backbone.

Before the computer lab incident, Vee and Alex had been on pretty good terms. Jessica's crowd and Alex's had never been all that close, but the line's separating the two cliques had been just blurry enough to allow for a relative peace between the groups. Alex and Vee had even been lab partners in chem class the previous semester.

But after Jessica's plans to steal herself a boyfriend resulted in a demolished computer lab and Alex's exile from Bay View High's social scene, Vee had stopped speak-ing to her entirely.

"Hey!" said Cassie. "What the heck is wrong with this thing?"

The camera in Cassie's hands was zooming in and out, apparently of its own volition. She set it down on the counter.

"Alex?" Cassie was eyeing the camera as though she expected it to blow at any moment.

"It's not me," said Alex. "I'm not doing anything this time."

The camera zoomed in on something across the street, snapped off a picture, zoomed out and then returned to the standby setting. Cassie picked it up gingerly, as though she were afraid that it might still shock her.

"Okay," Cassie mumbled as she inspected the view screen. "That's kinda creepy."

"What is?"

Cassie handed her the camera.

Standing in the center of the frame, leaning against the railing that lined the walkway, was Mr. Military Jacket. He was staring directly into the camera, a self-assured smile on his face... and he was *waving*.

Alex looked quickly out the window in the direction the picture had been taken. He was gone. Again. When she glanced back at the camera, the image had disappeared.

With one last beep, the camera turned itself off.

Alex glanced nervously out the window.

"Excuse me, miss?"

A heavy hand came to rest on her shoulder and Alex nearly jumped out of her skin. As she whipped around, she heard the barista's startled cry and the crackling sound of electricity arcing from a nearby socket. She didn't need to look to know that the espresso machine was toast.

People really needed to stop sneaking up on her like this.

The owner of the hand turned toward the commotion behind the counter and Alex let out a slow breath of relief.

It wasn't the guy in the military jacket. Just a middle-aged man with shoulder length salt-and-pepper hair and a neatly trimmed beard. He was dressed in dark jeans, a long-sleeved shirt and a brown vest. His thin, wire-rimmed glasses gave him the unassuming appearance of a college professor.

Somewhere behind her, the espresso machine ground to a halt with one final ratcheting death rattle. Alex cringed. That machine had probably cost more than her Jeep. The barista behind the counter unleashed a string of curses far more colorful than the ones the clothing-store clerk had employed.

The man smiled politely. "I believe you dropped this," he said.

Alex registered his Scottish accent with distraction and stared at his outstretched hand. He was holding her wallet between two fingers. She was positive that her wallet was still safe inside her satchel in an interior zippered compartment, where she always kept it.

Alex took the wallet from him and flipped it open. The mugshot she'd had taken at the local DMV almost a year earlier stared back at her. The wallet was hers alright. "Thank you. I didn't even realize I'd dropped it…"

In fact, she was almost certain she hadn't.

She unlatched the cover flap of her satchel and unbuttoned the tab that held the main compartment closed. The interior pocket was still zipped tight. She opened it.

Empty.

How had it fallen out?

"No trouble," said the man. "Saw it over there by the door. Lucky you were still here."

"Yeah," she said. "Lucky."

She returned the wallet to where it belonged and spun back around, intent on thanking him again.

The sitting area was empty. Alex's gaze swept across the coffee shop and then out the window to the now deserted, sun-drenched boardwalk.

"Where did he…?" Cassie trailed off. "Okay, that's it. I need some vitamin D if I'm going to be expected to deal with all this weirdness. It's time for the beach."

Vitamin D did the trick.

Alex spent the next three-and-a-half hours on a deserted strip of beach, listening to the sound of waves crashing against the shore and working on her tan lines.

No weird guys who were there one second and gone the next, no fried electronics, just a few hours by the shore with her best friend.

This was what she'd been hoping for when she agreed to a day at the boardwalk with Cassie.

She brushed a few errant grains of sand from her feet and slipped them back into her socks.

"You've got to be the only person on the planet who wears jeans and Chuck Taylor's for a day at the beach," said Cassie.

The soft rumble of thunder echoed through the air around them. In the distance, storm clouds were moving in as flashes of lightning lit the darkened sky a little farther off shore. Beautiful, but it meant an end to their sunbathing.

"I happen to love my Chucks, thank-you-very-much," said Alex as she tied the laces. "Besides. Sun will set in an hour or two. The temperature's already dropping. You can't tell me you're not cold in those shorts."

"Freezing," she admitted, handing Alex her messenger bag as she got to her feet. "But dammit, I look cute and we both know that's what counts."

"Naturally."

Cassie led the way back to the boardwalk. "Okay, so I'll meet you at your house just as soon as I run by the Red Box for movies and pick up the pizza. Should I order a small veggie for your aunt?"

"Better make it a medium," said Alex. "She was going to spend the day throwing pottery. You know how she gets when she's working. I doubt she stopped for lunch."

"One large pepperoni and mushroom, a medium veggie and whatever chick-flick I can find. I've got this!" Cassie started off in the direction of the parking lot and then turned to walk backwards. "You sure this errand for your aunt won't take long?"

"Just need to pick up a special order for her from Ballard's," Alex called across the promenade to Cassie's retreating form. "It's only a few blocks and then I'll walk home."

"Okay! See you in a bit!"

Alex left the boardwalk and turned down a little-used side street. It was only a short ways to Ballard's store from here and she knew the shortcuts well.

As she made her way down the empty street a gentle rain began to fall. She tugged a lightweight hoodie out of her messenger bag and slipped it on, flipping up the hood as she quickened her pace.

Rejoining the flow of traffic on one of the main roads, she had the uncanny sensation that someone was watching her. Casting a quick glance over her shoulder, she caught sight of Mr. Military Jacket, trailing her from a few yards back.

Unnerved by his sudden reappearance, Alex turned down a random side street.

After walking for another minute, she paused to look around. Her pursuer, if that's what he was, was nowhere to be seen.

Relief washed over her as she turned back onto the main road and approached her destination. The words *Ballard's Rare Books* were etched in faded gold paint on a green sign hanging above the door.

She walked inside.

Ballard's store wasn't all that wide, but it made up for that in its length, with five towering rows of bookshelves stretching endlessly to the back of the shop. Books lined every wall and every shelf. High above, a balcony ran the circumference of the large room, allowing access to an even higher set of shelves that reached toward the lofty ceiling.

Alex couldn't help but smile. She'd always loved this place.

As she stepped further into the store, she immediately noticed that something was different. The wonderful, musty aroma that seemed to be reserved solely for the yellowing pages of old books was missing.

Instead she'd been greeted by another scent entirely: the smell of something burning—of meat cooking.

She would have chalked it up to the smell of Mr. Ballard's dinner, except that the aroma was nearly overpowering.

"Mr. Ballard?" she called out.

"Hello, again."

Alex whipped around. The Scotsman from the coffee shop now stood behind the register. He leaned against the countertop with an air of nonchalance and smiled wide.

"Hope I didn't startle you," he said. Despite his smile, there was a baleful look in his coffee-colored eyes.

Alex glanced toward the door.

"And I *really* hope you're not thinking about leaving." He walked out from behind the counter, pushing open a waist-high swinging door.

Alex inhaled sharply and took a step backwards.

As the door swung open she had caught sight of a charred and blackened mass at the Scotsman's feet. After looking at it more closely, Alex nearly cried out upon recognizing the distinct features of a skull.

The dark shape was what remained of a human body.

"Oh, my god." Her stomach lurched. "Is that... Did you...?"

The man had come to a halt halfway between Alex and the store's entrance.

"It is," he said. "And I did."

Alex stood frozen in place despite every instinct she possessed commanding her to run. Run where? The man was blocking her only exit.

He pulled a lighter from his vest pocket. Alex took another step back, closer to the shop's wall.

"You know the wonderful thing about fire, Alexandra?" He flicked the lid open.

How had he known...?

Of course. Her wallet. He must have read the name on her driver's license before giving it back to her in the coffee shop.

Alex's grip tightened around the strap of her satchel. She had to get out of here.

"It's the perfect murder weapon, fire." He pulled the flame from the lighter into his hand, where it hovered, impossibly, an inch above his palm. "Persistent, resilient, ultimately untraceable… and entirely at my command."

He flicked the lighter closed with his free hand and slipped it back into his pocket.

Alex considered making a run for the door, intent on barreling into him and, with any luck, taking him by surprise.

Before she could put her plan into action, however, he hauled back his right arm and *threw* the blaze straight for her. Alex staggered aside and the flaming orb landed just to her left. The fire spread quickly, engulfing the bookshelf behind her in a matter of seconds.

She stepped away from the conflagration.

"Just a suggestion," he said, a sneer twisting the lines of his face. "You might want to *run*."

With one last, desperate glance at the exit, Alex turned on her heel and fled deeper into the shop.

FOUR

The fire swept toward her as if it had a mind of its own, a sentient being driven by a single goal: to consume her.

Alex reached the end of the row of books and turned left, the fire spreading, following, taking the corner and closing fast, licking at her heels as she ran along the bookstore's inside wall.

The only exit she knew of was at the front of the building, the area surrounding it now a veritable inferno. In desperation she fled to the rear of the building, hoping to find another way out.

A putrid gray smoke had thickened the air inside the shop, stinging her throat as it filled her lungs. The threat of asphyxiation now seemed as imminent as the flames trailing only a few feet away.

Reaching the back corner, Alex spotted a door leading to the shop's storeroom. She tried the handle with no luck, finally kicking the base of it in desperation.

Taking as many steps back toward the flames as she dared, Alex got up a running start and slammed her shoulder into the very center of the wood.

A blinding pain rocketed through her arm, spreading from the base of her neck to the very tips of her fingers. With a yelp, Alex bounced off the heavy door and fell to her knees before it.

The door was locked tight. It wasn't going to budge.

She looked to her left. Her only other option was a spiral staircase leading to the upper balcony. The second tier of the store offered more walls lined with books, but no visible exit.

Alex got to her feet. The glass-paneled bookcases set against the nearby walls were already alight. Soon even the staircase wouldn't be an option.

Realizing that the approaching flames had effectively made the decision for her, she started up the stairs, the handrails already hot to the touch.

Alex risked a glance upward and her heart sank at the sight of what awaited her at the top of the stairs.

Dirty blonde hair. Hazel eyes. Gray military-style jacket.

She came up short, four steps from the landing.

The look on his face held just a hint of amusement. "Well?" He offered her his hand. "You coming?"

She hesitated, weighing her options. Risk running back down the flaming aisles to find another exit? Or trust the guy who'd been stalking her all afternoon?

The fire had spread to the nearby shelves. The heat was growing unbearable.

"You cut me deep," he said. "You'd actually choose a fiery death over the prospect of my company. I have to admit, that stings a bit."

She didn't move.

His expression grew serious. "Trust me, Alex."

Still uncertain, but more fearful of the flames than of the stranger before her, she took his outstretched hand—and very nearly dropped it in surprise. The sensation was… electric.

Literally. There was an actual, live current passing between their joined hands.

The flames were closing in.

Dismissing the odd sensation, she gripped his hand tightly and climbed the remaining steps.

Upon reaching the landing, Alex looked quickly for the

exit through which the stranger must have arrived... and found nothing. How had he gotten there?

Alex came to a stop before him and tried to pull her hand from his. He wasn't letting go.

"Ready?" he asked. The self-assured smile he'd worn earlier was once again firmly in place.

"For what?" she choked out, the mixture of heavy smoke and utter panic causing her throat to tighten. "There's no door!"

"Door?" The smile grew wider. "Who said anything about using a door?"

Alex opened her mouth to reply—and instantly wished she hadn't.

Before she could form a word in protest, the world around them had fallen away. The sound of thunder roared in her ears as a sudden change in pressure knocked the air from her lungs and forced her eyes closed.

Just when she felt certain that her body would soon do the impossible and turn itself inside out, it was over.

The pressure was gone... and she was falling.

Alex's eyes burst open. She was eye level with the tree-tops and falling fast, heading straight for a dark body of water that stretched out below her.

A cry of surprise slipped from her throat.

The grip on her hand tightened.

Alex caught one last glimpse of her savior as they broke the surface of the water... He was still smiling.

"Is he back yet, Kenzie?"

"No."

"...How about now?"

"Brian, if you ask me about Declan one more time, I'm taking that book you've had your nose stuck in for the last couple of days and I'm torching it."

Stricken by the prospect, Brian covertly slid the large tome in front of him off of the table and into a backpack on the floor. Using his foot, he nudged the pack further from him, until it was well out of the older girl's reach.

Kenzie had a laptop opened in front of her and was typing furiously on the keyboard. Brian's gaze traveled between the girl and the bag.

They sat in silence for another moment.

"Are you sure he's—"

"*Brian.*" She glanced up from her work.

"Sorry! It's just that he should have been back to check in *hours* ago."

Her expression lost some of its severity when she registered the concern in the eyes of the bespectacled ten-year-old sitting across from her. She turned her attention back to her computer.

"It's Declan, Brain," she said, intentionally using his nickname and softening her tone. "He can take care of himself. You worry too much."

That didn't exactly make him feel better, but he stayed quiet all the same.

A moment later and the silence was broken once again, this time by Brian's father, a tall, well-dressed man who had materialized through a door that led to one of the adjoining rooms. He cleared his throat and Kenzie glanced up from her computer.

"Any news?" he asked.

Kenzie had a faraway look in her eyes as she raised one eyebrow. A smirk played at the corners of her mouth. "Perfect timing as always, boss. He's back. And it looks like he brought someone with him."

Brain's father looked around the room as though he half-expected them to be hiding behind the sofa. "Well? Where are they?"

Kenzie appeared to be fighting back laughter as she

hiked a thumb over her shoulder in the direction of the bay windows.

He walked to the casement.

From where Brian sat at the table, he could make out two sets of ripples spreading across the still waters of the lake.

Brian's father let out a sigh, grabbed a coat from the coat stand and headed out the front door, making for the winding path that led down to the water.

"C'mon, kid." The girl climbed to her feet and snagged him gently by the arm before he could bolt out the door. "Let's go get some towels. They're gonna need them."

Wanting to follow his father, but realizing it would probably be a bad idea, he settled for following Kenzie obediently through the living area and up the stairs.

They were definitely going to need those towels.

Alex reached the surface first and swallowed a lungful of icy air.

The frigid water and the cold, crisp air made for a jarring contrast to the oppressive heat they'd left behind in the bookstore.

Her mind reeled, a thousand different questions running through her head. Where were they? How had they gotten here? Better yet, how was she going to get *back*? If she didn't show up at home in the next twenty minutes or so, Cassie and Aunt Cil were going to freak.

Treading water was proving difficult. Her satchel and clothes weighed her down and her muscles had already begun to cramp in response to the cold. Fat lot of good that bathing suit was doing her under her layers of clothes. She hadn't exactly been dressed for a swim.

She scanned the shoreline for the closest way out of the water. Roughly one hundred feet to her right a dock jutted out from the tree-lined shore. It seemed as good a place as any and she started toward it.

Her rescuer surfaced in the middle of her path and she swerved to avoid him.

"Hah! What a rush." He ran a hand through his wet hair, grinning from ear to ear. "Why are you just sitting there? This water's cold."

She stared at him blankly. He started for the dock.

The rush of gratitude she had felt toward him for saving her from certain death in the bookstore was now warring with an uncharacteristic urge to *smack* that idiotic smirk off his face.

Grateful though she might be, he'd still just dropped her into the icy waters of a lake in the middle of nowhere, over a hundred feet from the shore.

And for whatever reason, he seemed to find it funny.

All around the lake, mountains towered high above, limiting the horizon to a blue circle of sky. The early evening sun was already threatening to dip below a distant prominence. Wherever they were, it wasn't Florida.

"Where in God's name *are we*?" she demanded. Cassie wanted moxie? Well, Alex was bursting with it right about now. "What just happened? Who was that fire-happy psycho in the bookstore?"

Her words came out at a stutter through chattering teeth. Great. She'd aimed for intimidating and hit cold and waterlogged instead.

"And who are you, anyway?" She tried her best to sound assertive. "Better yet, *what* are you? How did you bring us here?"

He paused mid-stroke and glanced back at her, his self-satisfied grin faltering, but only for a second. Instead of answering her questions he made for the dock again.

Alex continued to tread water for another moment and then resigned to following him. What choice did she have?

They were still a good fifty feet out when an angry voice echoed across the lake.

"Dammit, Declan!"

The smug smile was wiped from her dubious hero's face.

Declan? So he had a name.

A forty-something man in an immaculate black suit and gray peacoat was making his way down the dock. He was handsome, though not in any traditional sense. The man was tall and lean, lanky, but with an air of purpose and authority that made him appear larger than he was. His walnut-colored hair was going grey at the temples and his thin mouth and weathered features intensified the scowl on his face.

With a grunt of annoyance, Declan resumed his swim to the dock. His strokes sent him quickly through the water, despite being weighed down by wet clothes and a pair of boots.

He made it look easy.

Alex followed, her progress slow and awkward.

After nearly twelve years in Florida, Alex was well accustomed to being in the water. She'd even been on her school's swim team the year before, helping them to the state championship for the first time in ten years.

Then again she hadn't been doing laps in the school's swimming pool fully clothed with a satchel roped around her.

Her savior, not surprisingly, reached the dock first.

"The lake, Declan? Really?" The man knelt at the edge of the platform, offering his hand. Alex could hear the hint of an accent that she couldn't quite place. "You couldn't find a better spot to reappear?"

Declan took the man's outstretched hand and, bracing his other hand on the dock, hauled himself from the water and onto the platform in one fluid motion.

The younger man sat down with a thud and peeled off his saturated jacket. Alex gripped the edge of the dock, trying not to notice the way Declan's thin white t-shirt was now clinging to his well-defined torso.

She'd known the guy a grand total of five minutes and he'd already left her with a sour first impression. The last thing she ought to be doing right now was ogling his six-pack.

Alex shoved all musings about Declan's physique to the back of her thoughts and finally registered what the tall man had said.

They could have reappeared somewhere else? Declan *chose* to drop them in the lake?

Oh, yeah. Her first impression had definitely been the right one.

"Carson Brandt was there," Declan said, wringing the water out of his coat. "Had her cornered."

The twisting motion called her attention to his biceps.

Cursing her traitorous hormones, Alex tried to derail that train of thought with an attempt to pull herself from the water under her own weight.

Her arms gave out a few seconds in and she slipped beneath the surface.

Well, that was embarrassing. If she could look any more pathetic to these people, she wasn't sure how. Alex slicked back her hair. Declan was still wringing out his jacket and hadn't seemed to notice.

A cold breeze ripped across the surface of the lake and, suddenly, Declan's muscles weren't nearly so distracting. She needed to get out of this water before hypothermia set in.

The tall man nodded. "But the *lake*, Declan?"

"The building was going up in flames." He squinted up at the man in the suit, the glare of the sun in his eyes. "She could have been on fire."

The man chose to ignore this and turned to help Alex from the water, resigned.

"For the record," said Alex through chattering teeth, "I was not on fire."

She tossed her satchel onto the deck, took the tall man's outstretched hand and—in a maneuver that only slightly resembled the one Declan had just demonstrated—launched herself from the water and tumbled onto the dock.

"I knew I should have sent Nathaniel with you." The older man shrugged off his coat and placed it around Alex's shoulders.

"Hey, I got her out didn't I? She's here. She's in one piece."

More or less, she thought to herself.

Alex tried to wring some of the water from her hair, crinkling her nose as she plucked a slimy clump of algae from her dark brown tresses. She tossed the disgusting glob back into the lake and dropped the tangled, still-dripping mess that was her hair in resignation.

"She's fine," said Declan, defensive. "You're fine, right?"

She gave him a look. "*Peachy.*"

"See? Both Alex *and* her astounding wit have made it here intact. Her sense of humor seems to be M.I.A., but I'm pretty sure that was a pre-existing condition." Declan got to his feet and headed toward the shore. "Mission accomplished."

Alex glanced up at the man in the suit. His eyes followed Declan's progress, scowl still firmly in place.

"Um, hello?" said Alex.

The man in the suit turned to face her.

"Hi. Excuse me, but… what just happened? Where am I?"

His expression softened.

"Of course. I apologize. I'll explain everything once we get back to the cabin." He helped Alex to her feet. "My name is John Grayson. No need to tell me yours. I already know quite a bit about you, Alexandra Parker."

He ignored her look of surprise.

"You must be freezing. Let's get you inside. I know you have questions for us. I promise, I'll tell you whatever you want to know just as soon as you're settled. You'll be safe here for the time being."

"Safe? Safe from what?"

"Like I said. Once you're warm. I'll answer your questions then. Do you prefer Alex or Alexandra?"

"Alex," she said, gathering up her saturated messenger bag and adjusting the oversized coat that hung from her shoulders.

Alex wasn't about to wait until they reached the cabin. She wanted answers now. Figuring that by asking questions with a yes or no answer she might be able to wheedle a bit more information out of him, she tried again.

"Did you send Declan to follow me?"

"I did."

"To keep me safe?"

"Yes."

"He wasn't supposed to bring me back here, was he?"

Grayson's mouth was a thin line. "His job was to evaluate the situation and to ensure your safety. He wouldn't have brought you here if there had been another way. Although dropping you in the lake…"

"I'm guessing you don't welcome all your guests this way?"

His expression became rueful. "Declan's turned getting under people's skin into something of an art form."

"I get that." She tried to smile, but her teeth were still chattering too hard. It came out more like a grimace. "I've only just met him and already I'd like to shoot him."

Grayson offered her a watery smile and started off in the direction Declan had vanished.

Alex followed after him, hesitant, but freezing. Her Converse All-Star's squeaked, wheezed and oozed lake water with every step. "Inside" promised warmth and the potential for dry clothes. That won out over hypothermia any day.

FIVE

Alex huffed as she struggled to keep pace with Grayson's long strides, lungs burning as her exhalations formed hazy clouds of mist in the thin mountain air.

Sunlight trickled through the rustling branches of the trees above, creating dancing pools of light on the forest floor. As the wind picked up, Alex pulled her borrowed coat tighter around her shoulders.

The trail leading to the cabin snaked its way at a steep incline through the forest and she soon found herself focusing less on her guide, and more on her unsteady footing. Large amounts of melting snow had left the well-worn path slick with mud and pockmarked by puddles of standing water.

Alex stumbled along behind Grayson, her flat-soled Chuck Taylor's offering little in the way of traction.

"Not much further now," he said.

The rush of adrenaline that had flooded her system earlier was letting up, but this unexpected exercise had kept her blood pumping. She felt relatively warm despite the wet and the cold.

A short ways ahead of them Declan had paused to retie a bootlace.

Grayson had noticed him, too. Alex could tell, because the preoccupied expression he'd worn for most of the walk had morphed into one of vexation.

Declan straightened, picked up his canvas jacket and

continued walking, now only a few yards ahead of them.

Alex gasped.

They had emerged from the wooded path into the mouth of a small clearing. At the top of two stone staircases stood a sprawling structure that—Alex could only assume—was the cabin Grayson had referred to.

Cabin wasn't the word for it. *Mansion* came closer.

Alex had seen cabins before.

In fact, she was quite familiar with one in particular.

Every year during summer break, Aunt Cil would drag her to a tiny mountain town in North Carolina for two weeks to "get away" from the fast pace of the city. The cabin had two bedrooms, no phone, ropes on the bathroom doors in place of doorknobs, wood siding, a tin roof and a window air-conditioning unit that never seemed to cool a radius wider than three feet.

This was not her aunt's summer cabin.

Alex stopped in her tracks and took in the sight before her.

The massive three-story home stood flush against the mountain, paneled in richly stained dark cedar and marked with stonework accents. With its immaculate grounds and unique features, it looked like something straight off the cover of an *Architectural Digest* magazine.

Who *were* these people?

Declan was now almost twenty feet ahead of them, making his way up the first of the two stone staircases.

Where the first staircase emptied out there was an open area just large enough to accommodate a neatly stacked woodpile and a small, shed-like structure built in the same style as the house above.

Next to the woodpile, a guy around Declan's age stood splitting firewood. Despite the chilly weather, he was wearing only a pair of jeans and a black tank top. A gray, long-sleeved henley was tied around his waist. His olive complexion and short black hair set him apart from both Declan and Grayson in appearance.

When Declan reached the top of the first set of stairs he lowered the axe.

"Hey, you're back! How'd it go?" He took in Declan's soggy appearance with thinly veiled amusement. "…The hell happened to you, man? Why are you wet?"

"Oh, you know. Walked through fire, rescued the girl, went for a swim." Declan walked past him and started up the second stairway. "Just another day at the office."

Alex looked him over as she approached.

Like Declan, he was gorgeous. Unlike Declan, there was an obvious kindness in his dark brown eyes. Those weren't the eyes of someone who'd rescue her from the fiery clutches of death only to drop her into a frigid lake for a laugh and the sheer rush of it all.

She liked him already.

The dark-haired teen turned his gaze on Alex… and the axe slipped from his hand, falling to the ground beside him with a muted *thump*.

He stared at her, mouth open in a small "o" of surprise. Recognition blazed in his eyes.

He said something then that she didn't quite catch and the look of wonder was wiped from his face. Schooling his expression, he offered her a slow smile instead.

What was that about? She was certain she'd never seen him before. A guy like this, she would have remembered.

"You brought company," he said.

"So I did," Declan called over his shoulder. "Now put a shirt on, before your fugliness sends her screaming back into the lake."

Declan's joking aside, it was as though some perfectly chiseled Greek god had descended from Mount Olympus and now stood before her, chopping firewood. If Cassie had been here, nothing short of Armageddon would have prevented her from flirting with him.

Cassie.

She was probably wondering where Alex had disappeared to, right about now.

"Alex, I'd like you to meet Nathaniel Palladino." Grayson gestured toward the axe-wielding Adonis. "Nathaniel, this is Alex."

Alex glanced down, feeling self-conscious. Between her drenched clothes and Grayson's too-large jacket swallowing her petite form, she was likely exuding all the sex appeal of a drowned rat in a peacoat.

"Nice to meet you," said Nathaniel. He stuck out a hand as they approached.

"You too," she said. His hand was warm and his grip firm, but gentle. She could feel calluses on his palm.

Nathaniel jerked his hand back with a quiet curse. "I'm sorry. I shouldn't have—I mean, I... My hands are disgusting," he said finally. "You know... Tree sap."

"Oh," she said, surprised and a little confused. "It's fine. Really."

A flash of color caught her eye.

Up above, two figures peered over the railing that surrounded the patio balcony. The first was a girl who was probably as old as Alex, with flaming auburn hair cut in a drastic swing bob—longer in the front than the back. She smiled down at Alex and held up what looked like a towel.

The other figure was a young boy with mousy brown hair and bright blue eyes made owlish by the large glasses perched atop his nose. He waved at her. She waved back.

"That's Kenzie and Brian," said Nathaniel, following her gaze. He eyed the towel. "Looks like Kenzie knew you were coming."

Declan reached the top of the stairs and the boy, Brian, ran over to greet him, towel in hand. She watched as

Declan ruffled his hair and the two disappeared from her line of sight.

Nathaniel picked up the fallen axe and gave it one final swing, lodging it into a nearby stump.

"Are you all ... family?" she asked slowly. They were an odd bunch, with only Brian bearing any resemblance to Grayson.

"In a manner of speaking." He untied the arms of the henley and slipped it over his head. "Grayson sort of... took us in... when we were kids. All but Brian. Brian's his son from his second marriage."

"You mean you, Declan and Kenzie are all...?"

"All orphans?" He seemed unfazed by the question. "Yeah. We are."

He looked at her as though he wanted to say something more, but thought the better of it. "Come on. You must be freezing."

Alex glanced back over her shoulder as she mounted the first step and was rewarded with a beautiful vista of the forest and the lake below. The view would have been far more inviting had she not just gone for an unscheduled swim in those shimmering black waters.

"You must be Alex," came a voice from above.

At the top of the stairs, Kenzie stood waiting, her arm outstretched and a towel in her hand. Alex accepted it gratefully.

"I'm Kenzie."

"Nice to meet you," said Alex. "Thanks for the towel."

The girl quirked a smile. "I'd like to apologize for my idiot brother."

Alex couldn't hide her confusion. Which brother was she referring to, exactly?

"The moron that dumped you in the lake," she explained. "We really *don't* welcome all our guests that way."

The statement was a word-for-word echo of what Alex had asked Grayson earlier.

Kenzie's cheeks blazed the same color as her hair. "Yeah, suppose I ought to explain... I've sort of been eaves-dropping on your conversations since you got here."

Alex glanced back toward the pathway. The lake was nearly a five-minute walk from where they now stood. How could she possibly have heard their conversation?

"I didn't," she said, answering Alex's unspoken question. "Well, I mean I didn't technically *hear* you, per se. *Technically* I read your mind. I've sort of been spying on your thoughts since you arrived."

"*Kenzie*," Nathaniel admonished.

"I know, I know." Kenzie sighed. "Sorry, Alex. Promise to stay out of your head from now on. Curiosity got the better of me. When I heard Declan get back and I realized that he had brought you back with him... I couldn't help myself."

Alex probably should have felt violated—or at least a little incredulous—but after having been transported from Florida to god-knows-where in a brilliant flash of light... Well, a nosy telepath seemed about par for the course. This whole situation felt surreal.

"You can read minds?"

Alex conducted a quick inventory of the thoughts she'd had since arriving.

Oh, geez. Declan's abs. Nathaniel's god-like good looks. She'd heard all that?

Alex turned ten shades of red at the realization.

Maybe the whole thing *was* just some sort of parlor trick. Maybe Kenzie had just made a lucky guess. Any explanation would be preferable to the alternative right about now.

"Not to worry, chica." Kenzie winked at her. "Your secrets are safe with me. And I promise—no more going into your head without your permission. If you want, I can even teach you how to block people like me from getting in."

"Hey, Nate!" Declan's voice called from the cabin's front entryway. "Heads up!"

A bottle of Gatorade spiraled through the air, heading straight for the back of Nathaniel's head. He turned, but not quickly enough. There was no way he'd be able to get his arms up to catch it in time.

Alex's eyes widened in surprise.

The bottle of red liquid had come to a complete standstill and now hung suspended, frozen in place, a few short inches from Nathaniel's nose.

He plucked it from the air a moment later.

"For Alex," said Declan. "Grayson thought she could use it."

Alex blinked. Had she really just seen that? Or were her eyes playing tricks on her?

Nate offered her the bottle.

First Declan zaps her out of a burning bookstore and then Kenzie potentially reads her mind... Now Gatorade bottles were defying gravity and Newton's first law of motion?

Gingerly, she accepted the beverage.

"You're wondering what just happened." Nathaniel's smile was almost apologetic.

"Did you just...?" Alex couldn't find the words to finish her question. What, exactly, *had* he done?

"Suppose I ought to explain." He folded his arms across his chest. "You see, everyone here can do something kind of... special. Kenzie reads minds, Declan teleports, Grayson and Brian can see glimpses of the future—"

A gentle tug pulled the unopened Gatorade bottle from her hands and thrust it back into the air. It hung there for a moment before falling slowly back down to her.

"And I'm telekinetic," he finished. "I can move objects with my mind."

She stared at him dumbly, wondering if her day could possibly get any weirder.

"Oh," said Alex. She had no idea what to say. If she hadn't seen it with her own eyes, she never would have believed it. "Okay, then."

Kenzie laughed. "Come on, Nate. Let's get her inside before the cold air and all our weirdness sends her into shock."

Alex allowed them to lead her through the main entry-way and into the cozy warmth of the cabin. They stepped into a spacious living area, lined with hardwood floors, softly lit and filled with wrought-iron furniture. Comfortable-looking leather couches faced a large stone fireplace at the center of the room and a kitchen table sat off to one side. Against the left side of the far wall, an oval pass-through window offered a glimpse into the kitchen.

Her gaze traveled upwards.

A cathedral ceiling towered high above, one massive wrought-iron chandelier hanging from its center. The second floor was open to the living room, the banister-lined hallway offering those upstairs a birds-eye view of the downstairs living area.

Despite the intimidating beauty and size of the house, it was most definitely a *home*.

In the dining area, she noticed a backpack sitting next to the kitchen table, textbooks and a laptop spread out on the tabletop. A jacket was slung over the back of the loveseat, a variety of tennis shoes and boots were sitting next to the front door beneath the coat rack, pictures of the four kids and Grayson sat on the end-tables, and there was a fire roaring in the fireplace.

Fire.

Alex shivered despite the warmth, unable to look away

from the crackling flames. Had she really almost died in that bookstore?

It all seemed so impossible. The way the fire had followed her down the aisles as though it had come to life and was determined to envelop her. The way the man had controlled it so completely, the flame not even burning his palm as it hovered less than an inch above his skin. The way Declan had transported them from the bookstore to the lake in a blinding flash of light.

A creaking sound interrupted her thoughts and she tore her gaze from the hearth.

Grayson was coming down the staircase.

From the corner of her eye, Alex could see Declan and Brian standing in the kitchen.

"Kenzie, would you mind finding some clothes for Alex to borrow? And show her to one of the spare rooms upstairs. Prove to her we're not completely lacking in our hospitality when it comes to greeting guests." Grayson sent Declan a pointed look through the pass-through window.

Declan only smiled.

Kenzie took the now soaked peacoat from her shoulders and hung it on the coat rack. "Allons-y!" she said, making for the stairs. "Next stop: dry clothes and a hot shower."

Alex had a million questions still to ask about what had happened at the bookstore, about where she was and who they were and about how she was going to get home—but right now, the offer of a warm shower and dry clothes was too enticing to ignore.

The aching cold Alex had been experiencing since their splashdown in the lake had left her feeling weak and increasingly disoriented, her thoughts becoming harder and harder to organize. A chill had settled over her and she was starting to think that even the heat being produced by the large fire wouldn't be enough to warm her.

That worry she'd had earlier about suffering from hypothermia now seemed very real. She needed to get out of these wet clothes.

Shower first.

Then she wanted some answers.

SIX

The bathroom had become a sauna.

Alex sat on the tiled floor, wrapped in a terry-cloth robe she'd found hanging on the back of the door, wondering what she should do next and trying hard to feel warm again.

She was currently weighing the pros and cons of making a break for it.

Sure, Grayson and his family *seemed* nice enough... But who were they, really? And could she trust them?

A simple look around earlier had made it clear that she was far—*unbelievably* far—from home. They didn't make mountains like these in the Sunshine State.

So how was she going to get back home again, without Declan's help?

She could sneak out and pray that the others, Kenzie especially, failed to notice...

But then what?

The cabin was surrounded on all sides by an ocean of trees—a forest so vast she hadn't been able to see to the end of it. If she chose the wrong direction, she could end up hiking for days before she found help.

Alex frowned.

They'd given her no reason *not* to trust them. If anything, Grayson and his family seemed like they genuinely wanted to help. And she *liked* them. Especially Kenzie and Nathaniel.

As for Declan... Well, he might be an incorrigible jerk, but he *had* saved her life. That should count for something, right?

Her mind made up, Alex stepped out of the en-suite bathroom and back into the sizable guest room. Grayson had promised her answers, but she wasn't going to learn anything by hiding out in there.

Alex breathed a sigh of relief. Laid out on the bed were a pair of jeans, a black camisole, a hairbrush and a zip-up hoodie.

Dry clothes!

As she slipped into them she made a mental note to thank Kenzie... Then wondered if the other girl hadn't just heard her, anyway.

Moving to exit the room, Alex had made it halfway to the door before something caught her eye—ten feet away, standing upright in its charger atop one of the mahogany dressers, was a cordless phone.

By her count she was almost an hour late for meeting Cassie back at the house. Knowing her overprotective aunt the way she did, the odds were good that half the town had already taken to the streets in search of her. And if they knew about the fire in the bookstore...

On impulse Alex crossed to the phone, plucked it from the charger, and dialed.

Her aunt answered on the second ring.

"Hello?"

"Aunt Cil? It's me."

"Alexandra! Thank goodness! Where are you, honey?"

Alex hesitated.

She suddenly had no idea what to tell her.

"I'm... I'm not exactly sure," said Alex. "Before I tell you what happened, you need to promise me that you're not going to freak."

"Freak? Why would I freak, Lee-Lee? What's happened?"

Alex grimaced. "I went to Ballard's like you asked."

"I am aware of that, Lee-Lee." Cil's patience had obviously worn thin. "Cassie told me as much."

"Well, I was at the bookstore," said Alex, deciding in that moment to give her aunt the Cliff's Notes version of the story, "and this crazy Scottish guy started torching the place while I was in it—"

"*What*?"

Whoops. Definitely could have worded that better.

"But it's okay!" Alex said hurriedly. "This other guy sort of… well he *showed* up, out of nowhere, and he managed to get me out of the building before I was hurt."

"Where are you now, Lee-Lee? Why didn't you just come back to the house? Oh, god. You're in the hospital, aren't you?"

Alex could hear her aunt snatching up a set of keys on the other end of the line.

"No, no! *Imnotatthehospital*," she said in a rush. "I'm fine!"

This was definitely not going the way she'd hoped.

"Then where *are* you? Why haven't you come home?"

Alex let out a slow breath. How do you go about telling someone that you've pulled off the ultimate disappearing act and *teleported* to the middle of nowhere, with the help of some mysterious stranger… and *not* sound like a prime candidate for the psych ward?

Yeah.

Alex didn't know either.

"See, that's the thing. This guy… He can sort of disappear into thin air and reappear somewhere else." Alex winced.

Her aunt was going to think she was nuts.

"He took us someplace safe," she finished lamely.

Alex waited for her aunt to say something. When no reply came she kept going, the words tumbling out.

"I know it sounds crazy, but he sort of... *zapped* me here." She glanced around the elegantly decorated spare bedroom. Wherever *here* was. "I'm pretty sure I'm a long way from home right about now."

"Where are you?" Her aunt's voice had turned hollow.

"Some cabin." Alex wandered to the windowsill. "We're in the mountains. Near a lake. I'm still not sure where, exactly."

The line went dead.

"Aunt Cil?"

Silence.

Alex hung up the phone, turned it back on, and redialed. Halfway through the second ring the sound of raised voices carried up the stairs. Curious, Alex left her place at the window and walked out into the hallway. She came to a stop at the banister and stared wide-eyed at the scene unfolding downstairs.

The phone clattered to the hardwood floor, forgotten.

"What were you *thinking* bringing her here, Jonathan? Of all the idiotic, *irresponsible*—"

"And hello to you, too, Cecilia," Grayson sounded tired. "Long time."

"*Aunt Cil?*"

Declan and Nathaniel wandered into the living area from the kitchen. Alex barely noticed. Her eyes were glued to the frazzled form of her aunt standing in the room below.

Alex gripped the banister railing for support. "How did you...?"

Her aunt finally looked up. "Alex!" she cried.

Alex watched in disbelief as Cil took one step forward and disappeared in a ripple of violet light. A split-second later she had reappeared on the landing beside her.

Cil pulled her into a fierce hug before Alex could react. "Oh, Lee-Lee!" Her aunt pushed her back to arms

length, looking her up and down. "Are you alright? You're
not hurt are you?"

Alex's head was spinning. "I... You... *How did you do
that?*"

She heard Declan address Grayson downstairs. "You
never told me she had Variants in her family tree. Or that
she was *that* Alexandra."

Declan sounded angry. But why? Which Alexandra
was she supposed to be, exactly? And what was a variant?

"Need-to-know," Grayson replied. "You didn't."

"Oh, Lee-Lee," her aunt said again. She was staring at
Alex, a mix of grief and fear in her expression. "You
weren't supposed to find out. Not like this."

Cil reached for her arm, but Alex shrank back, just out
of her reach.

"Find out *what*, Aunt Cil?" Alex continued backing
away from her aunt, eventually running out of room and
bumping into the hallway wall. "What's going on? Since
when can you do... *that*? How do you know these people?"

Grayson was making his way up the stairs.

Cil looked helplessly from her niece to the dark-haired
man. Alex thought she could see tears welling up in her
aunt's eyes.

"There are some things you need to know, Lee-Lee.
Things I was hoping I'd never have to tell you."

"What are you talking about?"

Her aunt sighed. "I thought you'd be safe so long as I
stayed out of it and you stayed ignorant to the truth... But
I guess that's no longer an option." The look she sent
Grayson was icy. "Our family's a little... *different*. Your
mom and I, we were both born with the ability to teleport—to move instantaneously from one place to another."

Alex nodded slowly, trying to turn off the cynical voice
of reason that was loudly protesting this turn of events in

the back of her thoughts. This morning, such a declaration from her beloved aunt would have had Alex calling Dr. Moran—the psychiatrist Alex had been forced to visit for years after the death of her parents—and scheduling Aunt Cil for the next available appointment.

But now... She'd just seen the laws of physics shattered for the fourth time in a single evening.

The thing was, this time she couldn't write it off as some stranger with a parlor trick. This was family. This was *her* family.

And if her mom and her aunt were *different*, then what did that make Alex?

Declan was standing by the front entryway downstairs watching them, his hazel eyes intent.

Nathaniel walked up beside Declan and placed a hand on his shoulder. He nodded toward the door.

Declan's gaze didn't waver.

Nathaniel glanced upwards. Catching her eye, he sent her a brief, sympathetic smile before exiting. A few long, silent moments passed before Declan finally looked away and followed him outside.

Alex closed her eyes and tried to focus on what her aunt was telling her.

"Teleport," said Alex. "Like Declan. That's how I got here, right? Teleportation?"

"Yes, sweetie. Like Declan," she said slowly. "Declan and Mackenzie's parents, Nathaniel's mother, your parents... They all worked together when you four were kids."

"Parents?" she asked. "Plural? As in, my Dad, too?"

"Your Dad, too. He was telekinetic. He could move objects with his thoughts."

Like Nathaniel.

"Wait. If Nathaniel and Declan can do the same things as my parents, does that mean... Are we related somehow?"

Cil shook her head. "No. Teleportation and telekinesis are actually two of the more *common* abilities that Variants possess. And for the type of work your parents were doing... Well, those skills were very useful."

Alex swallowed the information, feeling numb. Eventually her thoughts circled back to the second part of what her aunt had said. The bit about all of their parents having worked together.

"What sort of work did they do?"

Cil pursed her lips and looked once more to Grayson. He cleared his throat.

"Twenty-two years ago, I'd just emigrated from England and was working for the NSA." He looked uncomfortable. "The United States government had been aware of people like myself, your parents and your aunt... of individuals with unusual talents, for quite some time. They referred to us as Variants—human beings whose DNA possessed slight variations from a normal human's genetic code. Variations that allow us to do incredible things."

He rubbed the back of his neck. "On account of my history with the NSA and my precognitive abilities, I was selected to head a newly formed bureau—one that would employ Variants in an attempt to aid the NSA, and other government organizations, with sensitive missions where our skills might prove... *useful.*

"The Agency started off small. Just a handful of us, really. Some paper-pushers to handle the bureaucratic affairs in the office and a single unit to work in the field, which I commanded. There were ten Variants on our team; four women and six men. We worked together for eight years. The unit was a great success. We were a bit like family."

Grayson paused, his jaw clenching. "They *were* my family," he said quietly. "Your parents were two of my very best friends."

Alex watched the older man pull himself back from the abyss he'd been peering into.

"One day, a powerful Variant named Masterson got it in his head that…" He appeared to be choosing his words carefully. "Well, let's just say he came after one of our own. The team tried to stop him."

Grayson paused again.

Realization dawned.

"My parents didn't die in a car crash," Alex whispered, "did they?"

It was more a statement than a question.

Cil blanched. Alex felt her knees give way beneath her and she sank slowly down the wall. Her borrowed sweater snagged on the cotton t-shirt underneath and hitched it up around her waist. She tugged it back down.

"All these years…" she heard herself say.

Alex had only been a kid when her parents had died. Just a little girl.

These days she was hard-pressed to remember a time before she had gone to live with her aunt. A time before the "accident."

A time when her family had still been whole.

She kept the few memories that remained locked away inside of her, to be brought out only when the darkness was at its worst… or any time she was feeling *particularly* masochistic.

The memories were few, but they were everything.

They were all she had.

She closed her eyes.

It was the smell of her mother's perfume—the light, flowery scent of honeysuckle mixed with the heavy sweetness of orange blossoms.

It was riding piggyback, high on her father's shoulders—so scared of slipping, but so certain that his strong arms would always be there to catch her, should she fall.

It was learning to swim in the chilly waters of the creek out behind their house. It was a picnic on a summer day. It was the smell of her mother's pumpkin pound cake in the fall.

And more than anything, it was love.

Every other thing she knew about her parents—all of the facts and anecdotes she'd collected like valuable treasures over the years—had all come from Aunt Cecilia.

And they'd all been lies.

Anger.

Betrayal.

Despair.

Alex couldn't quite name the feeling that had started to drain all the color and light from the world around her—that had caused her chest to tighten so painfully—but she thought that, perhaps, it was something entirely new. Some horrible combination of all three.

She glared at her aunt. "You said my mom was a school teacher… That my dad was an accountant! Now you're telling me that they were *spies*? That they were *murdered*? Was there *anything* you told me about my parents that was true?"

Her aunt's face crumpled. "Oh, Lee-Lee… Your parents loved you! They would have done anything to protect you! When they realized what was happening, they told me… They told me that if anything were to happen to them, that I was to raise you as normally as I could. They didn't want you to know about any of this, if it could be helped. They didn't want their life to be yours. They wanted you to be… *normal*."

The word hung in the air like a guillotine a thread away from a fall.

Nothing about her life would ever be normal after this.

She wasn't sure who was more deserving of her anger. The man in the bookstore for attacking her and forcing the truth out into the open? Declan for bringing her here? Her parents for insisting the truth be kept secret from her? Or her Aunt Cil for intentionally keeping her in the dark for so many years?

All this time... How had she not known? Not picked up on the clues?

"*Am* I normal?" she asked. "Or am I like you? Like my parents?"

Fear flickered in Cil's eyes for the briefest of moments.

Was this why Alex had suddenly turned into a walking electro-magnetic pulse, frying unlucky appliances any time she got upset? Had that been part of one of her parent's abilities?

Seemed pretty useless, if you asked her.

"Not all Variant offspring possess the traits of their parents," said Grayson. "Some are born completely human."

Her aunt nodded in agreement. "And some children who *do* inherit the variant genes from their parents never develop their powers, anyway. It just lies dormant."

They were quiet for a moment as the news sank in.

Alex narrowed her eyes as another thought occurred to her.

"What happened to the others?" asked Alex. "The rest of the unit—where are they now?"

Grayson leaned back against the banister. "Masterson killed the majority of my team." A shadow had fallen over his expression, seeming to grow darker with each word he spoke. "My wife. Your parents. All of our unit save for two: myself and one other, who I haven't spoken to for many years."

"So Kenzie, Declan and Nathaniel... ?" Alex couldn't find the words to finish her question. This must have been how they'd come to live with Grayson. Masterson had murdered their families. Just like he'd murdered hers.

Grayson folded his arms across his chest. "Orphaned.

Like you. I took them in because they had nowhere else to go. No family members left to take care of them."

"And you?" Alex asked, her eyes narrowing. There was a poorly concealed tone of accusation in her voice. "How is it that *you* survived?"

Later on, she would look back on this conversation and wish like hell she hadn't asked that question.

Grayson was quiet a moment. The look in his eyes suggested that he was no longer standing at the edge of that chasm...

The abyss had swallowed him whole.

"The last time I saw Masterson, he gave me two reasons for why I had to go on living. The first was that someone needed to look after the orphaned children." He unfolded his arms and stood up straight. "And the second was that killing me would have been an act of mercy. One he wasn't willing to provide.

"That night, Masterson died by my hand... And that is why I'm still alive," Grayson then turned and walked down the stairs, leaving Alex alone with her aunt.

The silence that followed Grayson's statement was absolute. She waited for the front door to close firmly behind him before she turned to her aunt.

"I don't understand," she said. "What did he mean by an 'act of mercy'?"

Cil was still staring at the door through which Grayson had disappeared. "One of Masterson's gifts was an ability to see the future," she said. "And while Grayson can see the potential future of any person, any place... he has never been able to foresee his own. When Masterson finally confronted Grayson, he saw something of Grayson's future. Whatever it was that Masterson saw... He felt that leaving Grayson alive would be a far crueler punishment than death."

SEVEN

Kenzie sat down in one of the whitewashed Adirondack chairs surrounding the patio's fire pit and glared at her brother.

"*What*, Kenzie?"

"You know what."

Declan ignored her, his attention fixed upon the pile of ashes resting at the center of the pit.

This attitude of his was getting on her nerves.

"Dammit, Decks, it isn't her fault and you know it."

He sent her a warning look. "Stay out of my head."

"I don't need to read your mind to know what you're thinking right now."

Nathaniel got to his feet. "I'm going to go finish chopping that firewood. You two try to keep it civil, would ya? There's enough drama around here tonight as it is."

Kenzie watched him disappear down the stone steps, then returned to her former activity of glaring at Declan. She kicked at the leg of his chair. "You can't hold what happened against her, Declan. She was a victim, too. She was just as innocent in all of it as we were."

"Innocent?" He snorted. "That's a laugh."

"That girl in there doesn't even remember what happened. And no one's told her. She's been lied to her entire life. You can't possibly hold her accountable for something that happened when she was *four years old*."

Declan fell quiet.

Kenzie fought back the urge to read his mind. Normally she didn't have to. Predicting her brother's thoughts and moods usually came as naturally to her as breathing.

And while Declan possessed a stubborn streak roughly a mile wide… Something about this felt different. It wasn't usually this hard to make him see reason.

"You weren't old enough to remember it either, Kenzie," he said bitterly. "You don't have those images burned into your brain."

"Oh, like hell!" she snapped. "God knows you replayed them enough times growing up. I saw them in your head whether I wanted to or not."

"I'm sorry, Kenzie." Her brother's face twisted with an emotion she couldn't identify. "I didn't… I would have saved you from that if I could have."

She sighed. This wasn't about them.

"You can't focus all of your anger on Alex, Decks. She didn't do it. Masterson did."

"It was *her* he was after, Kenzie. Not *them*."

"No," she said. "They were protecting an innocent child from a madman."

"Yeah. And they *gave their lives* doing that, Kenzie. Eight people. Dead. And for *what*? What could *possibly* be so important about that girl?"

"It's not her fault," she said again. "Declan, it's not Alex's fault our parents are dead."

Alex paced slowly around the spacious living room, unsure of what to do with herself and too wound up to sit still.

After their conversation, Aunt Cil had followed Grayson outside, apparently to discuss Alex's situation. She had reappeared ten minutes later, intent on leaving once more to carry out some damage control back home.

Cassie was still out driving around in search of her and something like half the town knew that she'd gone missing already. Okay, maybe it wasn't *half* the town, but it sure seemed like it after Cil finished listing all the people she had phoned while trying to find her.

Cil had also *insisted* that Alex stay at the cabin until she had things sorted and knew it would be safe for her to return home.

When she had asked how long that might take, her aunt's reaction hadn't been promising.

Alex sank into the corner seat of the tan leather couch, tilted her head back and stared up at the cathedral ceiling.

At this point, it wasn't a matter of *processing* all these revelations. It was a matter of *accepting* them.

Alex let her eyes drift closed.

Mutant powers—which Alex had always assumed to be the stuff of sci-fi movies and graphic novels—were not only *real*, they also appeared to run in the family.

Her parents had been spies and were murdered by a psychopath.

Oh, and in an attempt to kill her, a crazy Scottish man had *incinerated* Mr. Ballard and burned his bookstore to the ground.

Alex fully expected to wake up at any moment and find out this whole nightmare had been just that. It had all been just a dream.

And you were there, and you were there, and there's no place like home...

She opened her eyes to find a smiling face staring down at her.

"Hi, Alex."

"Hi, Brian." She smiled. She couldn't *not* smile at the kid. His grin was infectious.

"Are you going to be staying with us for a while?" he asked.

"I don't know," she said honestly. "I guess it looks that way, doesn't it?"

The boy's smile grew wider.

At least *someone* was happy about the arrangement.

The door to what Alex thought might be an office opened and Grayson stepped through it.

"How are you, Alex?" Crossing the room, he took a seat across from her at one end of the immense flagstone hearth.

"I'm alright," she said. "Just trying to sort through it all, I guess. Wondering where I go from here."

He nodded.

Brian plopped down beside Alex on the couch just as a blast of cooler air reached them from the front entryway. Nathaniel had appeared in the doorway toting a leather firewood carrier overflowing with small logs. He dropped it beside the hearth and set about building up the fire, using a poker to stoke the pile of glowing embers.

The front door opened again. This time, Declan and Kenzie strode through it wearing identical masks of exasperation.

"Ah, good," said Grayson. "You're all here. There are some things we need to discuss."

Nate paused in his work, stealing a glance in Alex's direction. He sent her another reassuring smile. This time, she smiled back.

There was a sudden blur of movement off to her left. Declan had collapsed onto the love seat adjacent to Alex's couch and was sinking back into the cushions.

"Hold up. If we're having a family meeting, I need coffee." Kenzie disappeared into the kitchen. "Talk amongst yourselves!"

"Girl's already wired for sound," Declan muttered. "She needs to do the rest of us a favor and switch to decaf."

"I heard that!" Kenzie's disembodied voice called from the kitchen.

"Homework, Brian," said Grayson, noticing the boy for the first time.

"But *Dad...*" Brian pleaded. Grayson shot him a look. The boy deflated. "Yes, sir."

He leaned toward Alex.

"Save my seat! I'll be back," he promised in a low whisper, then got to his feet and trudged off toward the kitchen.

As Alex watched him go, her gaze fell on Declan. He was staring at her as though she were some curiosity that he was trying to make sense of.

"What?" she asked.

"Nothing," he said, but didn't look away.

Nathaniel cleared his throat. "So Alex will be staying here with us, Grayson?"

"For the time being the cabin will be the safest place for her," said Grayson. "I'm afraid, Alex, you won't be going *anywhere* until we can determine how and why you managed to attract the attention of someone like Carson Brandt."

Her aunt had basically said as much, but coming from Grayson the announcement felt like a prison sentence.

"There's something I've been wondering," said Alex. "How did you know to send Declan to follow me? What exactly did you see?"

Grayson's thin mouth turned down at the corners. "The trouble with my gift is that my visions are sometimes rather lacking in specifics. At first all I could see was a glimpse of you and another young girl sitting on a restaurant patio. A few hours later, I saw a second image—one of you running through a burning bookstore."

He rubbed his hands together. Just as he had in the hallway earlier, he appeared to be choosing his words carefully.

"Cil and I haven't exactly kept in touch over the years. I knew you were alive and well, somewhere, but I couldn't be sure that it was *you* I was seeing," he said. "Eventually I got lucky and saw a flash of you and your aunt together. Once I knew who you were and where to find you, I sent Declan."

"Why didn't you just call my aunt and warn her? Stop me from going to the bookstore in the first place?"

"Doesn't always work like that," said Nathaniel. "Calling your aunt might have insured that you went, for all we knew. The best chance we have to change something is to actually *be* there when it starts to happen."

"So you sent Declan to follow me instead," she said.

"Yes," said Grayson.

"Did anything in your visions tell you *why* Brandt wanted to kill me?"

Grayson shook his head. "None of this makes sense. You'd never seen him before? Never met another Variant before today?"

"No," she said. "Not unless you count Aunt Cil. My life before today was pretty... normal."

Well, as normal as you could get when you were a walking power surge, anyway.

Brian reappeared with a backpack and a laptop and settled back onto the couch beside Alex.

Grayson sent him a look of disapproval.

"What?" asked Brian. He hoisted what looked like a calculus textbook. "Homework!"

The older man sighed, but said nothing more. Brian smiled triumphantly and opened the book.

"There's something to all this we aren't seeing," said Grayson, returning his attention to the group.

"You're right." Declan leaned back further into the love seat, folding his hands behind his head. "To start with, Brandt wasn't trying to kill her."

Alex raised an eyebrow. "Tell that to the wall of flames that chased me through the bookstore."

Declan shook his head. "The man's a trained assassin. He kills people *for a living*. If he wanted you dead, it would have taken him two seconds and a wave of his hand." Declan gave her a look of appraisal. Alex felt her cheeks flare under his scrutiny. "You're not exactly a threat to a guy like him. Or to anyone else, for that matter."

She found herself wondering if there was a power out there that would allow her to melt into the couch cushions.

"...No offense," he added as an afterthought.

Kenzie sashayed back into the room, coming to lean against the back of the love seat. Her arms hovered above Declan, a steaming cup of coffee clasped between her hands. Declan eyed the mug warily and slid a few inches to his left.

"As much as I hate agreeing with my brother," she said, "Declan's got a point. Carson Brandt doesn't toy with his victims. It's just not his style. He's ten shades o' crazy, but he's no sadist."

Nathaniel tossed one last log onto the fire, crossed the room and then claimed a seat next to Alex on the arm of the couch.

"Alex's parents were Variants," Kenzie continued. "Maybe Brandt *knew* that her mom's side of the family could teleport. Maybe he was trying to see if Alex was capable of jumping, too. You know, by frightening her into it."

"But I can't ... *jump*." Alex wondered if she'd used the verb correctly. "You said that not all Variants pass on the mutation to their children. And even if I *could* teleport like my mom, or move things with my mind like my dad... I'm almost seventeen. Wouldn't I know about it by now?"

Grayson looked about ready to agree with her when Declan interrupted him.

"She's a Variant."

He said the words with such assurance that every head in the room swiveled in his direction. Even Brian glanced up from his homework with a quizzical expression.

Alex felt her stomach drop.

"What makes you say that?" Kenzie asked in surprise.

Declan pulled himself back into a seated position and looked squarely at Alex. "Ever had a problem with electronics?"

For a split second she wondered how he could possibly know about that... And then she remembered what had happened in the clothing store that afternoon when Connor had startled her. Declan had been standing right there. He'd seen the whole thing.

"Ever accidentally short-circuited a microwave when you realized you were running late for something important? Or scrambled the television reception when someone pissed you off?"

"What does that have to do with anything?" Alex's mouth had turned as dry as the Sahara.

"Electricity," he said. The smug smile had returned. "Before I jumped on my own for the first time—before I learned to control it—I used to wreak havoc on nearby electronics. I don't know why, maybe Brain over there can explain it. There's something about the electricity we need to be able to harness in order to use our ability. An entry in one of my dad's journals said that we build up a powerful static charge right before we jump. Until I learned to control it, I had a habit of... frying things."

Somewhere beneath the smiling facade, Alex could sense Declan steeling himself, as if the mention of his father's journal and the tiny glimpse into his childhood were opening the door to other, more painful memories.

Alex felt lightheaded.

She wasn't a Variant. She *couldn't* be.

Kenzie snorted in amusement. "I remember those days.

You were public enemy number one to our household appliances for almost a year."

"Weren't we going through, like, four toasters a month at one point?" asked Nathaniel.

Declan rolled his eyes. "Wasn't half as a bad as you sending the toaster *flying across the room* every five minutes. If we're comparing cost of damages, you'd take the prize, my friend."

Grayson cleared his throat and tried to steer the conversation back on course. "Well, if that's the case, Alex, then—"

"Yeah and don't forget Nathaniel's birthday party when Kenzie locked Declan in the utility closet with Joanne Boathouse!" Brian interrupted. His face lit up in another thousand-watt smile.

Grayson groaned, sidetracked from whatever it was he had been about to say by the unpleasant memory. "Thought I'd *never* get that water heater working again..."

Declan scowled. "Brian, I don't know why you love that story so much. You weren't even old enough to know what was happening at the time."

Nathaniel leaned in conspiratorially. "Joanne *Bode*-house was a year older than Declan, built like a tank, with afro-like red hair, an unfortunate case of acne, the temperament of an angry Doberman and god-awful breath. She had a huge crush on Declan when we were younger."

Declan looked pointedly over his shoulder at Kenzie. "Still haven't forgiven you for locking us in there, by the way."

"It was for the greater good," she said.

"What? And how do you figure that?"

"You'd just melted my computer's hard drive! You needed to get your powers under control. I figured trapping you in a closet with the Boathouse might provide you with the motivation you needed to finally jump."

The sound of their bickering continued, but it was soon eclipsed by the escalating clamor of Alex's thoughts.

She flashed back to the hunted expression that had flickered across her aunt's face when Alex had asked if she, too, was different.

All these months of burnt-out hair dryers and crackling cell-phone calls, malfunctioning computers and broken appliances. All this time her aunt had known what was happening to her, but had never said a word.

In the end, she'd found out anyway.

Alex finally knew the truth.

She was like Declan. Like her mom and her Aunt Cil.

Alex was a Variant.

The revelation left her feeling like some giant rug had just been pulled out from beneath her. Her world had gone from mundane to impossibly complicated in less than three hours.

"You okay?" asked Nathaniel.

"Fine." The room started to spin. Alex took a deep breath. "I'm fine."

She tried for a smile. It felt like a lie.

Declan and Kenzie were still going at it.

"Have you known what I was since I first saw you in the store?" Alex asked Declan.

Their bickering came to an abrupt halt. The room grew quiet.

"I suspected it," said Declan. "My suspicions were pretty much confirmed after the coffee shop. I was watching when Brandt startled you. I knew from the way the barista was acting that something had just shorted out."

Alex winced at the memory. "It was an espresso machine."

Brian snickered. Grayson cleared his throat and the boy was silent.

The exchange called her attention to the computer in

Brian's lap. "How come I haven't fried anything since I arrived?"

If it was emotional upheaval that triggered the surge, why hadn't she been affecting any of the electronic equipment here at the cabin?

"I've been... *managing it* since you got here," Declan said slowly.

Alex raised her eyebrows in surprise. "You can *do* that?"

"So long as you're close by, yeah. Whenever I sensed an energy spike, I sort of siphoned it off." He shrugged. "Our mutation isn't just about teleporting. To some extent, it's also about controlling electrical current."

So Declan would always be able to tell when her emotions were heightened? She wasn't sure how to feel about that.

Sure, it wasn't the same as Kenzie having free access to her thoughts, but it wasn't far off.

Alex pushed that notion aside as she considered the events of the last six months. It rarely seemed to be a problem when Aunt Cil was around. Had she been doing the same thing?

Alex thought back to that afternoon with Cassie at the coffee shop.

"The camera," she said. "You did that, didn't you? You made it take the picture somehow."

His expression held just a hint of a smile. "Right now you're building up a static charge every time your mood fluctuates. Near as I can tell, it's tied in to our adrenaline levels. A fight-or-flight thing," he said. "Until you learn how to control it and channel the excess energy, you're going to keep on having problems."

Alex sighed.

Grayson, who'd fallen silent after the Joanne Bodehouse digression, finally spoke. "I suppose that settles it, then," he said. "Declan, I want you to start her training. Tonight."

EIGHT

Alex eyed Declan warily.

To say that he was less than thrilled with the assignment would have been an understatement. After the order was given, Declan had dropped all pretense of civility. He was now openly glowering at both Alex and Grayson.

What a grouch.

"Why can't her aunt train her?" he asked Grayson. "I've got plans tonight!"

"And Alex has a trained assassin after her. Something tells me that trumps your card game," Nathaniel argued. "What's the problem, Decks? I think the gang at The Corner Hole can go one night without your company."

"It's The Corner *Pocket*," he corrected. "And that's not where I was going."

Card game? And what sort of a place went by a name like The Corner Pocket?

"She needs to learn, Declan," said Grayson. "And time is most definitely of the essence. Whatever you had planned can wait."

"Why not let Nathaniel train her?" suggested Brian.

The boy had an excellent idea going there. She'd take Nathaniel's help over Declan's *any* day.

"He knows enough about the mechanics of how it works to teach her the basics," Brian continued. "Don't you, Nate?"

Alex appraised the tall, dark, handsome and *friendly*

guy in question. He seemed to be considering it. The look in his dark brown eyes was thoughtful.

The look in Declan's, on the other hand, was one of pure indignation. For whatever reason, he didn't like that idea. He wasn't about to let Nathaniel take the job.

Crap.

"It's going to take more than an understanding of the mechanics to get her to jump for the first time," said Declan. His expression wavered toward aggravation before settling on determination. "I'll train her."

"Good," said Grayson.

Crap, crap, crap.

"Uh... You sure about that boss?" asked Kenzie. Her stricken expression caused Alex's stomach to do a back-flip.

Even his *sister* thought this was a bad idea. Wonderful.

"I'm sure Nate could handle it," Kenzie went on. "And hey, maybe I can help, too."

"No," Declan stood. "I'll do it."

He disappeared into the shadows of a dimly lit hallway.

Nate turned to face her. "You'll be fine. Really. Just... try to keep on your toes."

Alex swallowed. "Okay."

Training.

The word brought to mind unpleasant images of five-mile runs in inclement weather, obstacle courses filled with mud, cumbersome climbing walls, martial-arts lessons and weapons coaching. Exercises that were meant to hone a person's fighting skills and strengthen their endurance...

But what would *Variant* training be like?

"Come on, Alex," said Declan. He'd reemerged from the darkened hallway and was striding quickly toward the front door. "Let's get this over with."

She scrambled to catch up, stumbling over the corner of an end table as she went.

Kenzie reached her brother first and snagged him by the elbow, bringing him up short. She didn't say anything. Just gave him a look.

"It's okay, Kenzie," said Declan.

Alex silently observed them as she worked her feet into her still-damp sneakers. What was that all about?

She wondered idly if Kenzie could speak into other people's minds in addition to being able to read their thoughts.

Declan pulled his arm back from his sister's hold and walked outside.

Alex scrunched up the sleeves of her borrowed jacket and wished she had an outlet for the nervous energy now coursing though her system. She stepped from the warmth of the cabin and out onto the flagstone-paved patio, following a few feet behind Declan as he made his way down the twin staircases and over to the winding path that led to the lake below.

The evening air held a chill, but she hardly noticed.

One thing she *had* noticed, however, was the fluffy blue object Declan held in one hand.

She studied the towel. "Planning to go for another swim?"

"Not if I can help it."

They continued on in silence for a while until the path grew steeper and they neared the lakeshore. Alex tried to focus on her footing. If it was bad working her way *up* the mountain in this muck, it was even *worse* trying to go down it.

And she wasn't about to start this training session off with a face plant in the dirt.

Although half of her felt like it was probably a lost cause, the other half was bound and determined not to look like an idiot in front of Declan.

If he could do it—if her mom and her aunt could do it—then she could too.

She was *going* to figure out how to teleport tonight.

…Or so she hoped.

The lakeshore here at the cabin was very different from what Alex was used to seeing. Where Alex lived, lakes and ponds were usually bordered with swampy fields of saw grass and an endless array of cypress trees. Reaching the water without a dock often involved trekking through the mud until the water deepened and the scattered cattails gave way to lily pads. Only then might you reach open water.

Here, however, the dark sand of the lakeshore could stretch for a hundred feet at a time before being interrupted by a rocky protrusion, or a mass of plant-life creeping out from the edge of the forest.

Declan passed the dock and continued on down the beach, finally reaching the fallen trunk of a massive spruce tree were it lay, half buried beneath the sand, blocking their path. The trunk stretched from the edge of the tree line out into the water.

Declan tossed the towel over it and then, bracing himself on a few of the sturdier limbs, climbed up and over.

Alex followed suit, landing softly in the sand on the other side. As she turned around to get her bearings, she found Declan standing in front of her.

He reached out, put his hands on her shoulders and pressed downwards. She fell into a seated position against the fallen tree.

"Sit," he said. "Stay."

"That's cute," she said. "Tell me to 'heel' and see what happens."

He smiled at her, genuine amusement shining in his eyes. All that protesting to Grayson aside, Alex wondered if he might actually be enjoying this.

"All part of the process." He turned his back on her and started down the empty coastline. "If I'm going to teach you how to teleport, first you have to know how to follow orders."

He disappeared into a stand of pine trees roughly ten yards away.

Alex dug the toe of her Chuck Taylor's into the dirt and resigned herself to waiting.

Seconds passed, then minutes. She stared out over the placid waters of the lake and fought back an urge to follow him into the woods.

Just as the sky overhead began to change from the bright colors of the sunset to the inky-blue shade of twilight, Declan materialized in front of her.

The sight was breathtaking. One moment she'd been staring at an empty stretch of shoreline, and the next, beautiful tendrils of violet-colored lightning arced from a singular point that hung suspended in midair—a blinding white fleck of light that grew to form the shape of a man.

In less time than it took for her to draw in a breath, Declan had appeared hovering before her. He dropped the last two feet to the ground in silence, any noise of his landing dulled by the sand.

She tried to hide the look of awe that had flashed across her face.

"You didn't move," he sounded vaguely surprised. "Good girl."

Alex chose to ignore that. "Why did you reappear a couple of feet up in the air instead of on the ground?"

In his arms, Declan was carrying a pile of rocks he must have picked up during his stroll through the woods. He readjusted his hold on them before he answered.

"I like the feeling of weightlessness, I guess. Plus, when I teleport, I'm going by the memory of what the place looked like when I last saw it," he said. "Never know when something will have moved."

He knelt near a shallow indentation in the sand and started arranging the rocks around it in the form of a circle.

The smell of ozone hung thick in the air, sweet and pungent, like it always did before the arrival of a summer thunderstorm back home. Alex could feel the tingle of static electricity on her bare forearms. She rubbed her arms distractedly as she watched him work.

"What happens if you teleport into a wall?"

"Can't," he said, moving more rocks. "You either wouldn't be able to jump in the first place, or you'd end up a foot or two away from the obstruction."

They were quiet for a long moment while he continued his work.

"What are you doing?" she asked when she couldn't take the silence any longer. "What are the rocks for?"

Declan finished the circle and, without bothering to answer her, disappeared into the woods again.

Alex tried not to groan in frustration.

What was the point of all this? When were they going to get around to the actual training?

Alex wondered what her aunt would think about Declan teaching her to jump, and then dismissed the thought entirely. Aunt Cil had given up any right she had to complain the minute she decided to keep the truth from her.

If training meant that she would eventually be able to control her gift—*control* her effect on electronics—then train was exactly what Alex planned to do.

Declan reappeared in front of her, this time with a bundle of branches in his arms. He made for the circle again and dropped the twigs in a pile beside it.

He started toward her. "Jacket, socks, and shoes. Off."

"What?"

"Take them off."

Suddenly wary, Alex complied. The temperature was dropping quickly in the half-light of the setting sun. Shivering, she tossed the jacket Kenzie had loaned her over the base of the fallen tree.

"Why? Is it more difficult to teleport with clothes on?" A sudden fear gripped her. "Wait. I'm not going to reappear *naked*, am I?"

Declan laughed. "Well, it would certainly make *my* job more interesting," he said. She felt her cheeks grow warm. "Don't worry about it. You'll take whatever's touching you along with you when you go. Clothes, some of the air around you... Even other people, if they're touching you when you jump."

"Alright. Good to know." She tugged at the hem of her borrowed black camisole, feeling self-conscious. "So then why am I standing here barefoot and jacket-less in fifty degree weather?"

There was that grin again.

"Your eyes. Close them."

"Yes, master." She'd been trying for sarcasm, but the unexpected sensation of warm hands on her bare shoulders caused her voice to catch. His touch held that same electric charge she'd felt when she'd taken his hand in the bookstore. She peeked one eye open. "What are you doing?"

His expression was serious again. "Eyes closed."

She curled her toes into the sand and tried to breathe normally. The heat radiating from Declan's hands and the faint scent of his cologne were making it difficult to concentrate.

"I want you to think back to when we teleported here from the bookstore." Declan guided her along the shore as he spoke. From the direction they were moving and the changing texture of the ground beneath her feet, she thought they were headed toward the water. Alex struggled to keep from stumbling in the loose sand. "Think about how it felt. Replay the motion of it over and over in your head."

He brought her to a stop at the waters edge. Alex could feel damp sand beneath her feet and the frigid waters of the lake lapping at the back of her heels.

"Okay," she said. "Insane pressure, tingly feeling, falling through the air…"

She let out a cry of surprise as Declan pushed her backwards. The shove was gentle, but with her eyes closed tight and the wet ground giving way beneath her feet, she'd lost any chance she had of maintaining her balance.

As Alex began to fall she found herself clinging to the memory from earlier. If she could just teleport herself away from the water, she could fall in the sand.

Acting on instinct, Alex braced herself. At first nothing happened…

And then time shuddered to a stop.

The world around her had come to a standstill. She was no longer falling, but the feeling of weightlessness remained.

Tendrils of violet electricity arced through the air and coiled themselves around her. Before she could react, a blinding flash of light engulfed her and the ensuing change in pressure forced her eyes closed.

As the pressure peaked and then abated, a tingling sensation surged through her, every muscle struck useless by the same prickling numbness she was accustomed to feeling when her foot went to sleep.

And then it was over.

Her eyes sprung open. She was falling, but not into the sand like she'd planned.

One second… Two seconds… Three…

Alex let out a curse as she sliced through the still waters of the lake.

She was going to *kill* Declan.

NINE

Alex surfaced and took a gasping breath. Cold. So very, very cold.

The still-setting sun provided her with just enough light to make out Declan's shadowy form standing on the beach.

Though it was too far away to be certain, she figured he was probably laughing.

Desperate to get out of the cold water, she attempted a jump… And nothing happened. Something about being in the water seemed to be stopping her.

Frustrated, she swam for the shore, the extra towel and Declan's order to take off her jacket and shoes suddenly making sense. He'd known before they started that she would end up in the lake again. But how? And why hadn't he said anything?

Her anger-fueled strokes propelled her quickly toward the shore. The sooner she reached it, the sooner she could strangle him.

As the sun sank fully below the horizon, a light blazed into existence on the beach. Declan had started a fire.

Alex dragged herself slowly from the water, shaking from the cold.

"You knew!" she spat. Once again, she'd aimed for righteous indignation and landed at a whimper. Stupid cold water. "You *knew* I was going to end up in the lake again, didn't you? You could have warned me, you jerk!"

Declan, to his credit, had lost the look of amusement he'd been wearing when he sent her back into the lake.

He tossed her the towel she'd asked about earlier and she fell to her knees beside the fire.

Alex wrapped the thin material around her, not caring that the sand was sticking to her borrowed clothes, or that her saturated camisole was probably leaving very little to Declan's imagination.

"It was a possibility, yeah," he admitted. "When you jump, you have to have a destination in mind. If you don't, you could end up anywhere you've jumped recently. It's like those paths are..." He searched for the word. "Like they're magnetized. In your case, that meant you were drawn to the path you traveled this afternoon."

"And it didn't occur to you to tell me about the destination thing *beforehand*? Or to maybe, I don't know, teleport me somewhere else before we started? Somewhere dry? So that I'd at least have a fifty-fifty shot of *not* ending up in the lake?"

"Huh." His forehead crinkled in contemplation. "I hadn't thought of that..."

Alex stared at him in disbelief. She was starting to think he'd taken the job with the sole intention of making her training as difficult as possible.

Why, oh why, couldn't he just have let Nathaniel teach her?

"Look on the bright side." Declan stoked the fire with a branch before dropping it into the flames. "Hard part's over. You've figured out how to teleport on your own."

Alex narrowed her eyes. Somehow, as she sat dripping and shivering on the lakeshore, muscles screaming in complaint, that didn't feel like much of a consolation.

He got to his feet.

The smile was back.

"Now you just need to work on sticking the landing."

Alex stood, dropped the towel, and smiled back at him. A mischievous gleam glinted in her steel-gray eyes. "Stick the landing, huh?"

Declan, rightfully, looked nervous.

"...Alex? What are you—*oof!*"

She'd cleared the few feet between them before Declan could react and, by using what she'd just learned, she managed to teleport mid-tackle, taking him with her as she disappeared from the campfire-lit shore and reappeared in the darkened sky above the lake.

They twisted as they fell through the air. Alex could feel Declan's strong arms wrapping around her waist as they neared the surface of the water.

They jumped again.

This time they reappeared, a horizontal tangle of arms and legs, inside a dimly-lit room Alex didn't recognize.

They landed on something soft, crashing into it with all the speed they'd picked up falling above the lake. There was a loud *crack*, followed by the sound of splintering wood.

The mattress they'd landed on dropped another foot and a half to the floor as the frame supporting it buckled.

There came the thundering sound of footsteps on stairs and the door behind them flew open.

Alex was lying nose-to-nose with Declan, their legs still entwined. She craned her neck around just in time to see Kenzie and Nathaniel burst into the room.

An overhead light flicked on.

Kenzie seemed amused; Nathaniel, annoyed.

"Hey guys!" Declan drawled.

"This isn't what it looks like," said Alex.

"This is exactly what it looks like," said Declan. "What's a guy got to do to get a little privacy around here?"

Alex managed to get in a good kick to his shin, despite being pinned to the bed.

"I am not *even* going to ask." Kenzie shook her head

and walked out as Brian appeared behind her in the hallway.

"Dammit, Declan." Nathaniel appeared resigned as he
took in the splinters of wood from the mangled bed frame
and the general disarray that their arrival had caused.

For a moment, he looked as though he were going to
ask about Alex's freshly-saturated clothes and sand-cov-
ered bare feet. Instead, he glared at Declan.

"What?" Declan asked, feigning innocence.

Nathaniel sighed. "You're paying for a new bed."

"It's alright," said Declan, cheeky grin firmly in place.
"Always wanted a futon."

Nathaniel turned on his heel and walked back out,
snagging a chuckling Brian by the shirt-collar and closing
the door behind them.

Alex tried to disentangle herself from Declan, but he
had her pinned with one of her arms trapped beneath his
side. His arms were still wrapped tightly around her. That
same electric sensation she'd felt when he'd touched her
shoulders earlier was now cascading through her in waves.

Declan smiled, his face only inches from hers. "Yeah,
I'd say you're *definitely* getting the hang of it."

His scent washed over her, a swirling mix of cinnamon
and woodsmoke. For a moment, Alex forgot how to breathe.

Was it her imagination? Or was Declan actually flirting
with her?

Alex tried to slow her racing heartbeat and worked to
ignore the tremble of butterflies in her stomach.

The cabin was warmer than the beach, but she was still
drenched. And still freezing.

Her eyes narrowed. She wasn't about to forgive and
forget so easily. He'd been nothing but a jerk to her since
the moment they'd met. Plus, he'd sent her for an unscheduled swim twice now. And for that, he still needed to pay.

Placing her free hand on his chest, she pushed him

backwards and with a little effort, managed to pull her other arm free.

"Where are we?" She sat up.

"My room at the cabin."

"Your room?"

He propped himself up on one elbow and shrugged his other shoulder. "Needed someplace soft to land. Besides... Now when you teleport without a destination you've got a fifty-fifty chance of either ending up in the lake, or in my bed. I have to say, I like those odds."

"Ha-ha." She started for the door.

"Where are you going?"

Alex cast a glare over her shoulder. "To ask Kenzie for more dry clothes. And to shower—again—because her idiot brother couldn't resist dropping me in the lake for a second time."

"Oh no you don't." He leapt from the bed, placing himself between Alex and the door and cutting off her exit. The action made her flinch.

Alex fought to calm her nerves. Her heart had started to race again, but this time Declan's close proximity had nothing to do with it. She flashed back to that afternoon with Brandt in the bookstore.

A crystal-clear image of the shopkeeper's blackened corpse tore through her thoughts.

That could have been her.

"We're not done with your... training... yet..." he trailed off. "Hey, what is it? What's wrong?"

She snapped back to the present.

Declan was staring at her, brow furrowed in confusion. "You haven't tried to draw that much energy since we met this afternoon. What's the matter?"

Damn.

She was starting to wish Declan couldn't read the changes in her emotions quite so easily.

"Nothing," she said, trying to push the awful image from her thoughts and quiet her sudden fear.

Declan's gaze traveled from the door back to where he stood, blocking her exit. A look of understanding crossed his face.

"The bookstore?" he asked softly.

Alex nodded.

This was Declan. He might be a jerk, but he wasn't Brandt. He wouldn't hurt her. At least, she didn't think he would…

He walked closer, tentatively placing his hands on her shoulders, the same way he had on the lakeshore. She could feel the electricity passing between them, a one-way stream, flowing out of her and into Declan.

Alex focused on the electrical currents she was affecting. Declan was right, she was calling up a large amount of energy as her anxiety intensified. Even before he had touched her, she could sense him siphoning off the excess. She'd never noticed it before. Had all this teleporting made her more sensitive to it?

Declan looked thoughtful. "Before you go, there's one more thing I want to try and teach you tonight." He guided her back to the bed. She perched on a corner of the mattress and he sat down beside her.

Her shoulders felt cold from the loss of his touch.

A moment passed. Alex looked at Declan expectantly. He was staring at her, but appeared lost in thought.

He scratched the back of his head.

"Well?" she said.

"I'm trying to figure out the best way to do this." His expression was sheepish. It wasn't a look she ever expected to see on him. The honesty in it was almost endearing. "Never exactly tried to teach this to someone before."

After another minute of contemplation, Declan held up both hands, palm out and gestured for her to do the same.

"Alright. Close your eyes."

She hesitated. "Last time you told me to close my eyes, I went for a swim."

He laughed. Alex couldn't help but smile. The low rumble of Declan's laughter was quickly becoming a sound that she relished hearing. And oh, that was *so* not good.

"No swimming this time," he said. "Promise. Just close 'em."

She complied.

Their hands were still a few inches apart, but Alex could sense the current flowing between them.

"Feel that?" he asked.

"Yes."

"Okay, I want you to concentrate on that sensation. Right now it's traveling one way. From you, into me," he said. "I want you to reverse it."

Alex opened her eyes. "How the heck do I do that?"

"Eyes shut," he said again. "Do you ever do as your told?"

She smiled and closed her eyes once more. "Not if I can help it."

"Stubborn..."

She could hear the smile in his reply.

Alex wasn't sure what it was about this guy. Declan seemed to be bringing out a side of her that, before tonight, she hadn't even known existed.

It was as though he'd somehow managed to light a fire inside of her. A fire that was now slowly starting to consume her, transforming her as the blaze grew brighter, searching for new ways to shine through.

Sure, he was driving her half-crazy in the process with his obnoxious attitude and that damned cheeky grin... But Alex's growing desire to prove herself to him was forcing her to be far more brazen than she would have, normally.

And to be entirely honest, Alex was rather starting to enjoy herself.

"You reverse the flow by drawing the energy back into you," Declan was saying. "You did it earlier when you teleported us from the lakeshore, and then again when you got upset, but you can affect the current without doing either of those things. You just need to recognize the electricity for what it is and learn to conquer it."

She wondered if he could possibly be more vague. Conquer it? How was she supposed to *conquer* an intangible force she couldn't see and could hardly feel?

"Think of it like water," he continued. "Stop the flow and then pull it back toward you."

Alex tried to do as he asked. She concentrated on the feel of the current, the way it flowed into her and then back out through her palms. She tried to interrupt the process and grab hold of the current.

The flow reversed. She could feel the energy pouring back into her.

"Perfect," he said. "Now comes the hard part."

Uh-oh.

"I want you to ground out the charge."

"You want me to what now?" Alex knew she was on the verge of sounding like an idiot, but she really had no clue what he was talking about. She was beginning to wish she'd paid more attention in Mr. Mulvaney's Physical Science class last year.

"You need to disperse the charge into something that can't be affected by it. Get rid of it by grounding it."

Alex pulled one hand back, stopping the exchange of energy. She held her palm up and followed her instinct, transferring the energy from one form to another. Moments later, a crackling ball of electricity, roughly the size of a golf ball, hovered above her palm.

Declan's eyes grew wide. "What did you just do?"

She was staring at the roiling mass of static, surprised. "I don't know! I just knew I wanted to get rid of the energy and… then there it was."

The sphere of electricity hovering above her palm made her think of a different orb she'd seen only a few hours earlier… one that had been made of *fire* and wielded so skillfully by Brandt.

Before Alex could stop herself, she tensed.

The sphere in her hand started to expand, her anxiety fueling the electrical charge building in her palm. If she didn't get rid of the ball soon, there was no telling how large it would grow.

"What do I do now?" she asked, panic edging into her voice. "How do I get rid of it?"

"I don't…" Declan was shaking his head. "I don't even know… How are you doing that?"

Someone knocked at the door.

The sound made her jump. Her hand jerked and the orb was sent spiraling toward the ceiling. It collided with the ceiling fan, blowing out the bulbs, shattering the ornate glass cover and plunging the room into darkness.

In a blur of movement, Declan lunged forward and covered her body with his, knocking her back to the mattress as he tried to put himself between Alex and the shower of sparks and falling glass.

The door opened. Grayson's lanky form stood silhouetted in the low light of the hallway. "Alex? Declan? What's happened?"

"Are you alright?" Declan asked quietly. She could feel the whisper of his breath on her cheek.

Cinnamon. Woodsmoke.

"Fine," she said. "I'm fine."

Alex, once again pinned to the bed, took in Grayson's upside-down form. Her eyes were slowly growing accustomed to the darkness.

"It was my fault," she said, trying to free herself and sit up. "I, um, sort of fried the ceiling fan."

"Ah," said Grayson. He seemed less concerned once he realized they were both in one piece and that nothing was, you know, on fire. "Not to worry. It's not the first time something like that's happened around here. Just need to reset a breaker or two."

His blasé reaction surprised her. Even her aunt, who was so laid back about most things, would have been up in arms over something like this.

Declan's room was littered with pieces of his demolished bed frame and hunks of broken glass, but Grayson appeared to be taking it all in stride.

Just how often did Declan and the others blow something up around here, anyway?

"I was just coming to let you know… I'll be leaving for Washington tonight."

"DC? Tonight?" Declan echoed. "Why?"

The shadows hid Grayson's expression and his voice remained monotone. "Business. I'm afraid it can't wait."

Declan got to his feet. "Need a lift?"

"No," said Grayson. "I need you to stay here. I want you and Nathaniel to keep an eye on the others. Monty's already at the airport prepping the jet."

The *jet*? They had their own *jet*?

Of course they did.

"I'll be back in a few days. Sooner if I can manage it. I want you all to stay here at the cabin while I'm gone. Keep Alex safe and out of sight."

"What about Kenzie and Brian? They have school tomorrow," said Declan.

"They won't be going. It's Wednesday. Their break starts Friday afternoon, correct?"

"Yeah, I think so."

"Well, until then, if anyone asks, they both have the

flu. I'll send their headmaster an e-mail later," he said. "While I'm gone, keep up Alex's training. And no looking into Brandt, Declan. I mean it. I'll handle it."

Declan scowled. "Yes, sir."

Grayson turned to leave. Almost as an afterthought, he added, "Call my cell if you need me."

"Yes, sir."

Grayson disappeared down the hallway.

As Alex got to her feet, she noticed a small cut on Declan' neck, just above his collarbone. "You're hurt," she said, reaching up.

He caught her hand in his.

"It's nothing," he said. He held on to her for just a moment longer than necessary. She started to say something, but he cut her off. "Better go flip that breaker."

Declan dropped her hand and walked out, leaving her standing alone in his darkened bedroom.

TEN

Alex woke to the smell of coffee and blueberry muffins.

She wasn't sure which one had convinced her to leave behind the blissful dream she'd been clinging to—a dream of Connor and a life before she fried the computer lab—but eventually she managed to pry one eye open and fix a baleful glare on the digital clock atop the bedside table.

6:27 A.M.

The events of the previous day came back in a rush. Alex found herself wishing more than ever that she could find her way back into last night's dream. She settled instead for pulling the duvet over her head and groaning into a pillow.

After the abrupt end of her training session the night before, she'd made her way back to her guest room and discovered two suitcases, filled to bursting with clean clothes, toiletries, and half a dozen books plucked from Alex's to-read pile back home, sitting on the edge of the bed.

Cil had apparently stopped by while she and Declan had been down by the lake.

The initial rush of gratitude she'd felt at the sight of her belongings was soon replaced by an even stronger wave of disappointment. Her aunt hadn't even bothered to leave a note, much less find her to discuss things again before leaving. She'd just gone.

Then again, what was left to say?

Alex pushed down the duvet. She could hear movement downstairs and a light shone in the hallway on the other side of the bedroom door.

Might as well join them. She certainly wouldn't be going back to sleep any time soon.

Throwing on a pair of jeans and a long-sleeved shirt (her aunt had obviously known about the weather here and packed accordingly), she padded barefoot out into the hall.

The sounds of movement from below were soon joined by the ringing report of a dropped metal pan.

"Oops," she heard Kenzie say.

"Well if she wasn't up before, she is now. Good going, Red," Nathaniel's disembodied voice carried up the stairs.

"Heh. My bad."

Alex made her way down the stairs and into the kitchen... and then stopped dead in her tracks.

The massive kitchen was a culinary war zone.

The beautiful black granite countertops were covered with potato peels, eggshells and what looked to be muffin batter. At the center of the long room stood an immense island, one end covered with discarded pots and pans of various size that someone must have pulled from the dark mahogany cabinets before deciding on the ones currently atop the stove. Some strange green liquid sat in a blender next to the stainless steel fridge... and in the middle of the chaos stood Kenzie, Nathaniel, Declan, and Brian, each occupied with a different task.

Kenzie noticed her first. "Morning, sleepy-head!"

"Sorry if she woke you," said Brian. He was standing on his tiptoes pulling dishes from one of the overhead cabinets.

"No, no. It's okay. I was up," said Alex. "Can I... help?"

"Nope," Kenzie replied, pressing down two slices of bread in the toaster. "This is a finely oiled machine we've got running here. You just have a seat."

Surrounding the hulking island at the kitchen's center were six barstools. Alex carefully made her way toward one of them just as Brian went whizzing past her with a stack of plates in his arms. She deposited herself on a stool facing the melee and took in the scene.

Nathaniel appeared to be manning two of the kitchen's three stovetops—alternating his attention between a pan of bacon, two pans filled with eggs, a skillet filled with hash browns and a covered pot Alex couldn't see the contents of—while Kenzie carried baskets of what looked to be toast and muffins into the dining area. They were both far too awake for this side of seven A.M.

Declan, meanwhile, just stood there, a statue amidst the chaos, staring into the open refrigerator. Judging from the intensity of his gaze, the secrets of the universe were hiding somewhere behind the orange juice and would be revealed to him if he simply glared at the container for long enough.

He looked… Well, to be honest, he looked a little hungover.

Like Alex, the others were already dressed for the day, but Declan was still sporting the pair of flannel pants and faded gray shirt he'd slept in. He'd obviously not bothered to glance in a mirror yet, because his hair was sticking up at weird angles. Somehow, despite the odds, even dazed and disheveled looked good on him.

Kenzie sidled up behind Declan and cleared her throat. He flinched at the sound.

"Either move it, Decks, or hand me the eggs. Your choice."

Declan let the refrigerator door close and stalked toward the island at the center of the kitchen. "There better be some coffee left."

Kenzie shook her head and retrieved the egg carton. "How do you like 'em, Alex?"

Alex, who had been staring thoughtfully at the rumpled form of Declan while he filled his mug, started at the question. Like who? Declan? At the moment, she was fairly certain he was an ass. But maybe that was just her.

"I'm sorry?"

"Your eggs," said Kenzie. "How do you like them? Scrambled? Over-easy? Up on the sunny side?"

"Oh! Um, scrambled, please."

Kenzie deposited the egg carton on the counter next to where Nathaniel stood frying bacon. "Adam and Eve on a raft and wreck 'em!"

Nate smiled. "Two scrambled eggs, coming right up."

Next to Alex, Declan stood savoring his coffee as if it were a lifeline. Definitely a late night for that one.

"You want some?" he asked, holding up the mug she'd been staring at. His voice was still a little rough from sleep. Alex tried not to find it attractive.

Honestly.

She tried.

"I'd love some," she said. "Thanks."

Declan filled a mug with coffee and nudged the cream and sugar in her direction.

On the other side of the room, Kenzie raised an eyebrow. "Well at least last night's bender at The Corner Hole didn't fry your brain to the point you completely lost your manners. I suppose that's something."

"Corner Pocket," he corrected automatically. "And I told you, that's not where I went."

"So then where *did* you go?" asked Brian as he wandered back into the kitchen.

"On a little fact-finding mission."

"Yes." Kenzie plucked the lid off of the large pot and stirred its contents. "Because you can learn so *many* interesting things from Jim, Jack, José and Johnny. Full of information, they are."

"I thought Grayson didn't want us looking into the Brandt thing." Nathaniel set the bowl of eggs he'd been whisking back onto the counter.

"Yeah, well." Declan shrugged. "What the boss don't know won't hurt him."

"Uh-huh." Nathaniel turned his attention back to the stove. "Cause that's worked out so well for you in the past."

Brian pulled out the barstool next to Alex and slipped onto the seat. He looked back and forth between Declan and the out-of-reach coffee pot.

With a resigned sigh, Declan filled another mug, dropped in a spoonful of sugar, and slid it toward the boy. "I'm telling you, kid, you keep drinking that stuff and it's going to stunt your growth."

Brian just smiled and sipped at his coffee.

"So what did you find out?" asked Alex.

"Not a lot. Brandt's been off the grid for the last few months. Near as I can tell, our run-in with him at the bookstore was the first time anyone's seen him since January."

"So what's he been doing in the meantime?" asked Nathaniel.

"That, brother, is the $64,000 question."

"Maybe he was on vacation," said Brian.

Everyone turned to look at him.

"What?" he asked.

"Psychopaths-for-hire don't take vacations, Brain," said Kenzie. "Not one's like Brandt, anyhow... Not without leaving a trail of charred corpses along the way."

"Oh," he said slowly. "Right."

"On that note," said Kenzie. "Who's hungry?"

Alex was stuffed.

Eggs, muffins, bacon, coffee... Oh, and the pot on the

stove with the mystery contents? Turns out, it was filled with grits. So naturally she'd had some of those, too.

Why hadn't someone stopped her? All sense of self-restraint had flown out the window after the first bite. Now she was miserable.

Her sudden voracity wasn't all that surprising, given that her last meal had been a latte at Bayside Brews the previous afternoon.

The others had invited her to have dinner with them the night before, but Alex had declined and gone to bed early. Or at least, she'd tried to. In the end she'd simply lain there, staring at the ceiling and over-analyzing everything until exhaustion finally claimed her around two A.M.

At least the coffee was helping with the lack of sleep. She was fairly certain she'd consumed enough of the dark liquid to fuel a small country for at least a week.

"Alex! Just the girl I've been looking for," said a voice from above.

She set down the book she'd been trying in vain to focus on and leaned back on the couch to get a better look at the upstairs hallway. Nathaniel was leaning over the banister with a smile on his face.

"In the mood for a walk?" he asked. "Figured I'd give you the ten-cent tour. I'll show you the rest of the house and then maybe we can walk around the property. Thought you might like to know where everything is since you're probably going to be stuck here for a while."

"Yeah, that sounds great!" said Alex, springing to her feet. She'd say yes to just about anything right now if it got her off of the couch and out of her own head for a while.

Tour the property with Nate? That one was definitely a no-brainer. Besides, this would be the perfect chance to get to know him a little better.

Couldn't argue with that.

"Just let me get my shoes and—"

"Sorry, bro," Declan interrupted. He was making his way down the stairs, hair still wet from showering, clad in jeans and a black t-shirt, with the jacket he'd worn yesterday hanging from one hand. "She's already got plans."

"I—what?" she sputtered. "What plans do I have?"

"Training," he said. "You've still got to work on sticking the landing."

"Can't it wait an hour or two?" she protested. "We've got all day and Nate was going to show me around."

Declan came to a stop next to her and slipped on his jacket.

"Yeah, Decks. There's no reason the training can't wait a little while," said Nate. Alex didn't miss the look that passed between the two of them. "You can have her back in a couple hours."

Declan just smiled and snaked an arm around Alex's waist. "Catch you later, Nate."

They jumped.

One moment she was staring at a vexed Nathaniel, and the next she was dropping clumsily into the sand by the lakeshore. She rose to her feet, but then doubled over when a wave of nausea hit her like a freight train.

She really should not have had that second muffin.

"Easy there, champ," he said. "Probably should have warned you. Jumping on a full stomach... Well, it takes some getting used to."

Alex flattened one hand against her torso and took a deep breath.

Declan patted her hard on the back as he made his way past her and down the beach. "Regretting that second muffin yet?"

Her hand flew to her mouth. Oh, geez. For the love of God. No more talk of muffins.

"No," she lied as she forced herself upright. "But I do

regret that I didn't get to put on a pair of *shoes* before being abducted."

She lifted one bare foot and wiggled her toes for emphasis.

"You'll be fine," he called over his shoulder. "It's the beach. So you'll get a little sand between your toes... You're from Florida. You should be familiar with the sensation."

Alex trailed after him. "Says the guy in the Doc Martins. Do you have any idea how cold this wet sand is?"

Her voice was whiny even to her own ears.

She couldn't help it.

She'd *really* wanted to take that tour with Nathaniel. Leave it to Declan to keep that from happening. Her list of reasons to get back at him was growing longer by the hour.

If she could only figure out how...

Maybe she could enlist Kenzie to help her. Something told Alex the redhead would be more than happy to take on the assignment.

Alex winced. Her toes were already going numb.

Oh, yeah. His payback was going to be hell.

A thick, early-morning fog blanketed the lake and limited her sight to only a few feet in any direction. Declan had vanished into the mist up ahead. Alex began jogging in an attempt to catch up... then nearly collided with him when he appeared out of nowhere, headed in the opposite direction.

"Come on," he said, walking past her and disappearing into the fog again.

She did an about-face and followed him. After a while, they came to a stop at the same site they'd used for training the night before.

Declan paused by the remains of their fire and stooped to retrieve the towel Alex had dropped prior to launching herself at him. He looked over at her with a wolfish grin.

Alex rolled her eyes.

The jacket she'd borrowed from Kenzie, her socks, and her shoes were still where she'd left them, laying next to the fallen tree. She marched toward them.

Socks! Warm, wonderful socks...

Ew. Okay. So they were damp, slightly chilly socks.

She didn't care. They were still socks.

As she finished tying her laces, she realized she should probably thank Declan for bringing her back to her shoes.

That was about the time he teleported, leaving her alone on the lakeshore.

Alex sighed, wondering if all of their training sessions were destined to leave her waiting alone on a beach for long periods of time.

Declan returned a moment later, minus the towel. He must have taken it back to the house. She wondered vaguely why Declan didn't just teleport everywhere. It sure beat walking.

"Better?" he asked her.

"Much. Thank you." Alex slipped into the jacket. "So what's the plan, Yoda? You're not going to make me stand on my hands while I try to levitate rocks, are you?"

"Was that a *Star Wars* reference?" Declan called over his shoulder. He was already off and walking down the shore again. "You are a complete dork, you know that?"

"Hey now. *The Empire Strikes Back* is a classic. Besides. *You're* the one who knew what I was referring to," she said, catching up and falling in to step beside him.

"Touché," he said. "No rocks just yet."

"Where are we headed?" she asked.

"Nowhere in particular."

"Nowhere?"

"Nope."

"Is this some sort of test?" she asked. "Some part of the training?"

"What, this? This is a walk down the beach." He shoved his hands into his pockets.

"But you said we were going to train." Alex stopped walking. After a moment, so did Declan. "What's so important about a walk on the beach that it couldn't wait for me to take a tour with Nate?"

He shrugged. "If you're so ready to leave, go ahead. I'm not keeping you here. Jump. You'll be back at the cabin in no time."

Alex considered it. Then she considered the dense fog covering the lake. If she jumped and ended up in the water, chances were good she wouldn't be able to see the right strip of shoreline in order to swim back. She could end up anywhere.

Her mind made up, she spun on her heel and started walking back in the direction of the cabin.

"Alex," Declan called.

"What?"

"I'll train you."

Alex hesitated. Declan closed the distance between them and held out his hand.

"Come with me," he said.

It was a request, not an order.

She thought of the bookstore. Of Declan's outstretched hand and his plea for her to trust him. The situations were entirely different, but for some reason, his eyes held the same weight of urgency now as they had then.

And just like in the bookstore, Alex couldn't say no.

She took his hand… and they jumped.

This time they landed in the middle of a circular clearing surrounded on all sides by towering spruce trees. For once, Declan had materialized relatively close to the ground and she was able to keep from losing her balance.

She took in her surroundings. "Are we still near the cabin?"

"About half a mile from it, but yeah." He let go of her hand. "This is where we usually go to train."

"Half a mile, huh?" she repeated. The figure made her curious. "Just how far can we jump?"

"As far as we want to."

"Really?"

"Really."

Declan appeared to be mulling something over. Before Alex could analyze what that look might mean, he took hold of her shoulders and they jumped again.

Eleven

It was too cold for April.

Grayson shifted his weight on the park bench, glancing up from the newspaper he wasn't reading to look across the rippling waters of the Tidal Basin. He was rewarded with a clear view of the Washington Monument through the blossoming cherry trees.

What was taking Bartlett so long?

Flipping the page, he pretended to focus on an article about the government's plan to subsidize alternative energy initiatives.

Grayson wasn't a man prone to fidgeting. The longer he sat there, however, the more restless he became. He needed this intel and Bartlett was the only one of his contacts who had access to it anymore. Everyone else had either died since he left the Agency, or retired to someplace tropical. He often wished he could do the same.

The Bahamas were probably nice this time of year.

Someone settled onto the seat next to him, leaned back, and propped their elbows on the back of the bench.

"Grayson," the fair-haired man said casually.

"Bartlett," Grayson replied.

This cloak-and-dagger bullshit was beyond ridiculous, but the younger man insisted on it. It left Grayson longing for the old days when he could have settled all this with a phone call.

"We didn't have anything recent in the system for

Parker," said Bartlett. "Just the standard profile and current address."

Grayson nodded.

That was good news. It was Agency policy to keep tabs on the offspring of known Variants, which explained the existence of a profile, but they wouldn't create an active file for Alex until she did something to warrant the attention. Or until her 18th birthday rolled around and they sent an agent after her to find out whether or not she'd inherited the gift.

Keeping it a secret after that would be pretty much impossible.

The question of *which* gift Alex actually possessed, however, was still up for debate. Until Grayson knew for certain, keeping her hidden from the all-seeing eyes of the Agency would be crucial. He just hoped the incident with Brandt wouldn't reach their attention before he could sort it all out.

Grayson folded his newspaper. "And the other name I asked you about?"

Bartlett had intentionally kept his gaze on the water up until this point, but now he turned and openly addressed Grayson. "That one's a bit more interesting."

Reaching into the messenger bag he'd set on the ground beside him, Bartlett withdrew a tablet. He flipped open the cover, turned it on and handed it to Grayson.

The older man read the screen and frowned. "That's not possible."

"You know how thorough they are. It's been confirmed six ways to Sunday," he said. "Are you sure you got your facts right?"

Grayson didn't answer. Setting the tablet on the bench, he rose to his feet and started for his car.

Declan managed a graceful landing.

Alex, not so much.

"You really ought to start warning me before you do that," she said, dusting off her jeans.

They were surrounded by a sea of green.

Undulating hills stretched out in every direction, speckled here and there with the brilliant yellow of buttercups in bloom, hedgerows, low stone walls and the occasional elm and alder trees. Above them, the sun was high in the sky—suggesting that wherever they were, it was probably early afternoon—and glinted off the waters of a small stream on the other side of the knoll on which they had landed.

A chilly breeze rippled through the grass. Other than a herd of sheep that dotted the hillside nearly half a mile in the distance, she and Declan appeared to be the only souls around.

It was beautiful.

"Where are we?" she breathed.

"Ireland."

"Wait... *What*? But... But I don't have my passport!"

That earned her a funny look from Declan. "I teleport you half-way around the planet, and your first reaction is to worry about your *passport*?"

"Well, what if we get stopped by a cop or something?"

"You plan on engaging in some sort of criminal activity while we're here?" Declan grinned. "Not that I mind, I'd just like a heads up."

"Very funny," Alex mumbled. "You may have forgotten, but some of us are still working on 'sticking the landing.' What would I do if I got stuck here and had no explanation as to how I arrived? How would I ever get back home?"

"And a passport with no entry stamp is going to help you... how, exactly?"

Okay, so he had a point. Damn him and his cunning use of logic.

He gave another low, rumbling laugh. "Would you just relax and enjoy the view? I can promise you the sheep won't report you for illegal immigration before we make it back home."

Alex smiled in spite of herself. Maybe she *was* being a little ridiculous.

And she had to admit. You really couldn't beat this view.

"Besides," he continued. "All you'd have to do is jump. Even if you didn't get the destination you aimed for, there's only a few places you could end up. Most of them would get you back to the cabin... One way or another."

Declan sat down, resting his arms on his knees as he gazed out over the scene. He plucked a blade of glass and began to roll it between his fingers.

"This used to belong to my family," he said after a while.

Alex sank into the grass beside him.

"After my parents died and Grayson took us in, the property went into probate. Grayson eventually tried to settle my parents debts and get it back, but by then it had been sold."

"So... this is where you were born?"

"Aye," he said, with a lilt to his speech and a hint of a smile. "This is where I was born."

"It's amazing."

"That it is." He dropped the accent. "I come here when I need to think."

She studied him as he stared off into the distance.

Alex had known him for less than 24 hours, but she was beginning to think that, even if she had the next 24 years, she'd probably never figure the guy out.

One moment, he was being a complete ass and doing

everything he could to get under her skin... And the next, he was offering her coffee and transporting them across an entire ocean just so he could share with her this magnificent place he'd once called home. The sudden changes in his attitude were giving her whiplash.

He plucked another blade of grass and began ripping it into smaller pieces.

"Declan," she said.

He turned to face her.

Alex grimaced. "I... I just realized I never said thank you."

"For what?"

"For saving me yesterday," she said. "For getting me out of the bookstore. I owe you more than I can ever repay you, Declan. You saved my life. And I never even *thanked* you... You must think I'm awful."

His mouth opened and closed, then opened and closed again. He couldn't seem to decide upon a reply. Finally, he gave up and became very interested in the herd of sheep grazing off in the distance.

No wonder Declan couldn't stand her. He'd risked his life to save hers, and she'd been so caught up in her *own* drama, that she'd failed to even acknowledge it.

"You ready to start training?" he asked suddenly.

"Train?" she said. "Here?"

The edge of worry that had crept into her voice had less to do with her fear of jumping and more to do with the possibility that she would end up in the middle of a fog-covered lake, three thousand miles from Declan, on her first attempt.

"We can practice here just as easily as we can at home, so why not?" he said, once more on his feet. "And as an added bonus, there's this really great pub in town we can hit up when we're through."

She looked at him askance.

"What?" He feigned innocence. "They serve food, too, y'know. By the time we finish, that second muffin's going to be a distant memory. Jumping tends to work up an appetite."

He offered her a hand. Alex tried to ignore the electric current that spilled through her palm as she accepted his help and climbed to her feet. She wasn't sure what was more unsettling—the sensation itself, or the fact that she was starting to enjoy the feel of it.

Not that she planned on admitting that to Declan.

Ever.

"Okay," he said, stepping back a few feet. "Jump."

"That's it?" she asked, incredulous. "Just 'jump'? No advice this time? No words of wisdom?"

"Try not to fall in the lake again."

"That's so helpful, Declan. Thanks."

Alex selected a location at the bottom of the hill and tried to call up the memory of how it felt when she teleported. The ensuing jump forced her eyes closed and she surrendered to the pressure.

As she started to disappear, she congratulated herself. See? She totally had this down.

That was easy enough, she thought.

Something was wrong. The cool, dry air of the pasture now held an added weight. Everything felt damp.

Alex landed with a stumble, opened her eyes and groaned. She was standing in the middle of the training field again. How was it that Declan made this look so easy?

Remembering what she'd been told about selecting a destination, she closed her eyes and tried again. This time she concentrated on making it back to Declan.

Seconds later, she landed in a heap on Declan's unmade bed.

Alex sat up, looked around, realized where she was and swallowed hard. She prayed Declan wouldn't find out about this little side-trip. The smug smile it would elicit wasn't something Alex wanted to see at the moment.

The room looked roughly the same as it had yesterday, minus the signs of destruction.

Band logos lined the walls, a mixture of punk rock, metal and alt-country. Among them, Alex noticed souvenir concert posters from bands like the Dropkick Murphys and Avenged Sevenfold, Flogging Molly and Lucero.

It was an odd mix, but somehow, it was all so very Declan.

The locations of the concerts ranged from Alaska to Ireland, from Tupelo to Tokyo. She supposed when you could zap yourself there in an instant, no concert could ever be *too far*.

The thought made her smile.

Her gaze traveled to the bookshelf next to his closet. Alex was of the belief that you could tell a lot about a person by the books they kept within reach, on the shelf closest to eye-level.

She skimmed a few of the titles. Pirsig's *Zen and the Art of Motorcycle Maintenance*, Sun Tzu's *The Art of War*, Milton's *Paradise Lost*... Definitely not what she'd been expecting.

The door to the adjoining bathroom stood open. She could still smell whatever cologne it was Declan had used after he'd showered this morning.

She closed her eyes and inhaled. It was dark, it was musky, and it smelled like... Like Declan. The scent was intoxicating.

It had his room smelling much better than most of the guy's bedrooms she'd been in, in the past. Not that she'd ventured into the bedrooms of all that many guys. Just quick sojourns into those of Cassie's brothers and Connor's, really. And their rooms had always reeked of gym clothes and stale pizza.

This was almost heavenly in comparison.

Alex snapped out of it. She was supposed to be doing something right now.

Jumping. Ireland. Right.

What was *in* that cologne? Geez. It was like a drug. She took another appreciative sniff before she could stop herself, nearly jumping out of her skin when Declan's bedroom door creaked open.

"Hi, Alex." Brian was smiling shyly at her from the doorway.

"Brian!" Alex scrambled off the broken bed, looking guilty despite her relative innocence. "Hi. I was just—"

"It's okay," he said, still hanging onto the doorknob. "I know you guys are training and that you got here by accident. I saw it all last night."

It took her a moment to realize that he was referring to one of his visions.

"Can you do me a favor and tell Declan that my dad called and wants him to call him back as soon as he can? He's called three times so far and he's getting angry about Declan not answering his cell," he said.

"No problem," she said. "I'll make sure he gets the message."

He started to leave, but then paused. Turning back around, he smiled and said, "I'm glad you're finally here, Alex. I always knew I'd like you."

"Finally here?" she echoed. It was obvious he wasn't referring to her sudden arrival in Declan's bedroom. "You had a vision that I was coming?"

Brian's grin faltered. "Erm. I mean… Well, yeah. It was a long time ago. Couple of years, I think."

Curiosity had taken hold. "Can you tell me what you saw?"

The boy shoved his hands into his pockets and looked down, swaying back and forth on his heels. "It wasn't much. I was in a park at night. You were there. So were Nate and Declan. We were… We were having a picnic!" he said. "That's what it was. A picnic."

"A picnic?" Alex repeated. "At night?"

Brian shrugged.

Whatever it was Brian had seen, it hadn't been a picnic. Alex was hardly a human lie detector, but it didn't take much to realize Brian had fabricated that last part. She decided to let it be. It was obviously something he didn't want to talk about.

"I didn't think you could see your own future," she said.

"Dad can't," he admitted. "But I can. I haven't seen much. And most of it hasn't come true yet. But I still see things sometimes."

Alex appraised the boy standing in front of her. He was, what, ten? Eleven, maybe? And his powers had started manifesting years earlier.

The others seemed to have a decent command of their abilities as well and Kenzie looked to be the same age as she was. What, exactly, did that make Alex? A late bloomer?

Well, that was embarrassing.

"You should probably get back to Declan before he starts to worry about you," said Brian

"Declan? Worry about me? Somehow I doubt that."

"I don't know. I think you're starting to grow on him."

She looked at the boy, bemused. "How can you tell?"

Brian's smile returned as he reached for the doorknob. "See you later, Alex."

"Bye, Brian."

The door closed and Alex once again found herself alone in Declan's bedroom. Time to go. Hoping the third time would be a charm, she readied herself to try again.

It's okay. You can do this. Just concentrate. Ireland… Green fields… A chilly breeze…

Alex jumped... and found herself on the lakeshore.

Crap.

This might take a while.

"Yo, Nate!"

Thunk!

"Son of a..." Nate rubbed his forehead. The sudden shout had caused him to drop the wrench he'd been holding—the same one that had just been hovering a few inches above his face as he tightened the final bolt of a newly installed exhaust tip. He reached for the fallen tool with a grimace. "Dammit, Kenzie."

A chuckle came from somewhere near the open garage door. With a sigh, Nate slid out from beneath the car.

Using his gift, he slowly lowered the rear end of the vehicle back to the ground. He was simply lucky he hadn't lost his concentration and let the car fall when Kenzie startled him.

From now on, he'd be doing his repairs the old fashioned way. With a floor jack.

Kenzie was resting on the hood of his half-restored, black 1970 Dodge Charger, arms crossed, looking way too amused for his liking.

"I'm sorry," she said, still grinning.

That's funny. She didn't *sound* sorry.

He looked pointedly at Kenzie. The Charger was the only thing in this world that was truly his own. It was his baby. His love. His pride and joy.

And Kenzie was sitting on it.

"Off the car."

"Sir, yes sir!" She gave a mock salute and slid off the hood.

"What do you want, Red?" he asked, making his way to the work bench and hanging the wrench back on the peg board with a little more force than necessary. "Shouldn't you be in the house doing homework right now? Surely Brian's in there somewhere for you to annoy."

She harrumphed. "I see *someone's* in a good mood."

Nate closed his eyes and exhaled. Kenzie wasn't the one he ought to be snapping at.

Declan, on the other hand...

He flashed back to that morning, to Declan slipping his arm around Alex's waist before teleporting them both to God knows where, and the smug smile on his face as he did it.

"Catch you later, Nate."

Jackass.

Nate opened his eyes again. "Sorry. I'm just a little... frustrated."

"I see. And would that frustration be of the emotional variety, the professional..." Kenzie paused for effect. He turned to face her and she waggled her eyebrows. "Or the sexual?"

Nate rolled his eyes. He was not having this conversation with Kenzie.

"Oh, come on, Nate," she said as she sidled up next to him. She snatched a lug nut from the worktop and threw it in the air.

Toss, catch. Toss, catch.

"I don't have to be a telepath to see that you like her."

Toss, catch. Toss—

He plucked the lug nut from the air and placed it back on the workbench.

Nate was finding himself more and more grateful, of late, that he'd mastered the art of keeping Kenzie out of his head. If she ever learned the truth about what he felt for Alex—if she ever found out what *really* happened during that year he'd spent in Seattle—they'd *all* be in trouble.

He busied himself with putting away tools. "Even if I did—and I'm not saying I do—it wouldn't make a difference. She'll just end up falling for Declan, anyway."

"Why, did Brian see something?" she sounded incredulous. "Or are you having visions now, too?"

If she only knew.

Kenzie shook her head. "Honestly, after the way he reacted last night when he found out who she was… Well, I don't think wine and roses are exactly on the agenda for those two. If anything, he'll probably do everything he can to drive her nuts." The look she gave him was beseeching. "You know how Declan can be. And I *like* Alex. I'd prefer to keep her around, not drive her away. Which is why *you* need to be the one to step in and sweep the little lady off her feet."

He gave a laugh.

There wasn't much humor in it.

"And how would I go about doing that, exactly?" He walked back to the Charger and popped the hood, trying to appear disinterested.

He probably shouldn't be humoring her. It wasn't like it could actually work.

Unfortunately for Nate, his treasonous heart couldn't resist the urge.

Kenzie smiled. "You just be your charming self and leave the rest to me."

Twelve

Nearly five minutes had passed and Alex still hadn't reappeared.

Great. Now Declan was going to have to go searching for her. He really hoped she hadn't landed in the lake again. The prospect of helping her back to shore in that dense fog wasn't exactly an enticing one.

Although... such an act of heroism wouldn't be without its perks.

A small voice in the back of his thoughts suggested that the sight of an angry, soaking-wet Alex wouldn't be *entirely* unwelcome. And she was kind of cute when she was annoyed with him. There was something about the way she held her mouth and the fiery look that shined in her eyes...

He smiled at the mental image before he could stop himself.

That was a road he really shouldn't be headed down.

Still, every moment that passed made it more and more likely she'd fallen in the lake during an attempt to return.

He sighed.

Why had he even brought her to Kilkenny in the first place?

It had taken him a grand total of five seconds to mull it over and a split-second to make the trip... Followed by the last twenty minutes, every one of which he'd spent trying to explain to himself *why* he'd done it.

These fields were his refuge. His home.

And she was…. Well, she was *Alex Parker*. The girl who'd destroyed his family. The girl who had taken his home away from him.

He'd spent the last twelve years hating her—a girl he hardly knew.

In that respect, it was easy to despise her. And it was even easier to blame her for what had happened.

He didn't know her. Could barely remember her, except as some whiny, pigtailed little girl that the adults always bent over backwards to please—and eventually laid down their lives to protect.

No, he hadn't known her. But he'd imagined what sort of girl she'd probably grown into. No doubt she'd become a spoiled princess who expected the world on a silver platter and pitched a fit when it wasn't handed right over. A girl who thought nothing of others and only of herself.

…A girl he was having trouble reconciling with the one he'd finally met.

Not that Declan was ready to let go of his resentment altogether. At least, not just yet.

The jury was still out on Alex Parker.

Besides. Dropping that particular grudge would require admitting that his sister had been right about something.

And that just wasn't going to happen.

Alex reappeared at the bottom of the hill—completely dry, much to the disappointment of that traitorous inner voice—with a triumphant smile on her face. She even managed to nail the landing without stumbling.

"I did it!" she said, thrusting her arms in the air. "*Yes!*"

"What took so long?" he called down to her. "Make a few stops along the way?"

"Hey," she said, defensive of her celebratory mood. "I made it here, didn't I? And I didn't even have to go swimming first!" Alex laughed. "I'd say that's progress!"

She started to climb the hill.

"Hold it!"

Alex came to a halt and sent him a questioning look.

"Jump."

Her smile faltered. "I was afraid you were going to say that."

Alex reappeared at his side with her eyes closed and a pinched expression that suggested she might be bracing for an impact. She peeked one eye open, caught sight of him staring at her, and let out a squeal of delight.

God help him.

"Back to the bottom of the hill," he ordered.

"What, again?"

"Again."

She jumped to the bottom of the hill and back again. "Satisfied?" she asked.

He crossed his arms over his chest. "Again."

She sighed and disappeared.

"How about *now*?" The shout had come from somewhere in the distance. Glancing toward the sound, Declan found her standing beneath an alder tree a few hundred feet away.

Alex reappeared at his side.

"Yeah, okay," he said. "Now I'm happy."

The triumphant smile returned.

"Tired yet?" he asked.

"Nope."

Huh. Well, that was odd. After making so many jumps, the girl ought to be exhausted.

"Oh!" she said suddenly. "Before I forget! Brian said Grayson wants you to call him ASAP."

"*Brian* said? When did you see...?" he trailed off.

It was still early. Brian should have been at the house working on schoolwork. And that could only mean one thing.

He smirked. "You ended up in my bed again, didn't you? Shame I wasn't there to see it."

The expression on Alex's face was priceless. She looked like she'd just swallowed a bug.

He fished his cell phone from the pocket of his jeans.

Three missed calls.

So much for lunch at the pub. Shame. He'd been looking forward to that pint of Smithwick's.

"Alright, we're going to have to finish this later," he said. "Back to the cabin. I don't need the roaming charges."

Alex snorted in amusement. Giving him a small wave, she disappeared.

Declan shook his head, smiling, and followed her.

There had to be an easier way to do this.

"Would you sit still?" asked Kenzie, exasperated. "You're acting like I'm about to suck your brain out through your ears."

For all Alex knew, that's exactly what was about to happen.

She stared uncertainly up at the redhead. Alex was seated cross-legged on the living room floor while Kenzie knelt before her, a hand on either side of Alex's face, index and middle fingers resting at her temples.

"Kenzie, I really don't think—"

"Hush," she said. "I need to concentrate."

After a moment of silence, Kenzie pulled a face. "This isn't working. Oh! I know!" She closed her eyes again and made the same 'om' sound Alex usually associated with meditating Buddhists.

Declan and Brian chose that moment to walk into the upstairs hallway.

"What... the *hell*... are you two doing?" asked an amused Declan from somewhere above her.

Kenzie bristled. "*I*, big brother, am attempting to do my good deed for the day. Alex, on the other hand, is resisting my efforts to help."

"I would, too, if it involved you digging around in my head," said Declan as he started down the stairs. Brian trailed a few feet behind him. "Alex, what were you thinking?"

To be honest, she was sort of wondering that herself at the moment.

"I was hoping she could—" Alex had turned her head to the side in order to answer Declan. Kenzie turned it back. Alex sighed. "Hoping she could help me remember a phone number."

Alex's cell phone had been ruined during yesterday's splashdown in the lake. She couldn't even get it to turn back on, much less access her contact list. Not that losing her phone bothered her all that much. To be honest, after frying the last three, she was really starting to wonder what the point was in even carrying one.

"Ever heard of a phone book?" asked Declan, making his way into her line of sight as he took a seat on the couch. Brian dropped down next to him.

"Cell phone number," she clarified. "And I know it... I just can't remember it."

"Got it!" Kenzie shouted. She reached for the notepad she'd set aside earlier and scribbled down a number. "Man, I'm good."

She handed the notepad to Alex. The number to Cassie's cell stared back at her. Huh. She'd actually found it.

"Wow, thanks," said Alex. "That was... impressive."

"Thank you, thank you. Really, now," said Kenzie. "Don't applaud. Just throw money."

"Who is it you plan on calling?" asked Declan. "You're supposed to be in hiding, in case you've forgotten."

"Of course I haven't forgotten," said Alex, grabbing the portable phone off of the end table. "It's my friend Cassie. If I *don't* call her, we'll have a much bigger problem on our hands, trust me. As it is, she's probably not buying whatever story it is my Aunt's using to explain my sudden disappearance. I just want to make sure she knows I'm fine and not to worry."

Declan still didn't seem keen on the idea, but he remained quiet as she dialed.

"So what did the boss want?" Kenzie asked Declan.

Ringing.

"He met with Bartlett this morning."

"And?" Nathaniel had walked in through the front door, his arms and clothes spotted with engine grease.

More ringing.

Come on, Cassie. Answer.

"And," Declan continued. "According to the Agency files, Brandt's been dead since January."

"What?" asked Alex, covering the mouthpiece. "How's that possible?"

"It's not," he said. "Someone obviously screwed up."

On the other end of the line, a voice answered.

But not the voice Alex had been expecting.

"Hello, Alex. So very nice to see you made it out alive. You'll have to tell me how you did that sometime."

She nearly dropped the phone. "B-Brandt."

Hearing the tremor in her voice, Declan's head swiveled toward her.

"Ahh, so you've learned my name!" Brandt sounded pleased. "I suppose I shouldn't be too surprised, given the sort of company you're keeping these days. Tell me. How *is* my old pal Grayson?"

"What have you done with her?" Alex asked in a whisper.

Realizing what was happening, Declan gestured quickly

toward Nate, then reached forward and snatched up the paper with Cassie's cell number scrawled on it. He pulled the cell phone from his pocket.

"Speaker," Nate ordered, moving swiftly in her direction.

Climbing unsteadily to her feet, Alex held out the phone and put the call on speakerphone. If Cassie got hurt over this, Alex would never forgive herself.

"You mean the beautiful Cassandra?" Brandt sounded smug. "Oh, she's safe enough for the moment, don't worry, my pet."

Alex could hear muffled sounds in the background.

Across from her, Declan was still glaring down at his cell. He held the phone in a white-knuckle grip as his fingers moved furiously across the screen.

"Prove it," said Alex with as much conviction as she could muster. "I want to talk to her."

She heard shuffling and what sounded like a gag being pulled from her friend's mouth. "Alex?"

"Cass!" Alex fought back a sob. There'd be time for that later. Not now. "Are you okay? Has he hurt you?"

"I'm fine," her voice was raspy. "But Alex… Whatever he wants… Don't give it to him. Promise me you won't—"

"See?" Brandt's voice came back on the line. "She's the picture of health. And she'll stay that way, just so long as you do as I say."

"What do you want me to do?"

"I want you to meet me at your favorite place. The one you like to escape to every night just before dusk," he said.

Declan glanced up from the screen of his cell phone long enough to send her a questioning stare.

He might have been clueless, but Alex knew exactly which place Brandt was referring to.

"When?" she asked.

"Why, at sunset, of course," he replied. "I can't think of a more picturesque place to spend the evening."

Alex grimaced. Sunset. Back home, that would happen sometime between seven-thirty and eight P.M. That meant Cassie would be with him for another six hours, at least.

I'm so sorry, Cass.

"Why not meet now?" she ventured. "Why wait until tonight?"

"Sorry, my pet," said Brandt. "I've got some rather pressing matters to attend to this afternoon. I'm sure you understand."

She scrambled for an idea... Something—*anything*—that would make Brandt move up the timetable.

"Speaking of which," he continued. "I really must be going."

"No, wait—"

"One last thing, pet," he said. "I'm sure you've read enough novels and seen enough action films to guess what my one stipulation for tonight's meeting is..."

Alex swallowed. "You want me to come alone."

"*Very* good, pet. Knew you were a smart one. Who says public education in this country is lacking? I'll see you tonight."

The line went dead. Alex dropped the phone and sank to her knees, her heart racing.

"Did you get it?" Kenzie asked Declan.

Declan cursed and looked up from his cell phone. "No. Narrowed it down to northern Florida. That's as far as it got."

Alex looked numbly back and forth between the two of them.

He held up his cell. "Tracing program. I was using it to track your friend's phone."

She probably should have been surprised that there was an app for that, but she just didn't have the energy.

Nathaniel knelt beside her. "Where is it he wants to meet, Alex? What place was he talking about?"

Alex didn't answer.

What was she going to tell them?

She couldn't risk the others knowing where she was headed. If they showed up... If Brandt thought she hadn't come alone... There's no telling what he might do to Cassie.

Remembering that she was sitting in the room with a telepath, Alex slammed up the mental walls Kenzie had taught her to create before she'd gone fishing in her thoughts earlier. Alex was suddenly grateful for the impromptu lesson. She'd taught her the trick so that Alex could hide from Kenzie anything she didn't want the other girl to see. She didn't think she'd be using it again quite so soon.

Alex looked up. They were all staring at her expectantly.

"The... the pier," she said finally. "I go there to watch the sunset."

Declan studied her. He wasn't buying it. "Okay. Now where does he *really* want to meet?"

Fearing she might drown beneath the weight of his stare, Alex did the only thing she could do. She jumped.

She landed in the middle of the training field. Lucky, she supposed, since she hadn't actually had a destination in mind when she'd left. But considering what she *did* have in mind, this location worked out perfectly.

Declan would probably come looking for her... She just hoped he would be operating on the assumption that she'd gone back home instead of sticking around. As much as she wanted to spend the next six hours searching for the place Brandt was keeping Cassie, Alex knew she'd be better served preparing for tonight's meeting instead.

At the moment, the only thing she had going for her was her ability to jump... But being able to run away wasn't going to help Cassie. What she *needed* was to hold her own offensively against Brandt.

She needed to keep training. With or without Declan.

And she knew just where to start.

Focusing her anger, frustration and fear into something a little more destructive, Alex raised both hands and channeled the currents into the same churning mass she'd created the night before in Declan's bedroom. In no time, the sphere expanded to the size of a basketball. With a little effort, she sent it spiraling across the field. It collided with one of the gigantic spruce trees that lined the clearing. The impact echoed through the forest, splitting the tree through the middle. The top half of the tree wavered unsteadily from side to side before falling to the ground with a thundering crash.

There was no way they hadn't heard that.

Smooth, Alex. Real smooth.

So much for her hiding place.

Declan materialized a few yards away.

"Are you okay?" he asked, taking in the destruction. "Wait... Did *you* do that?"

Alex didn't answer him. Instead she moved so that Declan wouldn't be in her line of fire and then started building up another charge. She let it fly toward the fallen tree. Its branches shuddered and cracked, reeling from the force of the blow. In the place where the sphere had made contact, there remained nothing but a charred patch of earth.

Declan looked at her sharply.

The strange feeling of detachment that had encased Alex's emotions the moment she'd heard Brandt's voice on the line, shattered.

Alex no longer felt numb.

She knew what she had to do.

"What do you think you're doing?" he asked. His tone was practically dripping with disapproval.

The rush of anger that washed over her was nearly overpowering. Alex could feel it coursing through her veins, searching for an outlet.

"Training," she said, as evenly as she could manage. "What does it look like?"

Declan's brow furrowed. There's no way he hadn't sensed the sudden change in her mood.

"It looks like you're planning to get yourself killed," he said slowly.

"I'm *planning* on getting my friend back," she replied, channeling her emotions into another charge. Instead of letting this one go, she focused on manipulating its size. Larger, smaller. Larger, smaller. It was amazing how easily all this was coming to her now.

"Not alone," he said. "You're no match for him by yourself, Lex."

Lex? She might have enjoyed the intimate sound of the name on his lips, under different circumstances. It felt wrong to hear it from him now.

It was going to take more than Declan to stop her from going through with this.

Brandt had Cassie. And it was all Alex's fault.

The thought sent another wave of anger coursing through her. With a cry of frustration, she sent the charge spiraling toward what remained of the fallen tree. It disintegrated with a deafening report.

Her arms fell to her sides and she turned to face him.

"I'm sorry, Declan," she said. "I have to do this. And I have to do it alone."

"Alex, no!" Declan lunged for her as she started her jump.

He wasn't fast enough.

As the light engulfed her, she registered the look of panic in Declan's eyes... and prayed she was making the right decision.

THIRTEEN

"Come on, Brian," Declan urged. "You can do this."

The boy's expression was pained. "I *want to*, Declan! Honest! I just can't see her!"

Declan clenched and unclenched his fists as he struggled to keep his patience. "Then try harder!"

"*Declan*!" Kenzie admonished. "Can't you see he's trying? What pre-cog have you ever met that can conjure a vision on command?"

Declan began pacing the length of the cabin's great room. Kenzie couldn't remember the last time he'd been this worked up. And it wasn't just him. Alex's disappearance had left them *all* on edge. Even Nate was rattled.

"We all want to find her, Declan," said Kenzie. "But yelling at Brian isn't going to get us to her any faster."

An afternoon spent canvassing Alex's hometown had resulted in no leads and two increasingly agitated brothers. They'd turned to Brian as a last resort. The poor kid had been trying to force a vision for nearly an hour with no results. It didn't help that Declan and Nathaniel had been hovering over him the entire time.

She cast a glance out the window. The sun was close to setting. They were running out of time.

Declan ceased pacing and followed her gaze. He seemed to reach a decision.

Kenzie watched as he approached the door to

Grayson's office and tried the doorknob. Locked. Declan narrowed his eyes and disappeared.

Grayson's office was *beyond* off limits. Surely he hadn't…

A crash echoed through the house. Her brother reappeared a moment later with Grayson's Beretta in his hand. The one the boss kept in his desk. His *locked* desk.

"Declan, what the hell?" said Nate, catching sight of the gun.

"Whoa. Not a good idea, Decks," said Kenzie, jumping to her feet.

Had he *completely* lost his mind?

"I'm not just going to sit here and do nothing while Alex is off somewhere getting herself killed," said Declan. He checked the chamber for a round, then tucked the pistol into the back of his jeans and pulled on his jacket. "If the meet's going to take place somewhere she goes every night, then it's probably within walking distance of her house. I'll just have to keep wandering around until I find it. Call me if you learn anything."

"Declan, wait!" said Brian. "Maybe… Maybe if I had something of hers. Something she touched recently."

Declan appraised the boy. "Fine," he said. "I'll be right back,"

He jumped.

"You really think that will help you see her?" asked Kenzie.

Brian shrugged. "It couldn't hurt… and it always seems to work for those psychics on TV."

They sat in silence while they waited for Declan to return.

"Someone needs to call Grayson and tell him what's happened," said Nate.

Declan reappeared with Alex's waterlogged cell phone in one hand.

"Oh yeah, Nate," said Declan, handing the phone to

Brian. "That's an excellent idea. I can hear the conversation now. *'Sorry, boss, but we lost Alex. Oh and by the way, she's about to get herself flambéed by the one guy on the planet you specifically told us to keep her away from.'* That should go over well."

Nate glared at him. "He should know, Decks."

"What can he possibly do from DC?" Declan continued. "Even if I went and got him, what could Grayson do in this situation that we couldn't?"

"I don't know," said Nate. "*Something.* He knows Brandt better than we do. Maybe he can help us figure out what his end game is."

Kenzie could feel the tension in the room mounting.

"Enough," she said, feeling like the lone voice of reason in a sea of testosterone and male ego. "Fighting with each other won't solve anything."

Declan ignored her. "Why is it, Nate, that you are always so quick to defend the man? Always so blindly following his orders? He's not perfect, you know."

Nate looked like he was struggling not to rise to the bait. Good for him. Her brother was being an idiot. And if there was one thing she'd learned by having Declan as a brother, it was that there was never any point in arguing with an idiot.

Besides. Kenzie was starting to get the feeling that this argument had nothing to do with Grayson and everything to do with Alex.

"Always the golden boy," Declan prodded.

"Guys," said Brian.

"Always the good little soldier."

"Screw you."

"Ever since you got back from Seattle. What the hell happened to you, man?"

"*Guys!*"

Three pairs of eyes turned toward Brian.

"I saw her," he said. His face was ashen behind his too-large glasses. "I know where they're going to meet."

As far as last sunsets went, this one was pretty spectacular.

The sky above was aflame with bright oranges, hazy pinks, and deepening purple hues. The still waters of the lake below reflected a mirror image of the spectacle, making for a truly breathtaking sight... And on any other night, Alex would have thoroughly enjoyed the view.

At the moment, however, all she could see was the empty dock that stretched out in front of her like a path to the gallows.

She tried to remember what had made her think going alone would be a good idea.

As she made her way slowly down the wooden ramp and across the large floating dock that jutted out onto the lake, she wondered where Brandt was and whether or not Cassie was still alive.

Burying that thought, Alex arrived at the end of the dock, turned to face the swampy shoreline and proceeded to wait.

Alex had discovered the spot on her tenth birthday.

Back then, the path to the disused and dilapidated dock had been nearly concealed by brush and overgrown kudzu vines. She only found it by accident after her new bike—a birthday gift from Aunt Cil—fell victim to a flat. As she'd bent to inspect the nail protruding from her rear tire, she happened to catch sight of the broken sidewalk that disappeared into a line of cypress trees surrounding the lake.

When she'd pushed her way past the foliage and discovered the jetty, Alex had been delighted. She'd spent the rest of the afternoon there, listening to the stillness of the lake and soaking up the sun. When night fell and she finally returned home, her aunt had asked her what she'd been doing all day.

Alex had smiled and said, "Sometimes the Universe gives the best birthday presents."

She'd been coming here to watch the sunset ever since.

It was her escape. Her sanctuary. The place she went when she wanted to leave the world, with all its problems and its disappointments, behind.

Declan had the fields of Ireland.

Alex had a disused jetty surrounded by marshland.

Someone was making their way through the brush at the end of the bridge.

No.

Oh, this was so not good.

"Alex!" Connor exclaimed happily. He jogged down the ramp. "Finally. I've been looking for you since yesterday. Knew I'd find you here."

"Connor, what are you doing here?" She felt a knot of panic forming in her stomach. She had to get him out of here before Brandt showed up.

"I told you," he said as he reached her. "I need to talk to you."

"You have to go," she said, shaking her head. "You can't be here."

"What?" he asked. "Listen, I just want to talk. Five minutes. That's all it will take."

"No! Connor, you don't understand." Her heart began to race. "*You can't be here.* If he sees you, he'll—"

"Did you forget the single condition of our meeting, pet?" An angry voice called from the other side of the jetty.

Alex whipped back around.

Brandt was making his way down the ramp, arms outstretched and a dancing flame in either hand. More terrifying than the flames he brandished, however, was the sight of who was marching obediently in front of him.

Making their way carefully down the dock, arms in the air, were Cassie, Nate, and—of all people—Jessica Huffman and Veronica Hudgens.

What the heck was Connor's girlfriend doing here?

The girls appeared unharmed, but Nate had a nasty looking burn across one forearm and a cut across his forehead that was sending a steady stream of blood into his left eye.

How had Nate found her?

And where was Declan?

Veronica stumbled. Cassie scrambled to help her stand. The petite, raven-haired girl was trembling so hard that she could barely walk, tears streaming down her face.

"Jess? Did you follow me here?" Connor called out. "I *told you*, it's—" He finally seemed to notice the flames Brandt held in both hands. "What the hell?"

"And there I was lauding the efforts of the public school systems," said Brandt as they approached. "What was my one proviso?"

"Please," Alex's voice broke. "Please. They didn't know—"

"Come *alone*," he continued, as if he hadn't heard her. "That's all I asked."

Alex swallowed hard.

"All of you," said Brandt, his accent thick with anger. "Step away from Miss Parker, if you please."

He came to a halt at the end of the ramp. Alex watched the others form a group on the opposite side of the dock, well out of her reach.

A thin, fiery tendril separated itself from one of the spheres and glided toward Alex before diving to the dock a few feet away. The flame dragged itself in a tight circle around her feet until she found herself surrounded on all sides by a quivering, waist-high wall of flames.

Damn.

So much for Plan A.

"Please," she said again, the heat of the flames licking at the exposed skin on her forearms. "It's me you want. I'll go with you right now if you'll just let them go."

There was an angry chorus of replies from off to her right.

"*What?*"

"Alex, no!"

"Like hell!" said Cassie. Out of all of them, her voice was the angriest. "You're not going anywhere with that bastard!"

"Let her go," Veronica said in a small voice. "I mean, if it gets us out of here, just let him take her."

Cassie and Connor turned to gape incredulously at Vee. Alex didn't take her eyes off Brandt.

The Scotsman pretended to mull over Alex's offer. "Very tempting, but I'm afraid I can't let them go just yet."

"Alright," said Alex slowly. "Then what is it you want?"

"What I want," he sighed heavily as he stepped from the ramp and onto the floating dock, "is to live in a world where justice is certain, rules are obeyed and everything goes according to plan. But since that will never happen, I suppose I will have to settle for teaching you an important lesson instead."

Brandt raised an arm, the sphere of fire in his palm aimed directly at Alex's throat. He smiled. "It's time for you to *wake up*, pet."

It happened too fast.

Before Alex could register the fact that Brandt had moved, an orb of fire went sailing through the air... and hit Veronica square in the chest.

She didn't even have the chance to scream. The flames engulfed Vee in an instant, burning white hot and super-heating the air above the dock.

Alex hit her knees in the middle of her fiery prison and

raised her arms to shield herself from the searing heat. The circle of flames that surrounded her was putting off plenty of heat, but it now felt like a warm breeze in comparison.

Nate, who'd been standing next to Veronica, pushed the others away from the blaze, sending himself, Jessica, and Cassie to the deck and Connor headfirst into the lake.

Brandt readied a second sphere and took aim at Cassie and Nate.

"*Now, Declan!*" Nate shouted as he moved to protect Cassie.

Declan materialized beside Brandt, the barrel of a gun resting against the older man's temple.

Brandt's hand twitched.

Declan cocked the gun.

"I wouldn't, if I were you," said Declan, his voice eerily calm.

Alex's eyes sought out Cassie. Her best friend was sprawled on the opposite side of the dock, staring slack-jawed at Veronica's remains.

"Put out the flames around Alex," Declan ordered.

The fiery circle dissipated and a cool rush of evening air settled over her. She sighed in relief.

"Alex?" Declan called over his shoulder. "You okay?"

Alex, still on her hands and knees, cast a sidelong glance at the pile of smoldering ashes and scorched bones that had once been a teenage girl. She could taste the bile rising in her throat and turned away.

No one deserved a death like that.

"*Lex?*" Declan asked again, this time taking his eyes off Brandt long enough to shoot her a worried glance.

"Fine," Alex forced out. "I'm fine."

"Guess we'll have to resume your lesson later, pet." Brandt gave an impish smile.

The smile made her nervous. He had a gun to his head—so why was Brandt talking like he had a way out?

A familiar charge began building in the air. She looked quickly to Declan and found her own confusion mirrored back in his puzzled expression.

…And then Brandt teleported.

Alex stared dumbly at the place where Brandt had once stood.

"What the…" said Nate.

"Huh," said Declan, lowering the gun. "I can honestly say, I didn't see that one coming."

Connor was clinging to the side of the dock. When he caught sight of what remained of Veronica, he started to gag.

"Are you alright?" Alex hurried to Cassie's side, pulling her friend into a fierce hug. "Did he hurt you? Cass, I am so sorry. This is all my fault. I should have—"

"It's okay," said Cassie as she pushed Alex back to arms length. She smiled weakly. "I'm okay. I'm confused and I want some answers… but I'm okay."

Alex chewed her bottom lip. Sure Cassie *looked* okay, but who knew what Brandt had put her through?

Connor pulled himself back onto the dock and sat down heavily beside Cassie. He couldn't seem to tear his gaze from Veronica's remains.

Already on her feet, Jessica looked back and forth between them, then made a break for it, sprinting toward the shore.

"Jess, wait!" Connor called. "Where are you going?"

Jessica bumped into Declan in her rush to get away. He made no move to stop her.

"Let her go," said Nate. "She'll be alright."

Alex watched the girl vanish into the brush that lined the shore. She hoped Nate was right. So long as Brandt was on the loose, she wasn't sure that *anyone* would be safe.

Declan and Nathaniel came to stand beside Alex, two looming shadows in the fading light of the sunset.

"She's dead," Connor mumbled to himself, his attention having returned to Vee's remains. He raked a hand through his hair. "She's really dead. Christ."

Alex knew she ought to be feeling something right now.

Shock. Anger. Remorse. Pity.

Instead she just felt numb.

"We should go," said Nate. "In case he comes back."

"Go where?" Alex heard herself ask. She fought to regain her focus.

"The cabin," answered Declan.

Connor and Cassie observed the exchange silently. Alex took Cassie's hand in hers. "They're coming with us."

Declan and Nate exchanged a look. Alex couldn't read their expressions in the dim light, but it was obvious they weren't keen on the idea.

"I don't care where we go," said Alex. "It doesn't have to be the cabin. I'm not leaving them here."

"Alex—" Nate began.

"I'm. *Not*. Leaving. Them. Here."

Declan sighed. "Fine, we'll bring them to the cabin. But only for tonight. After that they're on their own."

With his face in shadow Alex couldn't be certain, but Declan appeared to be glowering at Connor as he spoke. She tightened her grip on Cassie and reached across her friend to take Connor's hand.

"Cabin?" asked Cassie. "What—"

Alex jumped, transporting the three of them from the dock to the cabin's living room.

"—cabin?" Cassie finished. She blinked and looked around. "Ohmigod."

"Where are we?" Connor stood up. "How the heck did we get *here*?"

"Alex! You're okay!"

Alex, who had been kneeling next to Cassie when they

reappeared on the living room rug, was knocked sideways by a mousy-haired blur.

"Whoa!" The blur had his arms wrapped around her in a vice-like grip. "Easy there, Brian."

Brian grinned happily down at her. She forced a smile for his benefit.

A flash of light from the kitchen signaled Declan and Nate's return, just as heavy footsteps came thundering down the staircase. Kenzie paused mid-way down the steps to take in the scene. "You're alive! Thank God. Now please tell me Declan didn't shoot anyone."

Brian helped Alex to sit up.

"Declan didn't shoot anyone," said Declan as he walked into the living room. "Brandt jumped before he gave me a reason to pull the trigger."

Kenzie rounded the kitchen table. "I'm sorry, I must have heard that wrong. Did you say he *jumped*? As in, *jumped*-jumped?"

"Yep." Nate joined them from the kitchen, a bag of frozen peas pressed against the burn on his forearm. "He jumped."

"That's impossible," said Kenzie. "Brandt controls fire... That's it."

"Not anymore, apparently," said Declan. He pulled the gun from his waistband, set it on the coffee table and then collapsed onto the couch. Alex eyed the gun curiously, reminding herself to ask him about it later.

Cassie took hold of Alex's arm. "Who are all these people, where are we, how did you bring us here and what in God's name did that psychopath want with you?"

"I..." Alex trailed off, struck by how similar the string of questions were to the ones she'd posed to Declan after their splashdown in the lake the day before.

Had it really only been a day since all this started?

Cassie was staring at her expectantly.

Alex had no idea where to begin. She wondered if Declan hadn't answered her yesterday for the same reason.

"But he's *ancient*," Kenzie continued before Alex could reply. "You don't just live forty-five years of your life and then wake up one day with a second ability. That's not how it works."

"You can stand there and argue with me all you like, but that won't change what happened, Kenzie. The man jumped," said Declan.

At that point, Connor and Cassie both turned to Alex wearing identical masks of confusion.

"Explanation," said Cassie. "Now."

FOURTEEN

"**A**nybody ever tell you your bedside manner sucks, Kenzie?"

"Anybody ever tell you that you need to grow a pair, Nate?" she countered. "Seriously, son. Suck it up. I'm trying to help you here."

Kenzie applied another butterfly bandage to the gash on Nathaniel's forehead. He hissed in pain and gripped the edge of the dining room table.

"Baby," Kenzie mumbled.

Declan's gaze slid past them and out the bay window.

Alex and her friends were still seated in the adirondack chairs on the patio, awash in the orange glow of the exterior lights, talking. They'd been out there for nearly half an hour.

He'd been waiting for them to come back inside so that he could get Alex alone long enough to tell her what a colossally stupid idea it had been for her to try and meet with Brandt alone. If he and Nate hadn't found them, she and her friends might *all* be dead right now.

Declan felt Alex's emotions surge again.

It seemed to be happening every time the meathead seated to her right opened his mouth. He should do them all a favor and just keep it shut.

Honestly, though. What could Alex possibly have seen in that guy? He gave new life to the dumb-jock stereotype.

The day before, Declan had been forced to suffer

through Alex and Cassie's hour-long discussion about Connor while he'd watched over them sunbathing at the beach.

The view had been excellent. The girl talk had been torture.

Declan now knew more than he ever wanted to know about the relationship between Alex and Connor.

Cassie was right. Connor was a dick.

So why was Alex getting so worked up over having him here?

Up until tonight, she'd been doing a much better job at controlling the extra energy being generated by her fluctuating emotions. Now, for whatever reason, Declan had once again found himself having to be the one to handle the excess current.

Outside, Connor's mouth was moving again.

He really ought to look to that.

Declan sighed and siphoned off a bit more energy. Alex noticed that time. She turned to look at him through the window, the lines of her face painted in a frown. Whatever they were discussing, it had her upset.

He nodded toward the front door in an attempt to get her to come inside. She held up a finger.

Hold on, she mouthed, and then turned to say something to Connor.

Declan was trying hard not to take that personally.

It wasn't going so well.

"Pizza's ready," Brian said from the other side of the pass-through window. "You guys want a slice?"

"You, sir, are a gentleman and a scholar," said Kenzie as she closed the first-aid kit with a snap. "I would love one."

"Nate?" asked Brian.

"When have I ever said no to pizza?"

"What about you, Declan? ... Declan?"

"What?" He looked around. Brian was handing Kenzie a plate through the window. "Oh. I'll grab a slice later, kid, thanks."

It was obvious Alex wouldn't be making her way back inside so that they could have that conversation any time soon. Declan got to his feet and made for the front door.

Guess he'd just have to bring the conversation to her, then.

Declan stepped out onto the patio and approached the trio. "We need to talk," he said.

"I'll be inside in a minute, Declan," said Alex, sounding tired.

"*Now* would work better." He came to a stop beside her chair.

She shifted in her seat to look up at him. "You have less patience than a three-year-old, you know that?"

"So I've been told." Declan bent down, snagged her by the elbow and teleported them to his bedroom.

Alex—who had been in a seated position when they jumped—landed hard on her backside.

"Would you please stop doing that?" she snapped.

"Doing what?"

"Teleporting me someplace without warning me first." She put her hands on her hips and fixed him with a cold stare. "Once in a while, a little heads up would be nice."

What had *her* knickers in such a twist?

He was the one who ought to be angry right now.

"And in case you hadn't noticed, I was in the middle of a conversation," she added.

He raised an eyebrow at that. She hadn't looked to be enjoying that conversation very much. Really, she ought to have been thanking him for providing her with an exit.

"What was that pinhead saying that had you so riled up, anyway?" He crossed his arms. "I was getting tired of having to control the excess currents you were calling up every two seconds."

Alex opened her mouth to say something and then snapped it closed again. "It was nothing," she said finally.

"Riiiight. You realize you were summoning more energy talking to Connor tonight than you did in the *bookshop*? Apparently, for you, talking to that guy is more stressful than the threat of being burned alive."

And yet she'd been the one to insist on bringing him here.

Women.

"He's been wanting to talk for a couple of days now, so I decided to hear him out," she said, looking everywhere but at Declan. "Apparently he broke up with Jessica last week. He was trying to give me some half-assed apology for cheating on me with her back in January."

Declan felt the currents surge again, but this time Alex took care of it.

"He wants to get back together," she finished.

"And you said…?" he tried to keep his tone disinterested.

Surely she wasn't stupid enough to get back with him. Not that he cared, he reminded himself.

"I haven't said *anything*," she said. "You interrupted me before I could answer him."

He congratulated himself on his excellent timing.

"And after everything that's happened today," she said. "Well, it hardly seems like the time to be discussing failed relationships."

"See? You *are* grateful I hijacked your conversation."

Alex sighed and looked around, finally realizing where they were. "What are we doing in your bedroom?"

He shrugged. "Wanted someplace private to talk. It's cold by the lake right now, so it was either this or one of the bathrooms."

Alex sent him a look that walked the line between amusement and exasperation. She appeared to be struggling to keep her lips from curving into a smile. "What did you want to talk about, Declan?"

The hint of her smile had drained away the last of his anger.

Suddenly, Declan was at a loss. Lecturing her for being so reckless seemed kind of pointless in light of what had happened. Her classmate was dead. What more was there to say?

"You scared the hell out of me, you know. If Brian hadn't had that vision..." Declan swallowed and stared at the hardwood floor beneath Alex's feet. He wasn't sure what he'd planned on saying, but that definitely hadn't been it.

He glanced up. She met his gaze.

"Declan, I—"

A knock sounded at Declan's door.

Declan couldn't decide whether to be annoyed, or grateful for the interruption.

"*What?*" he called.

The door opened and Cassie walked in.

"I've come to reclaim my friend. You have this nasty habit of stealing her away from me when I least expect it." Cassie's voice was light, but Declan didn't miss the hint of accusation hiding in her words. "C'mon, Alex. That wonderful smell coming from downstairs is pizza. Trust me. You want some."

Whatever Alex had been about to say before Cassie knocked died unspoken on her lips as she followed the blue-eyed blonde out into the hallway.

"This... is so not good," said Cassie as she peered through the kitchen's pass-through window.

Kenzie, standing next to her, couldn't agree more.

Connor had Alex cornered at the bottom of the staircase. The hunky moron was talking to her in a low voice. He looked determined. Alex, on the other hand, looked as though she wanted nothing more than to flee.

"I think she could use a well-timed interruption," said Kenzie. She started for the living room, but Cassie grabbed her by the wrist and brought her up short.

"She has to do this on her own," she said. "Trust me, I'd like nothing more than to save the girl from herself and tell Connor *exactly* what a cretinous, pond-scum-sucking loser I think he is… But if she doesn't stand up to him now, she never will."

"Is the guy really *that bad*?" Nate asked from his spot at the island in the center of the kitchen. He'd poured himself a fresh cup of coffee and was nursing it slowly.

Earlier, he and Declan had decided that, until the boss got back, one or both of them would be awake at all times. Just in case.

Nathaniel had drawn the short straw. He'd wake Declan in another four hours.

"Yes, gorgeous," said Cassie. "He really is *that much* of a lowlife."

Kenzie liked this girl. She had spirit, style and just the right amount of attitude. Alex appeared to have excellent taste in friends. In guys, however, Kenzie was starting to think the dark-haired beauty could use some assistance.

Assistance she would be more than happy to provide.

Returning her attention to the living room, Kenzie found only a frustrated Connor glancing around in confusion. "Huh," she said. "Alex seems to have disappeared."

Cassie whipped back around to see for herself. "Crap! She still didn't tell him no. I can tell just by looking at him."

"Which means, wherever she is, she's probably upset," said Kenzie, an idea forming. "I bet she could use some consoling."

Cassie seemed puzzled. Kenzie jerked her head in Nate's direction and the other girl's eyes lit up.

"Yeah," said Cassie, catching on to her plan. "Someone should really go talk to her. Make sure she's okay."

Nate glanced back and forth between them.

"Oh no," he said. "No, no, no. I told you that wasn't going to happen, Kenzie."

"And I think the boy doth protest too much," she said, slipping onto the barstool next to him.

Nate's jaw clenched. It was obvious that he was having one hell of an argument with himself right now.

What Kenzie didn't understand, was *why*.

Alex was a sweet girl. He *obviously* liked her. So what was the hold up? Surely this wasn't about Declan. Her brother had never stood in the way of Nate going after a girl in the past. So what would make Alex any different?

He seemed to relent. But judging from the look on his face, he hated himself for doing it.

For Pete's sake… When did he get so emo?

"Alright, fine," he said. "I'll go talk to her."

Kenzie gave Cassie a high-five.

Cassie nodded to Nate. "I'll handle Connor and keep him from looking for her. You handle Alex." Under her breath she added, "God knows she's in desperate need of some good handling…"

With that, Cassie disappeared into the living room. It was so nice having someone around to help her in her scheming.

"I'm assuming this means you know where Alex went when she jumped?" said Nate.

"Sally forth, fair prince," Kenzie smiled. "Your princess awaits you on the patio."

He disappeared into the walk-in pantry.

"Uh, Nate," said Kenzie, leaning out of her chair to peer into the darkened storeroom. "I think you're mixing up your 'p's' there, kiddo. Didn't Sesame Street teach you anything? I said *pa-ti-o...*"

"Needed to grab some supplies," he said, reemerging with a red bag in his hands. "Can't show up to an emotional rescue empty handed, now can I? I'd make a pretty piss-poor prince if I did that."

"*Excellent* use of today's letter of the day, Nate," she said with a grin. "He can be taught!"

"I try," he said as he made to leave. "Wish me luck?"

"Nah. You don't need it, Charming. Just go put a smile on the girl's face. I know you can do it."

He would totally thank her for this later.

Kenzie was sure of it.

"Twizzler for your thoughts?"

Alex smiled. Nate appeared next to her, leaning against the wooden railing that lined the patio.

"And here I thought they'd only fetch a penny," she said.

He held up a cord of the candy.

"My favorite. How'd you know?"

"Lucky guess." He set the bag on the railing. Alex could just make out his grin in the darkness. "How you holding up?"

Her expression was wry. "I'm holding up?"

"Yeah," he said slowly and turned to look out over the lake. "Guess today's been a little rough."

Now that *might just be the understatement of the century,* she thought to herself.

She followed his gaze. The placid waters of the lake below glistened in the dazzling glow of the full moon as tendrils of low-lying fog stretched out from the lake-shore like misty fingers reaching out from the darkened edges of the forest.

Up above them, the murky haze that had swallowed the cabin earlier in the day had given way to a perfectly empty expanse of sky, covered only by a blanket of twinkling stars.

Where Alex lived, so close to the city, only a few dim constellations were visible on any given night. Here at the cabin, there were more stars shining brightly in the sky above her than she could count in ten lifetimes. She recognized the Milky Way, stretching out just to the right of the moon—a shining, cloudy belt marked by pinpricks of light, and lined on either side by bright strips of swirling white indigo, and a haze of red ocher close to the horizon.

Alex smiled. This view was fantastic. The company wasn't so bad either.

Maybe this day *wouldn't* be a total loss.

After everything that had just happened, she couldn't believe her ears, at first, when Connor had told her that it was their *relationship* he was hoping to discuss.

But that was Connor, for you.

He wasn't *all* bad. He could be a little self-centered at times, but that didn't mean he didn't care.

Alex had said as much to Cassie the day before. Her friend had merely sighed and said, "*I swear, Alex, if you tried hard enough, you could find the bright side of a black hole. Just promise me you won't spend so much time looking for the good in people that you ignore all the bad, okay? I'm sick of watching people walk all over you. And that little toad has done nothing but take advantage of your kindness since the first day you met.*"

Only… Alex was finding it difficult to take Cassie's advice this time.

Every lick of common sense she possessed was telling her to send Connor packing… but her heart was having none of it.

She was torn. And it was written all over her face.

Which was probably why Connor had cornered her after she'd finished her slice of pizza, once again eager to discuss where they stood.

She couldn't figure out how to answer him.

Instead, she'd snagged the only coat hanging on the coat rack—Declan's—and jumped... all the way to the patio. Let Connor think she was in Bora Bora somewhere. Just so long as she didn't have to look into those big brown eyes again tonight.

Just so long as she didn't have to be strong enough to say "no" for a little while longer.

Alex climbed up to sit on the railing. "Never did get that tour."

"First thing in the morning," Nate smiled. "I promise."

Something in the pocket of her borrowed jacket began to vibrate. Alex reached inside and pulled out Declan's cell phone.

"It's ringing," she said.

Nate took the phone from her, checked the caller ID, and answered it.

"Monty," he said. "It's Nate."

Monty's Brooklyn accent reached her loud and clear through the stillness of the night.

"Hey, kid," he sounded angry. "You know I don't mind flying the old girl back solo, but the next time you decide to have Declan pick up Grayson, you've *got* to give me a heads up. I've been waiting on the tarmac for almost an hour."

"Whoa, Monty." Nate pushed away from the railing and offered Alex a hand. She took it and hopped down. "What are you talking about?"

Still holding her hand, Nate led Alex around the left side of the house. They came to a stop at the end of the flagstone path and Nate fixed his attention on one of the darkened upstairs windows

"This afternoon Grayson called and told me to prep the jet and we'd leave for New York at ten," he said. "Then he never showed. I just figured you'd come and got him."

The window they'd been staring at shuddered open. It took Alex a second to realize that Nate had been the one to raise it.

"Yo, Decks!" Nate shouted.

"Ack!" Alex could hear Monty grumbling on the other end of the line. "Christ, kid, cover the mouthpiece when you do that. My hearing's bad enough as it is."

Nate pulled the phone away from his ear. "*Decks!*" he shouted again.

"What is it?" asked Alex. Nate seemed to have forgotten that he was still holding her hand.

"Something's wrong," he replied, and then shouted again. "Dammit, Declan, get your ass out of bed!"

A light flicked on and Declan stumbled into view through the open window. He looked to be only half awake and was missing his shirt.

Alex, on the other hand, was not missing that shirt in the slightest.

"*What?*" Declan snapped. His voice held that same low, rumbling quality that it had carried that morning. He squinted down at them, first zeroing in on their joined hands, and then on Alex. "Hey. Is that my jacket?"

"Did you pick up Grayson?" Nate asked before Alex could attempt an answer.

"What?" he said. "No. Why?"

"Monty, when did you last hear from Grayson?" Nate asked into the phone.

"Around four," he said. "I've been trying his cell since he didn't show at ten. Tried his hotel, too. They said he checked out a couple hours ago. If he ain't at the cabin, where'd he go?"

"I don't know," said Nate. "Listen, stay in DC another night, just in case."

"Alright, kid," he said.

"And Monty?"

"Yeah, kid?"

"Call me if you hear anything."

"Sure thing."

Nate ended the call.

"What's going on?" asked Declan.

"Put a shirt on and round up the others," said Nate. "We're going to DC."

FIFTEEN

The seven of them stood crowded together in the narrow hallway of the apartment complex.

"This is a bad idea," said Kenzie.

"Like we have a choice?" said Declan.

"If you'd just let us come with you, this wouldn't be a problem," said Brian.

Kenzie shook her head. "Not gonna happen, kid," she said. "You'll be safe here until we get back."

The hallway fell quiet.

"Is someone gonna knock on that door?" asked Cassie. "Or are we just going to stand out here in the hall all night and listen to Connor's freakishly heavy breathing?"

"Hey!" said Connor.

"Go ahead and knock, Decks," said Nate.

"How come Kenzie gets to go and I don't?" asked Brian.

"Because I'll be able to pick up on your dad's thoughts if he's around and we'll be able to find him more easily," Kenzie replied.

"*You're* our fearless leader, Nate," said Declan. "You knock on the damn door."

"Yeah and he's *your* cousin," Nate countered.

Brian craned his neck to peer up at Nathaniel. "I thought you guys were friends."

Nate shrugged. "Oklahoma," he said, as though the word were explanation enough.

"Oh, right," said Brian. "Forgot."

Cassie shared a look with Alex. Her friend simply shrugged in reply.

Boys.

Deciding that all the men present were not only idiots, but chickens as well, Cassie sighed, stepped forward, and raised a hand to knock on the door. She didn't get the chance.

The door swung open.

Cassie stepped back.

Looming over her in the doorway was a guy who appeared to be in his early twenties. Definitely not the elderly grandmother-type she'd been expecting after Declan had so infuriatingly used the word "babysitter" earlier.

She was also quick to note that the man staring down at her was built like a god, with wavy, dirty-blond hair that came to his shoulders and eyes the color of jade.

Cassie was starting to wonder if all the guys in this new world of Alex's were destined to be so ridiculously attractive.

When the powers that be were handing out mutant abilities, they must have decided to throw in perfect physiques and soulful eyes to go along with each of them.

It appeared to be a package deal.

"Down, girl," Kenzie whispered in her ear.

"What the *hell* are you four doing in Newport?" he asked. "Does Grayson know you're here?"

"Hello, Aiden," said Nate.

"Nate," said Aiden. "You want to tell me why there's a party going on in my hallway?"

The ruggedly handsome blonde appraised the group. When his scrutiny fell on Alex, his eyes widened almost imperceptibly and his gaze flickered toward Nathaniel. Cassie watched as Nate subtly shook his head "no" in answer to Aiden's silent question.

What was all *that* about?

"We need a favor," said Declan, cutting to the point.

"Has hell already frozen over?" Aiden asked, his voice droll. "I must have missed the memo."

"You know we wouldn't be here if we had another option," said Nate.

"Do you remember what happened the *last* time I tried to help you?" He leaned heavily against the doorjamb. "There's still bullet holes the size of dinner plates in the sides of Norma Jean."

Bullet holes? And what, exactly, had become of this Norma Jean person?

"Norma Jean's his truck," Kenzie explained in another whisper. "He named it after Marilyn Monroe. Aiden sort of has a thing for blondes."

A thing for blondes, huh?

"Grayson's missing and Carson Brandt..." Nate trailed off.

Cassie shivered. She'd spent the entire night trying to think about something—*anything*—other than that name.

If she didn't think about it, it hadn't happened.

"Well, he's been giving us some trouble," Nate finished. "We were hoping Brian and a couple of norms could stay here with you. Just until we find the boss."

"You have a supernatural hit man after you and you came to my apartment?" He didn't look happy.

To be honest, if a bunch of people showed up at Cassie's door with someone like Brandt after them, she wouldn't be too happy about it either.

That man had more than a few screws loose.

She wrung her hands as though the motion might somehow wipe clean the memories of that afternoon.

Of the cold cloth drenched with chloroform that had covered her mouth and nose. Of waking up alone in the pitch-black trunk of a car. Of the sweltering heat and the

dank smell of mildew which permeated the long-aban-
doned warehouse. Of Brandt and the fire he toyed with as
he sat for hours, just watching her.

He hadn't touched her.

He hadn't needed to.

His presence and that flame had been enough of a
threat.

When Cassie finally stepped foot on the dock and saw
Alex waiting for her at the other end, she'd been both hopeful and terrified. Part of her had wanted her friend to stay
away—far away—but the rest of her knew that it would
have marked the end of her usefulness to Brandt.

Now here they were, hours later, still running from him.

All the way to Newport, apparently.

Cassie attempted to distract herself from that line of
thought by trying to remember what state Newport was
in. This whole jumping-as-a-mode-of-transportation thing
was going to take some getting used to.

"Can you help us or not?" asked Declan.

Aiden's green eyes raked over the group in another
silent assessment. Cassie didn't miss the fact that his gaze
seemed to linger on her just a bit longer than anyone else.

"Fine," he said, stepping back to give them room to
walk inside. "But if my place gets torched over this,
Grayson's footing the bill."

Alex couldn't help but feel guilty.

"Are you sure the others will be safe with Aiden?" she
asked.

Leaving her best friend and her former love alone in
Oregon while Brandt was still on the loose really didn't
seem like such a great idea.

"Hon," said Kenzie, putting an arm around her shoulders as they stood on the lamp-lit sidewalk that lined the

deserted street. "There's no safer place for them right now than with Aiden. Trust me on this one."

She wondered what it was about Aiden that had Kenzie so confident in his ability to protect them.

Then again, he *was* her cousin. Bearing that in mind, the odds were good that Aiden was a Variant, too.

"You're sure this is the right parking garage?" Declan was staring up at the massive concrete structure looking less than pleased. "It's huge. This is going to take us forever to search."

"Yeah. This is the same one he used the last time we stayed at the Plaza," said Nate. "And you know Grayson."

"Creature of habit," Declan agreed. "Okay, guys, start walking."

Their trip to the Plaza had been a bust. Grayson's room had already been cleaned and no one on the night shift could remember having seen him. That's when Nate came up with the idea of searching for his rental car. It was a long shot, but they had no other leads left to pursue.

"What are we looking for again?" asked Kenzie as they made their way inside the garage at ground level.

"According to the guy at the rental agency, his car was a black BMW 6 Series Coupé," said Nate.

"And the guy tries to lecture *me* about flying under the radar," Declan mumbled. "Could he have picked a more conspicuous car?"

"Sure," said Nate. "He could have sprung for the convertible."

Declan sighed and stopped walking. "You know what? This will go a lot faster if we split up. Alex and I will start at the top and work our way back down. Call us if you find it."

Before anyone could speak a word in protest or suggest a better plan, Declan took Alex by the hand.

"Now I don't want you to freak," he said slowly, his

tone patronizing. "But I'm going to teleport us to the elevators. See the elevators? They're right over there. So you should probably prepare yourself."

"You're hilarious," said Alex. "You know, Declan, sometimes you can be a real—"

They jumped.

"Jackass," she finished.

"Hey," he said as he punched the button to call the elevator. "I was just giving you a heads up like you asked me to. No need to get pissy."

"If my brother keeps acting like an idiot," Kenzie called from the other side of the garage, "you have my express permission to smack him upside the head!"

"And you have *my* permission to kick his ass," Nate added.

"What, seriously?" Declan muttered. "Everybody's ganging up on me today."

The elevator to their left dinged and the doors slid open. Alex and Declan walked inside. As the reflective metal doors of the lift slid shut, Alex thought she heard something.

Whispers. Voices. Louder and louder and then... Silence.

She looked up at Declan. "What was that?"

"What was what?"

"That sound," she said. "All those people talking. Is there a speaker in here or something?"

"No," he said, bemused. "You feeling alright, Lex? No offense, but you really look like crap."

Alex caught sight of her reflection in the mirrors that lined the walls of the car. Dark circles were forming under her eyes and her skin glistened a sickly gray in the unforgiving glow of the fluorescent lights. To be honest, she didn't feel much better than she looked.

Ever since they'd arrived in DC her head had been *pounding*.

"I'm fine," Alex said as the doors opened. She wasn't about to let sleep deprivation and a headache stop her from assisting in the search for Grayson. He'd gone missing while trying to help *her* and she felt just as responsible for his disappearance as she had for Cassie's kidnapping. She started walking. "Come on."

Declan followed from a short ways behind her. As they rounded the corner to the next level down, the voices returned.

The whispers escalated to shouts and as the noise grew to a fever pitch, Alex covered her ears reflexively.

Silence.

"Okay, that's it," she said, whipping around. "Tell me you heard it that time!"

Declan nearly stumbled into her as she came to an abrupt halt in the middle of his path. He looked down at her, his brow furrowed. "Alex, no one said anything. In case you hadn't noticed, we're alone up here."

Alex glanced about in confusion.

Declan walked around her and continued on to the next level. "Let's go, Alex. That car's not going to find itself."

Resigned, Alex continued to help Declan look for Grayson's rental car through another two levels. As they rounded yet another bend, Alex spotted Kenzie and Nate twenty feet away, standing on the passenger's side of a black sports car.

"Is that it?" Declan called.

Kenzie looked up, a worried frown on her face. "Grayson's briefcase is on the floorboard of the passenger side. And on the driver's side there's…" she couldn't finish.

"There's blood on the driver's side door," said Nate. "There are dents in the rental and in the car beside it. He didn't go without a fight."

The sentence was punctuated by a sudden thickening of the static in the air around them. Alex felt the electrical energy surrounding her abruptly spike and then disappear altogether. A strange tightening in her chest caused her to suck in a breath as her heart skipped a beat.

What on Earth was *that*?

The lights went out. Alex stopped in her tracks as the garage was plunged into semi-darkness, the only illumination filtering in from street-lamps outside of the garage.

A shot rang out.

Alex felt something solid slam into her and she went crashing to the pavement between Grayson's rental and another parked car.

The "something solid" had been Declan. He was lying on top of her. Again. Only this time they hadn't landed on something so soft as his bed.

They really had to stop meeting like this.

Declan stared down at her. "Were you hit?"

A second shot. Alex winced as the report echoed through the garage. Between the blow to her skull from the rough landing and the crack of gunfire, her head felt like it was about to split in two.

"No," she replied.

Declan got to his knees and peered through the window of the car beside them, and then ducked down a second later as a third shot was fired. The rear window of a nearby car shattered.

"Nate? Kenzie?" he called out from his spot beside her. "You guys okay?"

"We're good, Decks," Nate replied.

From the sound of it, they were crouched on the opposite side of Grayson's rental.

"Hold on," said Declan. "Be with you in a second."

He grabbed her wrist and closed his eyes.

Nothing happened.

"*Shit!*" He dropped her arm. "Well, we won't be *jumping* out of here, that's for sure."

Alex gingerly pulled herself into a seated position, careful not to rise above the level of the car's windows. She tried to teleport... and couldn't.

"Why can't we jump?" she asked, fear sinking its teeth into her. "And who's shooting at us?"

"Both excellent questions, Alex," said Declan, risking another glance toward the source of the gunfire. "But I'm afraid I'll have to get back to you with the answers."

He jerked his head back down before whoever was shooting at them could get a clear shot.

The automatic locks of the coupé released. A moment later, both of the car's doors opened. Alex could see through to Nate and Kenzie kneeling on the other side.

"What's the hold up?" asked Nate. "We need to get out of here."

"Thank you, Captain Obvious," Declan hissed. He raked a hand through his hair. "We can't jump. Whoever it is that's shooting at us must have set off an EM pulse. It's why the lights went out."

"You think it's the Agency?" asked Nate.

"Unless you know someone *else* who has access to a suitcase-sized electromagnetic pulse generator," said Declan.

"A what?" Alex asked.

"A non-nuclear EMP," said Declan. "It's a weapon that disables nearby electronics by sending out a pulse. The Agency managed to shrink the machine down to a portable size a few years back, and now they use them to bring in Jumpers. It's like hitting a reset button on our abilities. Strips our powers, temporarily."

"But why in the world would they be *shooting* at us?" asked Kenzie. "The Agency knows we're not a threat!"

"Tell that to the guys with the automatic weapons, sis," he said. "Can you hear their thoughts at all?"

She shook her head. "No. They're blocking me. Whoever they are, they've had training in keeping out a telepath."

"Hate to cut short the confab, guys, but we need to start fighting back before they realize that they can just walk over here and gun us down," said Nate. "Operatives might be slow, but they're not stupid."

There was another crack of gunfire. Alex fully expected her ears to start bleeding any time now. The pain in her head was nearly blinding.

Declan leaned heavily against the coupé's open driver-side door. "Dammit, Nate. Why did I let you talk me into leaving the Beretta behind at the cabin?"

"How was I supposed to know that this would happen?" asked Nate.

Another shot. More shattering glass.

Alex cringed.

"What is this, Nate? The third time we've been shot at so far this year?" Declan's words were laced with annoyance. "It's *April*, man. Situations like this one are exactly why Grayson needs to let us carry guns."

Nate sent them a smile over his shoulder and started edging toward the rear of the car. "Relax," he said. "*I'm* the gun."

"Yeah, yeah. You're a badass," said Declan. "We get it. Now hurry up and get us out of this."

"What's he going to do?" asked Alex. "Throw a car at them?"

"The thought had crossed my mind," she heard Nate say from somewhere near the trunk. "Unless you have a better idea?"

Alex opened her mouth to reply and then startled everyone by crying out in agony instead.

The whispering voices from earlier had returned and were now screaming inside her mind, the bits of conversation having been joined by a flood of painfully sharp images and a roiling sea of emotions. Alex gripped the sides of her head, her own inner-voice suddenly drowning in an onslaught foreign thoughts.

And the thoughts *hurt*...

It took her a while to realize that the piercing scream cutting through the cacophony was her own.

Blinded by pain, Alex doubled over...

And everything went black.

SIXTEEN

"**W**hat happened?" Nate asked, coming into view on the other side of the car. "Why is she screaming like that?"

"I don't know!" Declan's hands gripped Alex's shoulders, trying to hold her steady. The harrowing sound of her screams had set his teeth on edge. What was happening to her?

Then it hit him.

Those voices she'd been hearing... He knew what they were. And if they didn't act soon, they were going to lose Alex. For good.

They needed to get her out of the city. Now.

"Kenzie," he said slowly. "I need you to knock her out... And whatever you do, don't look in her head."

"Are you *insane*? You know how risky that is!" she said.

"Don't argue with me, just do it!"

Kenzie hesitated.

"*Do it*, Kenzie!" he said again. "If you don't, she's as good as dead, anyway."

She seemed to relent.

"*Fine*," she said, climbing into the car. "But I swear to God, Decks, if this goes wrong and she ends up a vegetable, I'm never going to forgive you."

He'd never forgive himself, either.

Unfortunately, Kenzie's mental K.O. was the only way Alex was going to survive long enough for him to get her safely out of the city. They didn't have a choice.

Kenzie crawled into the driver's seat, careful not to raise up too high, and reached for Alex, grabbing hold of her upper arm. His sister's stare became vacant.

Next to him, Alex doubled over. Declan caught her in his arms before she could hit the ground.

Kenzie swayed in the seat before pulling herself together.

"Did it work?" asked Nate. He had a death grip on the headrest of the passenger seat and was staring anxiously at Alex.

Declan found himself wondering—not for the first time that day—exactly *what* was going on between his brother and Alex.

"Won't know until she wakes up," Kenzie answered.

As if to remind them all that there was still one more threat to be dealt with, four shots whizzed by in rapid succession.

Nate stood up. The sound of crunching metal and screeching tires filled the air.

Declan risked another glance toward their assailants and raised his eyebrows in surprise. Nate had created a barricade out of the parked cars, piling them on top of each other until the wall of automobiles stretched from one side of the garage to the other.

Sometimes, the things Nate proved to be capable of scared the hell out of him. Flinging two-ton cars around like they were bath toys happened to be one of those things.

Nate sagged heavily against the side of the coupé.

Declan looked down at the unconscious girl in his arms. She wouldn't be out for long. They were running out of time.

"Help me get her in the car," he ordered.

Kenzie flipped forward the driver's seat and assisted Declan in half-carrying, half-dragging Alex into the backseat. He didn't envy her the scrapes and bruises she was going to wake up with, but at least they'd managed to get her inside.

The driver's seat slid back into place, confining the two of them to the backseat. The bucket seats made moving around difficult, but Declan eventually managed to position Alex so that she was curled on the seat next to him with her head resting in his lap.

She looked oddly peaceful like that.

Declan, meanwhile, was getting a kink in his neck from being hunched down in the seat at such an odd angle.

A heavy thud reverberated through the garage and the wall of cars shuddered. That barricade wasn't going to hold them for much longer. And judging from the way Nate was still leaning heavily against the coupé, He-Man over there wouldn't be tossing around any more cars until he got his strength back.

Time to go.

"Nate," said Declan. "You drive."

"And how, exactly, would you like me to accomplish that, Declan?" Nate asked as Kenzie slipped back out of the car and he took her place. Nate grunted as he lifted himself over the center console and settled in behind the wheel. "The pulse disabled any car with electronic equipment in the engine."

"I'm working on it," he replied.

Declan felt around for nearby electrical energy, stretching his reach to the farthest periphery of his senses. If he could just tap into one of the still-working streetlamps outside of the garage...

Got it!

He began leeching the energy out of the light and into himself. It wasn't much, but it was a start.

Declan really wished Alex was awake right now to show him how she did that trick with the spheres.

He would just have to wing it.

What had she been doing when she created a sphere for the first time?

He'd asked her to ground out the charge. She'd been trying to give the current a place to go.

Right. Okay, then.

Here goes nothing, he thought.

Declan raised one hand, palm up, and channeled the energy through his arm and toward his fingers.

It worked. A crackling ball of pale violet light was growing in the palm of his hand. He gave a triumphant laugh.

"What the heck is *that*?" asked Kenzie. She was twisted around in the passenger seat watching him, her face illuminated by the dancing blue light of the sphere.

"A little something Alex taught me," Declan replied, smiling.

He placed his other hand on the metal frame of the car door. With a little concentration—and a lot of creativity—he was able to bypass the fried electronics that would have kept him from kick-starting the engine. Sending one last surge of electricity to the still functional fuel injectors, the car roared to life.

Nate looked at the coupé's dashboard in surprise. "Well, I'll be damned," he said. He and Kenzie slammed the car doors shut.

"You're welcome," said Declan as he used what was left of the energy he'd gathered to roll down the car's windows.

As Nate peeled out of the parking space, the wall of cars separating them from the agents exploded outwards.

Aiming for the opening in the barricade, Declan launched the sphere of electricity he'd formed through the open window. Nate sped the coupé around a corner before he could see if his attack had had the desired effect.

They careened out of the parking deck and onto an

empty side street before sliding into heavy traffic on the main road.

"We need to get out of the city," said Declan. "Faster the better."

"Interstate should be up ahead," said Nate. "It'll be the quickest way to go."

Something in the side mirror had captured Kenzie's attention. "Anybody else notice that black Challenger?" she asked. "Because I think it's following us."

Declan twisted in his seat. The Challenger was two cars back in the other lane and accelerating, weaving through traffic in an attempt to catch up with them.

"Better find that gas pedal, Nate," said Declan.

They sped up.

Ahead of them, a traffic light changed from yellow to red.

"Whoa," said Kenzie, pressing one hand against the dashboard and grabbing desperately for the door handle with the other. "Whoa, whoa, whoa! *Brake!*"

They sailed through the intersection… and only barely missed getting creamed by the cross-traffic.

Nate was smiling. "Did you *see* that?"

"Yes, Nathaniel." Kenzie had a white-knuckle grip on the door. "You have a bright future ahead of you as a wheelman for the mob. We're all so proud. Now focus on the road, please."

"I wouldn't celebrate just yet," said Declan, looking out the rear window. The Challenger had made it through the intersection and was following only a few car-lengths behind them. "We didn't shake them."

Nate hit the gas, turning onto the ramp that led to the interstate.

"I don't think we're going to be able to lose them," he said, threading the coupé through the lessening traffic. "Not like this."

"So what do we do?" asked Kenzie.

Nate caught his gaze in the rear-view mirror. "What's the biggest thing you've ever jumped with, Decks?"

He couldn't be serious.

"You want me to jump the *car*?"

"If we jumped without it, we'd still be traveling at the same speed we are now, right?" Nate asked. "I'd rather not reappear somewhere going a hundred-and-twenty miles per hour. Something tells me that wouldn't have a happy ending."

Declan's head slammed into the back of the passenger seat as the car pursuing them collided with their rear bumper.

"Son of a…" he mumbled, rubbing his forehead ruefully.

Seatbelts. They were more than just a fashion statement.

He glanced nervously at Alex. The impact hadn't been enough to wake her. She was still out.

"Hang on, guys," said Nate.

Declan looked past Nate and through the windshield. Up ahead, traffic was at a standstill. Nate swerved the coupé into the breakdown lane, flying past the stopped cars.

The black Challenger followed suit.

Declan continued to siphon energy from the passing cars and streetlamps, but he wasn't getting much. They were simply moving too fast for him to get a good fix on anything. At this rate, it was going to take ages before he'd have enough power to jump with all of them *and* the car in tow. That is, if he managed to jump at all.

Alex stirred in his lap and let out a whimper. Declan gently brushed aside the errant locks of hair that hid her face. She turned her head to look up at him.

She was awake. And from the looks of it, she was still in pain.

They were almost out of the city, but apparently it wasn't far enough to help Alex.

She turned away, closing her eyes tightly as her face twisted into a grimace.

Alex, look at me, he thought.

She didn't respond. He cupped the side of her face and turned it toward him. Warm tears spilled over his fingertips where they rested against her cheek.

Lex, he said again. Her gray eyes blinked open.

Focus on my voice, Alex, thought Declan, mentally shouting to be heard over the clamor of the voices in her head. *Can you hear me?*

She nodded mutely.

"Okay, that could be a problem," he heard Kenzie say.

He looked up. About half a mile ahead, the breakdown lane ended, branching off instead into an exit lane that continued on for another quarter-mile before curving to bridge the road they were traveling on. Unfortunately for them, it was still under construction.

Declan returned his attention to Alex.

You've got to shut out the voices, Lex, he said. *Imagine a wall separating you from them. A thick wall. Just like you did earlier when you wanted to keep Kenzie out.*

Nate drove the car through an opening between the water-filled plastic barricades and accelerated. As they rounded the curve, he muttered a curse. "Now would be a good time for that jump, Decks."

"Little busy here, Nate."

"Well, we're about to run out of freeway, so unless you want to teach this car to fly in the next ten seconds, I suggest you find the time."

Declan looked frantically out the windshield. The bridge up ahead was unfinished and they were fast running out of road.

Realizing he'd have to make do with what little energy

he'd gathered, he attempted a jump. Nothing happened. He needed more power.

In desperation, Declan drained the car's battery. The coupé's engine cut off.

They went over.

As they careened through the air, Declan tightened his hold on the back of the passenger's seat and wrapped his other arm protectively around Alex. Then, for probably the first time in his life, he prayed…

…and they jumped.

The front end of the car slammed into the blacktop, the undercarriage scraping against the pavement until the rear wheels finally connected. The coupé lurched forward a short ways before Nate hit the brakes and they screeched to a halt.

He'd done it.

"So much for the suspension," Declan muttered. "Hope Grayson listened to the rental guy about the optional insurance plan."

"I'm never getting in a car again," Kenzie said from the front seat. There was a funny waver to her voice. She opened the passenger-side door and tumbled out. "And if I do, so help me, it won't be with Nate."

"Hey now, my driving was excellent," said Nate. "Next time we're in a life-and-death style car chase *you* can drive and we'll see how well you manage." He peered into the backseat, frowning. "She okay?"

"She will be," said Declan.

Nathaniel nodded and climbed out of the car.

Declan felt a hand grip his arm. He glanced down to find Alex staring up at him.

"Hey," he said. "Feeling better?"

"A little," she replied, her voice small. "It's quiet again."

"Quiet sounds good," he said.

"Yeah," she agreed. "Quiet is good."

Alex gave a weak smile.

Declan stared down at the girl in his lap. She looked so frail. So easily broken. If he hadn't gotten her out of the city… Gotten her away from all those people…

She'd be gone right now. Everything that Alex was would have vanished in a sea of other people's thoughts.

That was twice today he'd almost lost her. They really needed to call it a night before she went for a trifecta. The girl was turning out to be more than a little jeopardy friendly.

"Where are we?" she asked, closing her eyes as if the words hurt. Then again, between Kenzie's knock-out and the psychic onslaught giving her the mother of all migraines, they probably did.

Declan took her hand in his before he realized what he was doing. She didn't pull away.

"Home," he said. "I teleported us back to the cabin."

"How?" she asked.

"I improvised."

"No, I mean… What happened while I was out?"

"Nothing much," he said. His thumb traced a lazy circle on the back of her hand. "We got shot at for a while, Nate tossed some cars around… Oh, and I managed to make one of those spheres of lightning you love so much. We ended the night with a high-speed chase and a long drive off a short bridge. Had some good times. You should have been awake, you would have loved it."

"I'm sorry I missed it."

The passenger seat flipped forward and Kenzie stuck her head in. "How's our girl?" she asked.

Declan let go of her hand.

Alex struggled to sit up.

"She'll be fine," said Declan, exiting the car. He turned around to offer Alex a hand in getting out.

He told himself he was just being polite. That it had nothing to do with the way he'd started to crave the electric sensation of her soft skin brushing against his.

Nope.

It had nothing to do with that, at all.

Alex took his outstretched hand and climbed carefully from the backseat. She managed to take only a few steps before her knees buckled.

Before Declan could move to catch her, Alex's body froze in place, leaning suspended in mid-air.

An invisible force gently pushed her upright. Kenzie rushed to help support Alex, wrapping her arm around the other girl's waist and draping Alex's arm over her shoulder.

"Nice catch, Nate," said Kenzie.

Their brother was leaning against the stone wall that lined the driveway, watching them with interest.

Nate pushed off the wall and approached them, shaking his head. "That wasn't me."

"What are you talking about?" asked Kenzie.

"I didn't do it. I'm still drained from moving around those cars in the garage."

Kenzie raised an eyebrow. "Well, who else could it have been?"

"I think…" Alex's voice was barely above a whisper. Her head was bowed and her gaze remained fixed on the ground. "I think it was me."

"Wait…" said Kenzie. "So Alex has *two* abilities?"

"Three," Declan corrected.

"What?" asked Kenzie.

"Alex has *three* abilities. She can jump, she's telekinetic… And she's a telepath. That breakdown she had in the parking garage? It was the telepathy manifesting."

Alex raised her head, two loose brown curls framing her face. Her eyes were filled with questions he wasn't sure how to answer.

"In the middle of a city? My god, no wonder she was in so much pain," Kenzie said quietly. "But three powers? Decks, you know that's not possible."

Alex's legs gave out again. Her full weight proved to be too much for Kenzie to support.

Declan moved to help, but Nathaniel reached them first. His brother scooped Alex wordlessly into his arms and carried her toward the staircase that led down to the patio.

He watched them go until they were out of sight.

"Three abilities," Kenzie repeated. "I don't understand it, Decks. Variants never have more than two abilities. It just doesn't happen."

"You know that's not true. It's happened once before."

Kenzie stared at him. "Once. And he wasn't born that way. The Agency *made* him that way."

"I'm just saying… It's happened before."

"Are you honestly suggesting that the *Agency* did this to her?"

"I don't know," he said, making for the stairs. "But we really need to find Grayson."

SEVENTEEN

"How's your head?" asked a loud voice.

Alex lay sprawled on the couch in the exact same place Nathaniel had set her down ten minutes earlier, her feet resting in Kenzie's lap and an arm slung across her eyes; a futile attempt to block out the low light shining down from above.

She attempted a reply, but the sound that escaped her throat was something between a grunt and a whimper.

"That good, huh?"

Alex heard Declan settle onto the coffee table across from her. She lifted her arm and squinted in his general direction. The pounding in her head had caused her vision to dissolve into an indistinguishable mix of light and color.

Even without a clear view of him, she knew that he was smirking down at her. She could hear it in his voice.

It was nice to see he found her situation so amusing.

Three abilities. According to Kenzie, it was impossible. Variants could only ever have, at most, two abilities—inheriting one from either parent. And even that was incredibly rare.

To have three abilities made Alex a freak amongst freaks.

She felt Kenzie's leg kick out in Declan's direction, heard the subtle *thunk* of her foot connecting with his shin, followed by the much louder sounds of Declan's grousing.

"*Quietly*, Decks," Kenzie chided. "You'd feel like crap, too, if a thousand different voices just had a shouting match in your head."

She spoke just above a whisper, her voice low and soft.

Not like Declan, whose voice would have been better suited for an outdoor sporting event. Or maybe talking over the sound of a jet engine.

She was pretty sure those extra decibels had been intentional.

Jerk.

"Is that what happened?" Alex's voice was raspy. "I was starting to think someone had just used my head for a soccer ball."

"Nah," said Kenzie, patting her leg gently. "Trust me. That would have hurt a lot less."

"Good to know," she said, covering her eyes again.

"Most telepaths develop their ability slowly, over time," said Kenzie. "We're not very strong at first. The things we hear and see... they're fuzzy. And quiet. Like barely heard whispers. Or like a radio that's tuned to the static between stations."

Alex could feel Kenzie fidgeting with the frayed edges of her jeans.

"Eventually, it gets louder, and as the thoughts become clearer, we learn to control what we let in. That way we aren't overwhelmed by the thoughts and emotions of the people around us." Kenzie paused. "And then, sometimes, the ability hits you all at once."

"When that happens," said Declan, "you're pretty much screwed."

"Judging from the amount of pain you were in, I'd say you were probably tapped into the inner-thoughts of every person in a ten-block radius," said Kenzie. "All of them, all at once."

"That's... a lot," she said.

"Honestly, Alex? I'm amazed you're sitting here talking to us right now," said Kenzie. "Most people don't recover from what you experienced. They just check out. Get lost in the chaos and never make it back to the surface."

Alex swallowed.

There'd been a moment in the car earlier when she'd almost done just that. The pain had been so intense. The darkness that lurked beneath the voices had felt so enticing. At the time, she'd wanted nothing more than to surrender to it and never feel anything again.

And then she'd heard Declan's voice, familiar and reassuring in the midst of the bedlam, and felt his warm hand gently graze her cheek. His touch had amplified the sound of his voice, causing his words to ring out crystal clear through the ocean of thoughts competing for dominance in her mind.

The wall she'd created at his urging hadn't helped much, but his voice, steady and persistent, had kept her from giving over to the darkness.

Declan's voice was the only reason she was still here. The only reason she was still whole.

When they finally made it back to the cabin, the voices had vanished as quickly as they had appeared. Alex had been sent reeling by the sudden return to silence.

"How come I haven't heard anything since we got back?" she asked.

"Because we all keep walls up," said Declan.

"The guys do it to keep me out," explained Kenzie. "And I do it to keep from accidentally hearing anything I shouldn't. Speaking of which. You're going to want to keep one up all the time, at least until you get the hang of things."

Alex heard someone flip first one light-switch, then another.

"It's safe to open your eyes, Alex." Nathaniel's voice

had come from somewhere behind the couch. "I turned off the light."

Cautiously, Alex raised her arm and blinked her eyes open. The painful glare of the chandelier overhead had been replaced by the dim glow of the light above the front entryway. She could just make out the shadowy form of Nate as he approached and knelt beside her.

He took her hand and turned it over, shaking a pill from a small bottle onto her palm.

"Only one?" Kenzie sounded dubious.

"Two?" asked Nate.

"Three," said Kenzie.

"*Three*?" echoed Declan. "The girl is five-two and thin as a rail. What are you trying to do? Knock her out for the next week?"

"Three," Kenzie insisted. "She'll be lucky if that even takes the edge off."

"How about we start with two and if she needs more, we give her another one later?" Nate suggested.

"Uh," said Alex. "What exactly are you giving me?"

"Pain meds left over from when I broke my leg last August," said Nate, shaking out another pill. He handed her a bottle of water. "They're not all that strong. Especially with our metabolism."

"What's wrong with our metabolism?" she asked, staring down at the bleary outline of the pills in her hand.

Generally speaking, she didn't make it a habit of taking other people's prescription medications. Then again, generally speaking, she didn't usually find herself suffering from excruciating pain that showed no signs of letting up, either.

She swallowed the pills.

"Variants' metabolisms tend to run a bit faster than the average," said Nate. "We burn things off more quickly than most people."

Well that explained why she never seemed to gain weight, despite her aunt's valiant efforts and Alex's borderline-unhealthy obsession with junk food. Cassie often joked that Alex could eat more than all four of her brothers combined.

"Speaking of overactive metabolisms," said Declan, climbing to his feet. "Getting chased by bad guys all night made me hungry. Is there any pizza left?"

"Fridge," said Kenzie.

With that, he and Nate disappeared in search of a food, leaving Alex and Kenzie alone in the living room.

"I know you don't want to hear this," said Kenzie, "but you've got some things to learn before it will be safe for you to leave the cabin again."

Alex sighed.

"Now that we have both Brandt *and* the Agency to worry about, it would be better if I started your training tonight. You're going to need to know how to keep out the voices before you even *think* about going anywhere populated."

Closing her eyes, Alex grudgingly admitted that Kenzie had a point. The wall she'd tried to put up when they were in DC hadn't done a thing to help her.

"When we were in the car earlier, Declan told me to put up a wall to block out the voices," she admitted. "I did it just like you taught me this afternoon, but it didn't work. I was certain I was just doing it wrong."

"Wrong or right, at that point it wouldn't have made much difference." Kenzie shifted on the couch, drawing her legs up under her. "You'd already let them all in. Hard to hold back the water when the dam's already busted, you know?"

Alex thought back to the sound of all those voices talking over each other and the amount of pain it had inflicted. The memory alone was enough to make her anxious...

The thought that it might happen again absolutely terrified her.

The lamp sitting behind Kenzie launched itself off of the end table and shattered as it collided with the wall, causing both girls to jump.

Hand over her heart, Kenzie took a deep breath. "Spending a few minutes training with Nate tonight probably wouldn't be a bad idea, either."

"So," said Declan as he popped open the BMW's trunk. "Alex has three abilities. Only one other Variant has *ever* possessed more than two powers... And if Alex *is* like that psycho Masterson, then that means she's able to absorb another Variants' powers through touch."

Nate paused in his inspection of the documents inside Grayson's briefcase.

He could tell by the tone of Declan's voice that his brother was working his way up to asking a question.

"We can assume that she got her jumping ability from being around her aunt," said Declan. "And she probably absorbed Kenzie's ability this afternoon when Red went digging in Alex's head for that phone number..."

Here it comes.

"But how did she get *your* ability, Nate?"

And there it was.

The question had been laced with innuendo... and just a hint of accusation.

"Grow up, Decks." Nate closed the briefcase.

Declan already knew the answer. He'd seen Nate holding Alex's hand earlier when they were standing outside his window. He was only asking the question to be an ass.

What Declan *didn't* realize was that Nate had known exactly what he was doing when he'd taken Alex's hand earlier. With Brandt still out there and Grayson missing, he'd wanted Alex to be as prepared as she could be—and that meant giving her his telekinesis.

Nate had been relieved when the truth about Alex's unique ability had finally come to light.

It made for one less secret he had to keep.

He only wished that someone would have mentioned the mental spelunking expedition Kenzie had taken into Alex's thoughts that afternoon before they left for DC. Maybe then he would have been prepared for what had happened to her in the parking garage.

The image of Alex screaming in agony wasn't one he'd soon forget. And it killed him to think that he might have been able to prevent it.

"Hey, it's a legitimate question," said Declan. "If it's physical contact that triggers the transfer, then how did she end up with your powers?"

"Grayson's stuff isn't telling us anything," said Nate.

Declan slammed the trunk closed. "No," he said. He seemed to have accepted that Nate wasn't going to answer him. "And this car was the only lead we had."

"You know what that means," said Nate.

"Yep."

"For the record?" said Nate. "This is an awful plan."

"You have a better suggestion?"

Nate started for the stairs.

"Where are you going?" asked Declan.

"I want to check on Alex again before we leave." Nate could practically feel the heat from Declan's glare. "And unless you want to settle for jumping back to the hotel or the parking garage, we're going to need a little help from Kenzie."

He made his way down to the cabin and walked inside. Kenzie and Alex were still seated on the couch in the living room. Alex had her eyes closed.

"You're doing great, Alex," said Kenzie. "See? I told you it was a piece of cake."

Declan walked in behind him.

Nate opened his mouth to speak, but his sister held up a hand and gestured for him to stay quiet.

Those pain meds must have done the trick if Kenzie had already started her training.

Eyes still closed, Alex gave a wry smile. "Yeah, well. It helps when the person teaching me actually gives me a little instruction on *how* to do something instead of just telling me to do it."

"Yeah," Kenzie agreed, fixing Declan with a look of amusement. "My brother could definitely stand to work on his people skills. You'd be better off with Nate training you. At least then you wouldn't end up in the lake as often."

Kenzie gave him a wink. Beside him, Declan mouthed the words "bite me."

Alex laughed. "A girl can dream."

Nate smirked.

Declan cleared his throat.

Alex's eyes sprang open. She caught sight of them standing at the front entryway and her cheeks blazed crimson.

"In case you were wondering," Declan sounded pissed. "We didn't find anything useful in the car. Nate and I are going back to DC to see what else we can find out from Bartlett and—"

"You can't honestly be thinking about going *back* there," said Alex.

"Apparently my brother isn't only lacking in people skills," said Kenzie. "He's also lacking in common sense. Stupidity, however, he appears to have in abundance."

"—And you two are staying here," Declan finished. "Don't even try to argue with me, Kenzie. It's the only choice we've got. We have to go."

Kenzie glared at them. "You're idiots," she said. "The both of you."

"Hey, you won't get any argument from me. I happen to think it's a terrible idea," Nate smiled. "We'll be careful, Red. I promise."

Kenzie's expression softened, but Alex still seemed worried.

"Before we leave," Nate continued. "We could use a little help."

Kenzie nodded, having already guessed at what he was about to request. "Come here," she said. "We might as well let Alex do it."

Nate hesitated.

The idea of giving Alex access to his memories when she didn't know what she was doing made him more than a little nervous. He could trust Kenzie not to look beyond the memory he offered her.

Alex might not have enough control yet *not* to look beyond it.

There's no telling what she might see.

"Can't *you* do it, Kenzie?" he asked.

"What difference does it make?" asked Kenzie. "She's got to learn sometime."

Declan had already crossed the room and was standing behind the couch. "You waiting on a written invitation, Nate? Come on. We need to get moving."

Alex chewed at her bottom lip and tucked a stray curl behind her ear. She looked nearly as anxious as he felt.

"What is it you want me to do?" she asked.

"Tonight was the first time Declan had been to DC," explained Kenzie. "So the only places in the city he can jump to are the places we visited tonight. Seeing as how those sites are probably crawling with Agency goons by now, they need a new location. Nate's been there plenty of times with Grayson, so they'll use his experiences to pick a different destination. Nate's going to focus on a memory—a picture of a place he's been before. You're going to find it in his thoughts and memorize it as best you can. Then you're going to give the image to Declan. That way he'll know the place well enough to teleport there."

"Finding the image sounds easy enough. I just read his thoughts, right?" asked Alex. Kenzie nodded an affirmative. "But then how do I give the image to Declan?"

"It's easier than you think. All you have to do is concentrate on Declan and the image at the same time," said Kenzie. "Oh, and I hate to say it, but until you know what you're doing, you'll need to touch him for it to work. Sorry about that."

Declan rolled his eyes. "Can we just get this over with?"

"Yeah, yeah," Kenzie huffed. "You're in a rush. We know. I've never seen anyone in such a hurry to get shot at. It's not natural."

Before the comment could spark an argument, Alex interrupted. "Have you got that image ready, Nate?"

"Yeah," he said. "Ready when you are."

He tried his best to clear his thoughts of anything he didn't want her to see and keep his focus solely on the image of the park.

But that was a little like telling someone *not* to think about a pink elephant.

Alex's stare became vacant, then sharpened as she met his gaze, her eyes narrowing in confusion.

Shit.

What had she seen?

He slammed his mental walls back into place, shutting her out before she could stumble across anything else.

"You get it, Alex?" asked Declan.

"Y-yeah," she stammered. "Yes. I've got it."

She shot another cautious glance toward Nate before

shifting on the couch and reaching up to press her fingers to Declan's temple. He pulled back a second later and Alex dropped her hand.

"Got it," he said, grabbing Nate by the arm. "Let's go."

Declan's cell phone rang.

Releasing his hold on Nate's jacket, Declan pulled the phone from his pocket. He checked the caller ID and then answered it in a blur of movement.

"Grayson!" he said brusquely. "Where the hell have you been? We've—"

Grayson's reply was muffled to the point that Nate couldn't make it out. He risked another glance at Alex. She was staring back at him, looking puzzled.

Whatever it was she'd seen, he'd have to deal with it later.

Next to him, Declan's eyebrows had shot toward his hairline in an almost comical look of surprise.

"You're *where*?"

EIGHTEEN

"Honestly, Johnny-boy. Did you have to hit me quite so hard? I think you might have cracked a rib."

"And can you blame me? You snuck up behind me in a *parking garage*, for god's sake." Grayson rubbed his aching jaw. "Not to mention the fact that, at the time, I'd been convinced you'd lost what few faculties you still possessed and attacked Alexandra. Incidentally, I'm not entirely sure I *believe* your claim that you had nothing to do with it. Declan's description of the man he saw in Florida matched you perfectly."

Brandt shook his head and took a seat at the bar. Grayson settled onto the stool next to him, grabbed a cocktail napkin from behind the counter and pressed it against his still bleeding lip.

Brandt motioned to the bartender. "As if I would ever harm that girl," his tone was indignant. "After everything I did to help you lot keep her safe back then, why in heaven's name would I try to kill her *now*?"

"I don't know, Carson," said Grayson tiredly. "Maybe because you've spent the twelve years since then killing people for a living?"

It was difficult to keep their voices low and still be understood over the roar of conversation and country music. Grayson glanced around at the peanut shells littering the hardwood floors, the row of pool tables off to one side, and the primarily blue-collar clientele in their faded flannel shirts and worn-in trucker hats. He looked down at his own Savile Row tailored suit and Burberry trench.

Bloodstained collar or no, he was definitely over-dressed.

The bartender, an attractive young woman in her mid-twenties, came to a stop in front of them. Taking their disheveled appearance in stride, she greeted them with a smile. "What'll it be, boys?"

Brandt returned her smile with something bordering on a leer.

Nice to see *some* things never changed.

"Glenlivet," said Brandt. "Neat, please."

"And for you?"

"Just water, thanks," said Grayson.

"He'll have the same, love," said Brandt, causing Grayson to raise an eyebrow. Brandt tossed a crumpled bill onto the bar. "Trust me. You're going to want it once you hear what I have to tell you."

The bartender slid two glasses of amber liquid in their direction.

"Oh? And what might that be?" asked Grayson.

"Thank you, love," said Brandt to the bartender's retreating form. He raised the glass to his lips. "That twelve years ago we screwed up."

A chill ran the length of Grayson's spine. "What are you talking about?"

"Back in January I was…" He searched for the phrase. "*Tending to some business* in Belfast."

"You mean you were there to kill someone."

"You make it sound so crass," said Brandt. He swirled the whisky in his glass. "I'm merely a means to an end. They'll end up dead one way or another. You know I only take the job if I feel the person deserves it."

"Yes. Because you're more than qualified to serve as *anyone's* judge, jury and executioner."

"I'm not here to defend my career choices to you, John."

"Then get to the point."

Brandt sighed. "I'd been hired by a party that wished to remain anonymous. Nothing unusual about that. What *was* unusual was that I'd been given a specific time and location where the job was to be completed."

"Would this location happen to have been a cheap motel on the east side of town?"

"Been checking up on me, have you?" Brandt smiled. "When I got there, I knew something was off. I found the bomb stashed in a closet and managed to shimmy down a fire escape a few seconds before it went off."

"How is it that everyone came to believe you'd been killed in the blast?"

"You're not the only one who still has a friend or two at the Agency," said Brandt. "Had them falsify some dental records for me."

"What does all this have to do with what happened twelve years ago?"

"I'm getting to that." Brandt took another sip of his drink. "I've spent the last few months trying to figure out who it was that hired me. I'd gotten nowhere until about a week ago when someone in the States accessed one of my Zurich accounts. I traced the transaction back to a bank in—of all places—a coastal Florida town."

"And?"

"And I hacked into the bank's security footage. Imagine my surprise when I saw my own handsome face walking around inside of a bank four-thousand miles away."

"Are you suggesting it was a Mimic that tried to kill you in Belfast?" Grayson asked, surprised.

Mimics were a type of Variant that could take on the physical features of any individual they touched. Shapeshifters. Brandt would have needed to have come into contact with one for his likeness to have been absorbed by them.

That still didn't explain how the Mimic had been able to control fire, unless that person had somehow inherited two abilities. And the odds against *that* one... Well, they were astronomical.

"That's what I thought too, at first, so I went to Florida and tracked him down. Yesterday afternoon I followed him to a bookstore." Brandt looked haggard. "I watched him attack the girl. And then I watched him teleport."

Three abilities. For that to be possible...

"No," said Grayson. "He's dead, Carson. I made sure of it."

"Well, apparently, you didn't make *damn* sure, because the man is still very much *alive*," said Brandt. "And if what happened in Belfast is any indication, he doesn't appear to be too happy about what we did to him. I don't know where you're hiding the girl, Jonathan, but it had better be someplace he won't think to look."

Grayson reached for the glass on the bar. He downed its contents in one gulp.

"Masterson's alive, John," said Brandt. "And if we don't figure out how to kill him properly this time, that prophecy of yours might just come to pass after all."

"You know, I used to own a pit bull. As I remember, he slobbered a lot less than your friend. Smelled better, too."

From her spot on the balcony, Cassie peered through the cracked sliding glass door and into Aiden's living room.

Connor lay sprawled on one end of the L-shaped couch, snoring like a buzz saw and drooling onto the cushions. Brian was asleep on the shorter leg, Connor's bare feet inches from his face.

Cassie shook her head, wondering what Brian's reaction would be when he woke to an eyeful of Connor's size 12's. She was surprised the aroma of Eau de Feet hadn't already woke him.

"You'd be wrong to assume that he's any friend of mine," she said, turning back around and leaning her weight against the railing.

Cassie had migrated to the apartment's balcony after trying, unsuccessfully, to fall asleep in one of Aiden's two recliners. Connor's thunderous snore would have been enough to keep her awake all by itself, but she was soon facing a second problem.

Every time her eyes closed, she found herself somewhere else.

Blink.

The warehouse.

Blink.

The trunk of Brandt's car.

Blink.

The dock.

Continuously reliving the events of the day had turned the prospect of sleep into a cruel joke. When Aiden had slipped quietly through the living room and out the sliding door to the balcony, the choice to follow him had practically made itself.

"That sounded distinctly bitter." Aiden's green eyes shined with mirth. "Is he an ex?"

"Not mine." She pulled the borrowed blanket tighter around her shoulders in a futile attempt to stave off the chill of the evening. A salty gust of wind dragged her long blonde hair behind her.

"Surely he's not *Kenzie's* ex?" Aiden arched a brow. "I wouldn't have guessed him to be my cousin's type."

"Alex's," she corrected.

The sound of waves crashing against the shore drifted up from somewhere below.

Aiden smiled. "Ah, the mysterious *Alex*. She of the wavy hair and endless trouble."

He spoke the words as though he were already familiar with Alex's particular brand of trouble.

Cassie focused on the moon's reflection on the water, the way the long column writhed and danced upon the crown of each breaking wave.

Aiden's place might not have been all that big, but his view of the Pacific Ocean was to die for.

At least, she thought it was the Pacific. She really ought to ask someone which Newport they were in.

"Do you usually get mixed up in these things?" she asked.

"More often than I'd like," he said. "Anything for family and all that… But one day I'm gonna start charging them hazard pay."

"You guys pretty close?"

He shrugged. "With Nate, I guess. He lived with me out in Seattle a couple years back. I got him a job on a fishing boat," he smiled. "Had some *interesting* times, before he decided to go back to work for Grayson."

"So is Nate your cousin, too?"

"In all the ways that matter. Nate's mom died just after my aunt and uncle did, so he went to live with Grayson at the same time as Kenzie and Decks. To me, he's family. Same with Brian in there. And Brian's dad, too." Aiden looked out over the water. "Grayson was more like a father to me than my *own* dad was."

They stood there for a long while, side by side against the railing, lost in a companionable silence.

"So tell me, Cassie."

"Hm?"

"How did *you* get mixed up in all this?"

This blanket wasn't nearly warm enough. She stared down at her hands.

Blink.

The warehouse.

Cassie swallowed hard.

"I was Brandt's leverage," she said. "He wanted to draw Alex into a meeting... so he... so he kidnapped me to ensure that she'd show."

Aiden's good humor evaporated. She could feel him studying her in the low light as an uneasy silence settled over the two of them. Not knowing what else to say, Cassie gazed out over the water.

Her vision blurred.

Blink.

The trunk.

Something warm was dripping onto her forearm. Crap. She wiped furtively at her cheeks. She'd been able to hold it together *this* long. Falling to pieces in front of a guy she'd only just met was *not* an option.

It wasn't.

She was stronger than this.

...So why were the tears still coming?

"Want to talk about it?" he asked.

The question caught her off-guard. "You know you're the first person who's asked me that? Everyone else just wanted to know if I was 'okay.' What kind of question is that, anyway? Am I *okay*? A crazy man snuck up behind me in a parking lot, held an awful smelling rag over my face until I passed out, shoved me in the trunk of a car, and then left me tied up in an abandoned warehouse for the *longest* ten hours of my life. After that he burned my classmate alive right in front of my eyes." Tears spilled down her cheeks. No stopping them now. "Oh, yeah, I'm okay. Life's a friggin' *peach*."

"Hey," said Aiden, his voice soft. Lifting one hand, he caught her chin and gently turned her face toward his. "Hey, it's okay. You're safe here."

With a subtle wave from his free hand, Aiden summoned the tears cascading down Cassie's cheeks into the space between them. The droplets swirled above his palm and then disappeared, evaporating into the cool night air.

Just as Brandt had controlled fire, Aiden could control water.

There was a hint of worry in his eyes, as though he wasn't sure what her reaction might be.

She surprised both of them by taking a step forward, wrapping her arms around him and burying her face against his chest. After a moment's hesitation, Cassie felt Aiden return the embrace, holding her tightly against him.

Safe.

For the first time since Brandt had taken her, she felt *safe*.

Arms still wrapped around Aiden, Cassie closed her eyes... and saw nothing.

Maybe she wasn't so broken after all.

NINETEEN

When Alex had mentioned earlier that she'd rather be trained by Nathaniel, this wasn't what she'd had in mind.

"Arm up," said Nate. "What are you doing? I said to hold it taught, not to dislocate your shoulder."

Nate was acting weird.

And, okay, Alex had only known the guy for two days. There was always an outside chance that he got moody and secretive about things *all* the time, and that this sudden turn for the pithy was nothing out of the ordinary.

But she didn't think so.

"Tensing up like that won't help," he was saying. "Your arm is simply a tool to help you visualize and narrow the direction of your focus. It's your *mind* that does the work. Now try again. Move the can."

The can shuddered, teetering on the edge for one long moment before slipping off the wall and clinking against the flagstone. It continued to roll until it met with the toe of Nate's boot.

"Is that what you were trying to do?" he asked doubtfully, staring down at the can.

Alex was starting to understand why sleep-deprivation was considered a form of torture. "Actually, I was trying to levitate it."

"Huh," said Nate. "Well, it's a start, I guess."

Alex couldn't get the image out of her head.

She'd only stumbled across it by accident. It's not as

though she'd *intentionally* gone digging into Nate's private thoughts. One moment, she was memorizing the image of the sun-drenched park in DC he'd offered her—and the next, she'd found herself somewhere else entirely.

Somewhere in the realm of his memories.

Nate bent to retrieve the can.

Alex had asked him about it, of course. How could she not?

When you stumble across a memory containing a crystal clear image of yourself—dripping wet, decidedly unconscious, and sporting a blue-lipped look of death—in someone else's mind...

Someone you'd only just met...

Well, it's going to raise a few questions.

Questions that had been met with a look of blind panic from Nathaniel. Oh, he'd tried to hide his reaction, but the damage had been done. He knew exactly which memory it was that Alex had been referring to. And his response told her that the image she'd glimpsed had a story behind it.

A story that Nate wouldn't be sharing with her *any* time soon, no matter how many times she might ask.

Alex returned her focus to the task at hand: figuring out how to move that stupid can. She'd get the truth out of Nate eventually. She'd just have to work out the logistics of *how* to do it later.

"So is Grayson coming back tonight?" asked Alex.

She sized up the soda can Nate had once again placed on the stone wall that lined the patio. He stepped back and she obediently raised her arm, preparing for her sixth attempt.

"Declan said Grayson would check in with us again tomorrow, but that he and Brandt had an errand to run," said Nate. "Whatever that means."

The idea that Grayson was out there somewhere with

that monster—and that he was there *willingly*—had taken them *all* by surprise. There was something very strange going on and Alex was desperate to find out what it was.

Grayson had hinted that the man he was with might not have been the same man that she'd met. But if the man coming after her wasn't Carson Brandt, then who was he?

"Come on, Alex," said Nate. "Where's your head right now? Focus."

Alex pulled a face. No matter how hard she concentrated, she couldn't move the lousy hunk of tin more than an inch in any direction.

Next to her, Nate's shoulders quaked with silent laughter. It was the first time he'd cracked a smile in over an hour. *"Relax*, Alex. You look like you're about to strain something. Remember what I said: you're moving it with your thoughts, not with your actual muscles."

Why was this so hard for her?

Telepathy had been a cinch, once Kenzie had shown her the ropes. Even her lessons with Declan hadn't been this challenging.

It didn't matter what she tried—the stubborn can simply wouldn't move the way she wanted it to.

Someone yawned behind her. She turned to find Kenzie wrapped up in a blanket. Alex hadn't heard her approach.

"And how's our prodigy doing?" asked the redhead.

Nate gave a noncommittal grunt. "She'd probably be better with a full night's sleep."

"You'll get no argument from me," said Alex. Her eyelids were growing heavier by the minute. "What time is it, anyway?"

"A little after two A.M.," said Kenzie.

Geez. No wonder she was so tired.

"Has Declan made it back with Brian yet?" asked Nate.

Declan left shortly before Alex began training with

Nathaniel, intent on taking Cassie and Connor home and bringing Brian back from Aiden's.

The decision to send her friends back to Florida hadn't been an easy one for Alex. After what had happened with Cassie, Alex wanted to keep her friends and family as close to her as possible—close enough that she could keep an eye on them.

Eventually, the others had convinced her that Cassie and Connor would be safer at home with their families and Alex had relented. She still wasn't certain she'd made the right decision.

Before Declan left, Alex had asked him for two favors.

The first was to have Cassie call her at the cabin as soon as he dropped her off at home. After everything Cassie had been through today, Alex wanted nothing more than to hear the sound of her best friend's voice and make certain that she was alright.

The second request was that Declan stop by Alex's house and check in on her Aunt Cil.

She wasn't answering at the house or on her cell phone and it was making Alex nervous.

Worry had started to sink its gnarled teeth into her, causing a tight knot to form in her chest. What if Brandt had come after her? Or the Agency? What if she hadn't been able to jump in time?

A thousand different scenarios, each one worse than the last, had played themselves out in her mind.

"They're not back yet," said Kenzie. "But Declan left ages ago. They ought to be home soon."

Alex sure hoped so. She wasn't sure her nerves were going to hold up much longer.

How did people in high-stress situations do it? Cops. Superheroes. Bruce Willis in all those Die Hard movies… How did they stay so cool and collected while the world was going mad all around them?

"Alright, Alex," said Nate. "How about you give it one more go before we call it a night?"

Too tired to argue, Alex raised her arm and prepared for one last attempt.

A flash of light drove back the darkness. The orange glow of the patio lights had been replaced by an electric blue flash heralding Declan's arrival.

Alex jumped to one side as four bodies appeared in the air next to her and tumbled unceremoniously onto the flagstone. Wisps of smoke surrounded them, filling her nostrils with an acrid stench.

Declan, Brian, Aiden and Cassie lay sprawled on the patio deck, coughing fitfully and looking rumpled. For whatever reason, Declan was the only one of the four that was dripping wet.

"*What happened*?" asked Alex. "Are you guys alright?"

She knelt beside Cassie as the other girl struggled to sit up. She was fighting to catch her breath, but other than that, she appeared unharmed.

"I'm okay," said Cassie, waving her off.

"We're fine," Aiden managed between coughs.

"Speak for yourself." Declan sat with his arms resting on his knees, water leaking steadily from his clothes into a slowly expanding puddle beneath him, his face haggard.

"Wait." Alex did a quick headcount. Their group was one short. "Where's Connor?"

"I took him home," said Declan.

Alex looked from Cassie to Declan and back again. He'd taken Connor home, but not Cassie?

"Honestly, Alex," said Cassie, her voice droll. "Did you *really* think that I was just going to go back home and leave you here all alone? Mind you, I didn't realize it would mean I'd come so close to getting *roasted* twice in a single day."

Declan glared at Cassie. "I tried to take her home, but

she seemed to have other plans. Your friend can be quite persuasive when she wants to be."

Persuasive? Declan wasn't the sort of guy you reasoned with. And she was pretty sure that the two of them couldn't stand each other. So how had Cassie convinced him to let her stay?

"Cassie stole his wallet," Brian explained. "Said she wouldn't return it until Declan brought her back here."

"That reminds me." Declan held out a hand. "Wallet. *Now*."

"Seriously, Cass?"

"Hey, it got me here, didn't it?" she said, fishing a battered leather wallet from the back pocket of her jeans. She threw it at Declan's head. "Think fast, Grumpy."

He caught it with one hand and opened it to check the contents before slipping it back into his pocket, mumbling, "*Klepto.*"

"You okay, kid? You look a little… singed," Kenzie was staring at Brian in concern.

Brian rubbed the top of his head, causing a handful of ash to fall from his hair. "All in one piece. No worries. Although we can't really say the same for Aiden's apartment. Pretty sure that one's a total loss."

Next to Cassie, Aiden rubbed his hands across his face and groaned. "I knew… I freaking *knew* I'd regret helping you guys. If that asshat so much as *touches* Norma Jean, you're the first one I'm coming after, Decks."

Declan stopped coughing long enough to stare daggers at his cousin. His wet hair was still dribbling water into his eyes. "How the hell was I supposed to know that Brandt would be able to follow me from Florida back to Newport?"

"*Brandt?*" Alex echoed.

The soda can took off like a shot and embedded itself in the trunk of a nearby tree. The others flinched.

"Whoa!" said Kenzie. "Breathe, Alex. *Breathe*. Before

you take someone's head off with an adirondack chair or something."

"Okay," said Cassie, staring in surprise at the can's remains. "That's new."

Alex tried to relax, but her nerves were becoming increasingly frayed around the edges.

It seemed ridiculous, but she was actually starting to miss the way things used to be, back when she only had to worry about the odd appliance getting fried.

Now she'd added flying projectiles to the list. What would she have to worry about next? Spontaneous combustion? Earthquakes?

Alex did as Kenzie suggested and sucked in a deep breath.

"I thought Brandt was with Grayson in Virginia?" said Nate.

"He is," said Declan. "Or at least he was. When Grayson called earlier, he said that he was about to get some answers... But I'm still waiting on a phone call to find out what those answers were. All I know is that this was *definitely* the same guy that torched the bookstore and kidnapped Cassie."

"Alright, but if Brandt's still with Grayson... Then who just came after you? Brandt's even-more-evil twin?" asked Kenzie.

Declan shrugged.

"How did this happen?" asked Alex. "How did he even find you, Declan?"

"He was waiting for me at your place," he said. "After I dropped Connor off, I went to see your Aunt, like I'd promised. Nobody was home. I was stepping off your porch when I saw him standing at the end of your driveway, so I teleported back to Aiden's. I thought I'd lose him with the jump."

"Yeah." Aiden's voice was laced with bitterness.

"Instead he rode your coattails back to Newport and started torching my apartment. Excellent plan, Decks. You're a genius."

"*Dammit*, Declan," Nate spat. The anger Alex had sensed simmering quietly within him for the last hour had finally bubbled to the surface. "If he can follow you, then why the hell did you jump back *here*? You could have led him right to Alex."

Brian shook his head, causing more ashes to fall from his brown hair. "We should be okay. Brandt jumped first," he said. "Aiden had him pinned in a corner with this really big, really *sharp* chunk of ice."

Alex eyed the soggy blonde sitting next to her, unable to contain her curiosity any longer. "Declan, why are you all wet?"

Instead of answering, Declan glowered at Aiden.

"So what happened to the apartment?" asked Kenzie. "Is it still burning? What about the other people in the complex?"

"Pretty sure that won't be an issue," said Cassie.

His anger momentarily forgotten, Aiden fixed Cassie with a rueful smile.

"Oh?" said Nate.

Aiden's smile grew wider. "I, uh… Well, I sort of put the fires out before we jumped."

His bad mood momentarily forgotten, Nate grinned. "Is there any water left in Newport? Or is it all in your apartment?"

Aiden gave a lazy shrug. "Probably safe to assume that I won't be getting my deposit back."

Nate and Cassie laughed.

"I don't get it," said Alex.

"Aiden can control water," said Cassie, matter-of-factly, as though that were a completely normal thing for someone to be able to do.

Her friend seemed to be handling all these revelations with surprising alacrity. Alex wished she could say the same.

"Yeah," Declan grumbled, shrugging off his moisture-laden coat. "And he can't aim for shit."

Aiden climbed to his feet and held out a hand to Cassie. "Hey, I told you to get out of the way, Decks. It's not my fault you have the reflexes of an eighty-year-old woman."

"Next time you need a quick escape, cousin, I'm going to remember you said that."

Alex reached for Declan's discarded coat and fished his cell phone from the pocket. It was damp, but it looked alright. She turned it on and dialed.

"Who are you calling?" he asked.

The others were headed inside, but Declan remained, watching her movements with interest.

"Aunt Cil," she said. "I want to make sure she's okay."

Brandt had been at Alex's house. Was *that* why her aunt wasn't picking up the phone?

There was no answer at home or on her aunt's cell. Alex left messages on both machines and wondered if there was anyone else she could call.

The phone buzzed in her hand. A text from her aunt.

DWBH, Lee-Lee. Am fine. Will call soon.

"D. W. B. H.?" asked Declan.

She gripped the phone.

When Alex had first gone to live with her aunt she'd been a wreck. For days Alex had cried nonstop, had refused to eat, and had been unable to sleep for anything more than an hour or two at a time.

Aunt Cil had been at the end of her rope, desperate to find something that would stop the deluge of tears.

And then, one night after tucking Alex tightly into bed, Aunt Cil had started humming a song.

Alex had recognized it instantly. The song had been one of her mother's favorites. She'd started humming along and, within minutes, had fallen into the first night of restful sleep she'd had since her parents' death.

"It stands for 'don't worry, be happy,'" she explained. "You know. Like the song. It means that she's okay."

Alex stared at the phone for a long moment before trying a third number. Declan was still watching her. She turned away from him and waited for an answer.

"Hello?" came a groggy voice.

"Connor!" she breathed. Alex ignored Declan's derisive snort. "Are you okay?"

"Alex?"

The sound of rustling sheets reached her through the phone and she knew she'd woken him. Alex could picture him there in his darkened bedroom, sitting upright in bed, hair tousled from sleep, clutching his cell phone as worry set in and he struggled to wake up.

She hated that he'd been dragged into the middle of all this.

Was this what it was going to be like from now on? Always worrying about the ones she loved? Always fearing for their safety?

How was she supposed to keep them all safe when she could barely hold it together herself?

"I'm fine, Lexie," he said. "Declan brought me home. Why? Is everything alright? Are *you* okay?"

"No, no," she said quickly. "Everything's fine. I just... I just wanted to make sure you got home alright. That's all. I'm sorry to wake you."

Declan was mumbling something under his breath.

"Goodnight, Connor," she said softly, then hung up.

Alex handed the phone back to Declan. His expression was unreadable.

"What?" she asked.

Instead of answering, he jumped.

Exhausted, Alex got to her feet and trudged back inside.

TWENTY

Her cell was ringing again.

Cecilia Cross stared at the phone vibrating in her right hand, frowning as she recognized the area code. The phone stilled and the call went to voicemail.

Not answering was growing harder every time the phone rang.

Trouble was, she still hadn't decided on what she would say when she finally found the courage to answer it. She couldn't seem to come up with anything that wouldn't potentially make the situation worse than it already was. So instead, she'd opted for silence.

She felt like a coward.

The light turned green and she hit the gas, dividing her focus between the rain-drenched roads and her cell phone, waiting impatiently for the message alert. Two minutes passed and still no notification. With a small sigh of relief, she slipped the phone back into the cup holder beside her.

If something had happened, Alex would have left a message. Cil was banking on the notion that no message meant there was nothing to worry about.

Well.

Nothing *new* to worry about, anyway.

Cil chewed at her thumbnail as she drove, squinting to see the blacktop through the torrential downpour and wishing, for the millionth time, that she'd handled all of this differently.

To hell with what Nora and James had wanted. Alex should have been told the truth about the family months ago.

Cil spent twelve years waiting for the day when her lies would fall apart. Waiting for the day when Alex would discover who she really was and what she was capable of.

When Alex hit sixteen, Cil had stopped worrying.

Sixteen years old and not a hint of either of her parents' abilities. No electrical disturbances, no mysteriously moving objects... Just a beautiful young woman with a budding social life, a bright future ahead of her and an unwavering determination to make something of herself.

At first, Cil couldn't believe her luck. She wasn't sure what the odds were against two Variant parents giving birth to a child without abilities, but somehow, they appeared to have done just that.

Alexandra was wonderfully, impossibly, *average*, and Cil couldn't be happier.

She was going to have that normal life her parents had wanted for her from the start—and she would never have to learn the truth.

In this instance, ignorance truly was bliss.

And then came the accident at the school.

Cil had hovered over her niece for the next week while she healed, under the pretense of keeping her still so she wouldn't pull the stitches in her side. In reality, she'd had a second motive for sticking close to her niece: she needed to know for certain if the accident had been Alex's fault.

For the first three days, nothing happened.

On the fourth day they had an argument. What it was about Cil couldn't remember.

What she *did* remember was that bitter moment of surprise and the intense pain she experienced when, after laying a hand on Alex's shoulder to calm her, her niece absorbed her energy and used it to short out every piece of electrical equipment in the room.

She should have told Alex the truth, then and there.

Instead, she'd kept her mouth shut. Cil told herself that she was keeping up the facade of normalcy for her sister's sake, because it was what she and James had wanted so badly for their little girl.

But that was a lie.

In reality, she'd been afraid of how Alex would react to learning the truth. Afraid of how Alex would feel about the fact that she'd been lied to for so many years.

Cil was afraid of losing her.

And now?

She turned the car into the driveway of their home and cut the engine. The blue, two-story Victorian that she shared with Alex glistened black with rainwater in the pre-dawn gloom. Sighing, she stared up at the empty house.

Well, she might just have lost her, anyway.

The phone shook violently against the sides of the cup-holder, startling her. Only one pulse—she had a message.

Heart in her throat, Cil checked the phone.

It wasn't Alex.

Grayson had sent her an image.

Before the image could be downloaded completely, there was another pulse. A text message appeared below the image, reading:

WE NEED TO MEET. BE HERE AS SOON AS YOU CAN.

The image finished loading and she scrolled up to examine it... And very nearly dropped the phone in surprise when she recognized where the picture had been taken.

The photo was of the dilapidated entrance of a disused

mineshaft, burrowed into the side of a mountain and lit harshly by the flash of Grayson's camera phone.

No, she thought desperately. *Please, God, don't let this be happening.*

Phone still clutched in one hand, Cil was out of the car in the next instant. She took a breath to steady herself... and jumped.

The muggy coastal air had been replaced with the dry chill of a Virginia night in early spring. Cil crossed her arms over her chest as a breeze rushed through the branches of the trees overhead and realized, belatedly, that she really ought to have grabbed a jacket before she left.

Thoughts of outerwear fled her mind when she registered that there were, in fact, *two* figures waiting for her at the entrance. Grayson hadn't come alone.

A flashlight was aimed in her direction. Cil raised a hand to cut the glare and tilted her head to see below it as she hesitantly approached.

"Grayson?" she called out. "Who's—"

"Cecilia!" a familiar Scottish brogue replied. "Well, well... It *is* a night for surprises."

"*You!*"

"It's alright, Cil," Grayson's voice called. He pointed the light at the ground, illuminating her path as she approached. "Brandt's not the one after Alex."

She wasn't sure whether to be relieved by that announcement, or terrified.

Judging from the fact that she was currently approaching the entrance to a place she only ever visited in her nightmares, she was leaning toward terror.

"You're looking good, Cil," Brandt drawled as she came to a stop next to Grayson. "The years have certainly been kind."

"Stuff it, burnout," she replied. Brandt was *definitely* the same letch she remembered.

"Lost none of that dazzling charm, I see," he quipped.

How Grayson and the others had tolerated him back when they'd both worked as consultants for the Agency had been beyond her. Working with scumbags like Brandt was *exactly* why she'd only consented to work with the Agency on an as-needed basis. And even then, she'd only agreed to do so to appease her sister.

Brandt, on the other hand, had simply been in it for the money.

Cil had never trusted the Agency, even when the organization had still been in its infancy.

As it turned out, she'd been right not to.

"Alright, you two," said Grayson. "To your corners. We're all on the same side here."

Grayson had swung the flashlight around to focus on a patch of brush near the gate. He pushed aside the branches to reveal a hidden keypad.

"How's Alex?" she asked as he typed in the code.

A heavy metal click resonated from the rust-covered door that sealed the entrance. Grayson swung it open. Only darkness lay beyond.

"Fine," he said shortly. He led the way into the black, vanishing completely before being illuminated by a motion-activated florescent light. "At the cabin. Same as she was when I called to update you earlier."

Cil followed Brandt across the threshold. The stone walls of the passageway seemed to insulate the cold, making the cramped entryway feel a good twenty degrees cooler than the air outside. She shivered.

Up ahead was a second door, this one equipped with a retinal scanner. Grayson ducked down to peer into the device.

"And after what happened with Cassie, do you really blame me for asking again?" She rubbed her arms in a futile attempt to warm them. "I just spent the last two

hours apologizing to her poor mother, who called me—
frantic—at midnight tonight, wanting to know where her
daughter was. Do you know what I told her? That they
went camping. *Camping*! Cassie hates camping! They *both*
do! And it's *pouring down rain*!"

Cil was aware that she was rambling. She couldn't help
it.

She knew what was waiting for them on the other side
of that door. And she had a sinking suspicion that what
they were going to discover when they finally made it past
all the security protocols would be far more frightening
than the wrath of Cassie's irate mother.

"So this is a nice little reunion," said Brandt, shoving
his hands into the pockets of his jeans. "Had I known we'd
be getting the gang back together, I would have dressed
for the occasion."

Cil took a moment to look at him—to *really* look at
him—and then appraised Grayson as well.

Brandt had a rip in his jeans and dried blood spattered
across his wrinkled black dress shirt. Even Grayson looked
worse for wear in his Burberry trench and designer suit,
though he'd at least attempted to pull himself back
together. His lip was split and he had the makings of a real
shiner blossoming around his left eye.

"What on *Earth* happened to you two? Jesus, Grayson,
you look like you just went five rounds with Mike Tyson."

"I'll take that as a compliment," said Brandt. "She's
right, you know. You really do look like hell."

Grayson didn't answer. He was too busy glaring at the
retinal scanner, arms akimbo and a scowl on his face.

"What's the matter?" asked Brandt.

Grayson sighed. "They must have changed my clearance
level. I no longer have access. And we've got maybe ten minutes to find a way in there before someone at the Agency
figures out what we're doing and comes to investigate."

"Well, Miss Cross?" said Brandt. "It *is* still Miss, correct? Not Mrs.?"

Cil glared at him. "They've still got the EM shield up, Brandt. I can sense it from here. We can't teleport inside." She narrowed her eyes at the scanner. "But maybe we can try something else."

Placing her hand on the side of the scanner, Cil began studying the inner-workings of the device, searching for the door control. Twenty seconds passed, then thirty.

"Not to trouble you, my dear," said Brandt. "But we *are* operating under something of a time constraint here."

Okay, so she was rusty.

The last time she'd attempted to use her powers to manipulate an electronic device had been two presidential administrations and a lifetime ago.

Another minute passed.

She couldn't find the damn door control.

What she had found, however, was the component that would have been triggered had Grayson's security clearance been high enough.

"Grayson," she said. "Look into the scanner again."

He did as she requested. Cil forced the approval and the door lock released with a hiss of air.

"Finally," said Brandt, pulling the door wide.

"You're welcome," she shot back, following them through the entryway—and into a world she'd hoped never to see again.

The place was a tomb.

Cil stood frozen in place, just a foot inside the door. Fluorescent lights were coming on, panel by panel, gradually illuminating the long hallway as Grayson and Brandt forged ahead, making their way toward the silver elevator doors that glinted in the darkness at the end of the passageway.

The air was stale. Cil wondered how many years had

passed since anyone had actually been down here. The entire complex was supposed to have been sealed up for good that snowy night, twelve years ago. The same night she'd helped Grayson and Brandt put an end to the horror that was Samuel Masterson.

As if reading her thoughts, the air filtration system in the ceiling above whirred to life, pumping in fresh air from above ground.

Glass partitions took the place of walls, demarcating the rooms on either side of the long hall. She supposed the glass had been selected in an attempt to curb the feeling of claustrophobia that came with working beneath countless tons of solid rock. Instead, it gave their former headquarters all the homeyness of a fishbowl, the contents of each room laid bare for all to see.

Desks, computers, file cabinets, a coffee pot on the counter in the break room… In its appearance, it was no different than any other office.

To look at it, you'd have no idea that their line of work had been anything but ordinary.

Her gaze lingered for a moment on a plain black picture frame that sat on a desk in an office to her right. James's desk.

In the image, her sister knelt in the grass out front of their former home, arms wrapped tightly around a three-year-old Alex, as they both smiled up at James behind the camera.

"Coming, Cil?" called Grayson. He and Brandt were already at the end of the hall and stood waiting for her at the elevator.

She started walking, the sound of her heels clicking against the linoleum floors, echoing in the quiet space. Cil found herself remembering a time when these offices had been filled with noise and movement and—more often than not—the sound of laughter.

Before Masterson's reign of terror incited the higher-ups at the Agency to change their methods (quickly making them the bane of Variants everywhere), Grayson's team had been a real force for good in the world.

Cil had worked with them often enough to see just how close the group had become in the eight years since the unit had been formed. Grayson had hit the nail on the head when he'd described their bond to Alex earlier—they weren't just co-workers. They were family.

The elevator opened.

It took every ounce of her resolve to step inside.

The doors slid closed. No going back now.

As they began their slow decent, Cil broke the silence. "Are you going to tell me what we're doing here, Jonathan?"

Grayson's choice to remain silent only served to confirm her fears.

"I should think the reason why we're here ought to be fairly obvious by now, love," said Brandt. "God knows we didn't come back for the sheer nostalgia of it all."

"It's not possible," she said quietly. "He's dead, Brandt. Masterson is *dead*… We *made sure* he couldn't come back."

"You two are like broken bloody records, you are," said Brandt. "You know, I never asked what measures you took to *make sure* he was truly dead… And honestly, I could have cared less *how* you did it, so long as the dog had finally been put down. But now that some bastard is out there masquerading with my face and sullying my good name—" Cil snorted at that. '*Good name*,' indeed. "Well, personally, I'd like to know for certain that your measures were effective."

The elevator dinged and the doors slid open.

One final blast door stood between the trio and the resting place of nothing less than pure evil.

Cil stared up at the massive metal door, curling her

hands into fists to fight the trembling in her fingers. It was a scene from her nightmares, made all too real.

Doors like this one weren't meant to be opened.

Another retinal scanner. Cil and Grayson repeated the process and, far sooner than Cil would have liked, she found herself walking into a massive room, empty except for a row of cryogenic chambers, standing upright at the center of the room.

Masterson's numerous gifts had made killing him nearly impossible. Accelerated healing and a myriad of other defensive abilities meant that, even if you *could* stop his heart, he wouldn't stay dead long.

In the end, a chemical cocktail, a little subterfuge, and a loaded gun had put him under just long enough for Grayson and Cil to transport him back to the mountain and place him in cryo-stasis—leaving him forever frozen in his temporary state of death.

Cil came up short. She wasn't sure what was more surprising. That one of the formerly empty units was now active—containing the body of a man she couldn't identify, because his face lay in shadow—or that Masterson's unit *wasn't* empty.

Samuel Masterson was still locked in his icy prison.

Grayson came to a stop in front of the unit, eye-to-eye with Masterson's sleeping form.

"Well, now," said Brandt. "There's a twist."

A pair of strong arms grabbed Cil from behind. One arm around her waist, the other reaching up to grip her by the throat. The arms were nearly translucent in the dim light, slowly shimmering into form. Another heartbeat, and the figure's materialization was complete.

Cil craned her neck to peer up at her now visible captor.

Samuel Masterson's face smiled down at her. "Hello, lovely," he said in a quiet voice. "Been a while, hasn't it?"

"Samuel!" Grayson said with a start. His gaze traveled

quickly from the man holding Cil, to the unit, and back again. "But how…?"

"I suppose I ought to start out by *thanking* you," he said. "Been trying for ages to get in here. Couldn't have done it without those magnificent eyes of yours, Jonathan. Much obliged."

"You followed us in here," said Brandt.

"Invisibility sure is a neat trick, isn't it?" he laughed.

"How are you *here* and in there at the same time?" asked Brandt.

"*Christ*, you three got old," said Masterson, giving Cil a once-over as she struggled in his arms. "Especially you, John. I suppose raising four kids on your own will do that to a man. Oh, but then you *weren't* alone the entire time, were you? There was that beautiful second wife of yours… The one you found to replace Mary. Now, what was her name? Lillian, wasn't it? Pretty name for a pretty lady. You always did have a weakness for the pretty ones, didn't you, John?"

"Shut up," Grayson forced out through clenched teeth.

"Such a shame what happened to her," he continued. "*Nasty* bit of business, that. Tell me, John. Did they ever find all the pieces?"

Masterson's smile could have chilled the noontime desert.

Grayson gaped at him, the color draining from his face.

"No," he continued. "No, I don't suppose they could have. I scattered bits of her in places even *you* wouldn't have thought to look. What can I say? I pride myself on my creativity."

"God damn you," whispered Cil. Masterson tightened his grip on her throat.

An alarm echoed through the large room. The blast door slammed closed and a locking mechanism clicked into place, sealing them inside.

The Agency had arrived.

"That would be our cue to hurry things along," said Masterson. "Jonathan, if you would please assist me by opening up my cryo-unit? There's a good chap.... And if you want Cil to live to see the dawn, you won't get too creative with the reanimation sequence. It doesn't need to go all the way through the cycle. You know as well as I do the body will start healing, no matter what state it's in when you pull it out of there."

Grayson walked slowly to the cylindrical towers. He punched something into the computer attached to Masterson's unit and the glass case of the container slid open.

"Excellent, Jonathan. Thank you," said Masterson. "Now, undo the restraints, lay the body on the floor, and step away."

Grayson did as he was told.

Masterson released Cil, shoving her toward Brandt. Carson held out a hand to steady her.

As Masterson knelt to examine the body, Grayson pulled a gun from the inside of his coat.

"Please," said Masterson, sounding bored. He raised a hand and, without bothering to look up, yanked the gun from Grayson's grasp using telekinesis, turned it in midair and aimed it at Cil.

The gun fired, the report echoing through the empty space.

Cil fell to the ground as the bullet tore through her right thigh.

"Cil!" cried Grayson, moving toward her.

"Not another step," said Masterson, finally glancing up. The gun floated through the air until it came to rest in his right hand. "That was very stupid, Jonathan."

Grayson addressed Masterson, but his eyes never left Cil's. "Are you going to kill us now, Samuel?"

"I told you, John... What fate has in store for you is far

worse than anything *I* could whip up. Not that I don't intend to give destiny a helping hand every once in a while. Lillian found that out the hard way, I suppose. Anyhow," Masterson pulled his half-frozen duplicate into his arms. "We'll have plenty of time to catch up in the months to come. I have something quite special in store for all of you. If you'd be so kind, please tell my pet I'm looking forward to her next lesson."

With that, the two Masterson's disappeared, vanishing not in a flash of light, but instead fading like a mirage, until the space they'd once occupied stood empty.

Brandt was the first one to pull himself together. He strode quickly to Cecilia, putting an arm around her waist and hauling her to her feet. She cried out in pain.

"I'm afraid, love, that you're our one and only ticket out of this place," said Brandt, by way of an apology. He guided her, limping, to a control panel set into the wall beside the blast door. "Can you disable the EM shield from here?"

She put a hand to the panel. The exterior controls hadn't offered her access to the security measures... But the computers *inside* the complex were a different story.

Cil found the shield's controls and powered them down. Easy as flicking a switch.

"Done," she said, still leaning against Brandt for support. The pain in her leg was excruciating, but the bullet had only grazed her. She'd definitely seen worse.

"Grayson," said Brandt.

Grayson was still staring dumbly at the place where Masterson and his doppelgänger had disappeared. "He played us," he said. "From the beginning... He planned for *all* of this."

"*Grayson!*" Brandt barked. "For god's sake, Jonathan, snap out of it and get your boney arse over here, before we leave you behind."

Breaking from his reverie with a determined look on his face, Grayson moved to join them.

Cil grabbed hold of his arm and jumped, leaving the scene of her nightmares behind. She was fairly certain she'd just collected enough new material to fuel new nightmares every night for the rest of her life.

TWENTY-ONE

"I was wondering where you'd disappeared to."

Aiden O'Connell sat on the stone edge of a large rock waterfall, positioned at the very center of the atrium. It was rare that he found his way to the cabin these days. Rarer still that he found himself a welcome guest.

He returned the mass of water he'd been toying with to the fountain beside him. "Alex still asleep?" he asked.

"Fourteen hours and counting," Nate answered, his shoes crunching on the gravel path as he approached.

"Yeah, well," said Aiden. "We both know that's nothing, for her."

Nate smiled, handing him a mug filled to the brim with steaming black liquid.

"Coffee," said Aiden after taking an appreciative sniff. "Thanks. I needed this."

"Careful," Nate replied. "Kenzie made it."

Aiden frowned warily at the mug. He'd had Kenzie's coffee before. It gave new meaning to the phrase "high octane."

"So what happened to the roof?" asked Aiden, nodding toward a ten-foot stretch of blue tarp that covered the glass ceiling above them. It crinkled loudly as it whipped about in the wind outside of the enclosure.

"Declan happened," said Nate. "Although I suppose I helped a bit."

"Uh-huh," said Aiden, taking a sip of coffee.

Nate settled onto the fountain's edge beside Aiden, rested his elbows on his knees and hung his head low, staring at the ground. Aiden recognized the look—he was losing himself in the memories of days gone by.

The last rays of the evening sun filtered through the trees that surrounded the enclosure, creating an army of shadows that danced upon the gravel pathway as the leaves above them trembled in the breeze.

This had been his home, once.

It hadn't lasted long, but it had been the most peaceful six months that Aiden had ever known. Nate wasn't the only one guilty of wishing he could go back in time and relive the past.

"I thought it'd be different, man," said Nate, looking up.

"Different how?"

"I don't know. Just... different. Easier."

"You told her anything yet?"

"How could I?" he asked, a bitter edge to his voice. "I say the wrong thing, and he dies."

"Yeah," said Aiden. "Or you say *nothing*, and *she* does."

"We don't know that," said Nate. "Not for certain. Besides, how do we know what the wrong thing to say even is?"

Silence settled over them. They'd had this argument before. Aiden wasn't sure if they'd ever agree on what action to take. One thing was certain, though—now that Alex had finally arrived, they were running out of time to make a decision.

"She saw something in my head last night," said Nate. "Kenzie had her digging around for a location for Declan. Somehow she managed to glimpse an image from Seattle."

"What did she see?"

"Probably the worst thing she could have." He heaved a sigh. "She saw herself on the deck of the *Misty Rose*."

"*What*? What did you tell her?"

"I didn't tell her anything... I just refused to answer her and then I changed the subject as fast as I could."

"Well, shit." Aiden raked a hand through his hair. He was all-for telling Alex what he thought she needed to know, but that particular piece of information he'd planned on leaving out.

The door to the house opened and Kenzie stepped through. "Yo, Nate!" she called over to them. "The boss is back. Family meeting in five."

Aiden and Nate got to their feet.

His cousin walked on for a short ways, then turned when he realized Aiden hadn't followed.

"What is it?" he asked.

Aiden smiled. "Think now would be a bad time to ask Grayson how he plans on paying for my apartment?"

"Alex, wake up."

"Mmpff."

Alex recognized the familiar tug and click of a ceiling fan cord being pulled. Light flooded the room and Alex burrowed deeper beneath the pillows in protest.

"*Alex*," said an insistent, distinctly feminine voice from somewhere above her. "So help me, Lex, if you don't get your butt up *right now*, I'm coming back with the ice water. It will be Rebecca Anderson's third-grade slumber party all over again. Do you really want that?"

"That sounds like a fun story. Let's hear about that," said a second voice.

Declan.

"If she tells you anything, I'll have to kill her," Alex mumbled into a pillow. "Then I'll have to kill you. So if she knows what's good for her, she won't say *anything*."

When Alex finally pushed aside the pillow she was greeted by the sight of Cassie, hands on her hips, glaring down at her. Declan stood across the room, leaning against one of the dressers with his arms crossed.

He looked bored.

How long had he been standing there?

"Look at that," he said. "Issuing death threats and she's not even fully awake yet. Impressive."

"Finally," said Cassie. "You've been dead to the world for ages."

"How long was I asleep?" It felt like she'd only laid down a few minutes ago. Surely she couldn't have been out for *that* long...

"Well, seeing as how it's nearly six in the evening here in the lovely state of New York... If I were to guess? I'd say, roughly fifteen hours."

"*What?*" Alex bolted upright, resulting in a rather painful rush of blood to her head. She fell back against the bed. "Ungh... Why did you let me sleep so long?"

"Trust me, it wasn't my first choice." Cassie sat down on the mattress beside her. "The others said you needed it, though, so I let you sleep. We're only waking you up now because Mr. Grayson's back and he wants to see everyone downstairs."

"Family meeting," said Declan, the words coming out at a crawl. She looked up. Declan was studying her from his spot across the room. His expression of boredom had morphed into one of confusion. "You feeling alright, Lex?"

"I'm fine. Why?"

Cassie appraised Declan. "What's with the look?" she asked.

"Something's... different," said Declan. "Alex?"

"Yes?"

"If I told you to jump right now, could you?"

She'd managed a jump last night, just before she went to bed. Whatever that pulse had done to her in the parking garage, it appeared to have been temporary.

"Sure, I..." she trailed off.

Declan was right. Something *was* different.

The soft thrum of electricity she'd grown so accustomed to these last few days was missing once more. Her connection to Declan had been severed.

But it wasn't just that.

Her thoughts were entirely her own again. Even without the mental walls in place, she couldn't hear Cassie, or sense the presence of anyone else in the house. No matter how hard she concentrated, Alex couldn't feel or hear any of them.

And even though she hadn't made much headway practicing her telekinesis last night with Nathaniel, Alex was fairly certain that that had disappeared as well. For the first time in months, Alex felt almost.... *normal*.

She sucked in a ragged breath as panic set in.

"That's what I thought," said Declan.

Three days ago, Alexandra Parker would have given anything to be normal again.

Now, on the run from the government and a psychopath who'd already killed two people and kidnapped her best friend, Alex's only means of protecting herself and the people she cared about had just vanished.

She was defenseless.

"It's gone," she whispered. Icy tendrils of fear were coiling inside her chest. "All of it... Just *gone*. How can it be gone? Declan, what do I do?"

"*What's* gone?" asked Cassie. "Alex, what is the matter?"

"Hop up, Cassie," said Declan.

For once, Cassie didn't argue. She moved aside and Declan took her place, sitting down on the bed next to Alex.

Without saying anything more, he reached up and placed his hand on the side of her face, cupping her cheek.

"Declan? What are you doing?" Alex asked, but didn't

pull away. She sat perfectly still, transfixed by the look of worry in Declan's hazel eyes.

After a few seconds, the heat radiating from Declan's palm was joined by a second sensation—the familiar quiver of electricity.

It was back. Declan's touch had reawakened her ability.

The look of relief that flooded his expression caused Alex's breath to catch in her throat, but it was the smile that followed that threatened to do her in entirely.

"That's better," he said. "For a moment there, I thought I'd lost you."

His gaze journeyed south, fixing on her mouth, before flickering back up to meet her eyes.

"Will one of you please tell me what's going on?"

Declan dropped his hand, but made no move to get up.

"I don't understand, Decks," Alex's voice was barely above a whisper. "What just happened?"

He surprised her again by offering his hand. "Just in case," he said with a shrug. When she still didn't move, he added, "You're getting your abilities from touching other Variants. I don't know how it works—or how long the contact needs to last—but I figure, better safe, than sorry. Now, hup to, princess. Grayson and the others are waiting."

Alex looked down at herself, suddenly self-conscious. She'd collapsed into bed the night before in a pair of yoga pants and an oversized sweatshirt. Not exactly her best look. She swept her unruly hair up and into a messy bun using the elastic band around her wrist, stealing a quick glance at her disheveled reflection in the dresser mirror.

Great. She looked like an extra gone AWOL from the set of a *Flashdance* remake.

Alex supposed it could have been worse. At least she hadn't ended up in the lake yet today.

Accepting Declan's outstretched hand, Alex slid from between the sheets, cringing when her bare feet met with the frigid hardwood floor. For a split-second, she gave serious consideration to diving back into the warm, comfortable bed, settling in beneath the duvet, and spending what was left of the day hiding from the world outside her bedroom.

It seemed like a perfectly acceptable response to the mess she was in.

World got you down? Discovered you're a mutant? Pesky psychopath on your trail?

The solution was simple: Go back to bed!

Alex was fairly certain that she could solve all those problems and more, if she could just have five more minutes of sleep.

Cassie led the way into the hall. Declan followed just a step ahead of Alex, arm twisted behind him, long fingers still entwined with hers. The longer the contact lasted, the more clearly she could sense the electrical currents in the people, objects, and air surrounding her.

Alex wondered, briefly, if Declan's offer to keep hold of her hand had been given solely to ensure the return of her ability, or if he might have had another motive... And then promptly decided that that line of thinking couldn't lead *anywhere* good.

Whether it was from the chill in the air, or the tingle of electricity flowing through their joined hands, Alex wasn't certain, but she couldn't hold back a shiver.

The currents surged.

Declan cast a quick glance at her over his shoulder. When their eyes met, the corner of his mouth quirked upward in a crooked grin.

Nowhere good.

As they reached the landing, Alex gazed down upon the living area below.

Brian and Nate were seated on the couch on either side of Kenzie, laughing at something the redhead had said. Grayson, meanwhile, stood near the front door, arguing in a low voice with Aiden. It was the most dressed-down she'd seen the patriarch thus far, in a pair of dark jeans and a pressed, white button-down shirt. He turned his head when he heard them descending the stairs.

The skin surrounding his left eye gleamed a nasty shade of purple, and had nearly swollen shut. Alex felt a wave of guilt wash over her. That one *must* have hurt.

"Ah, Alex, you're awake," said Grayson.

Aiden's black look was replaced with a soft smile and a nod in Cassie's direction.

Well *that* was an interesting development. She'd have to corner her friend later and grill her for details.

"How are you feeling?" asked Nate.

The trio reached the foot of the stairs and everyone moved to find a seat in the living room.

"I'm alright," she said, releasing Declan's hand and settling in next to Nate in the last open space on the couch. Declan sat on the arm of the couch beside Alex, as Cassie claimed the love seat, Aiden the ottoman in front of it, and Grayson returned to his spot on the hearth. "I had an unpleasant surprise waiting for me when I woke up, though."

"What, you mean my brother?" said Kenzie. "I suppose waking up to his face would be a shock to *anyone's* system."

"Kenzie," said Grayson. It wasn't so much a warning as it was a subtle reproach. "What happened, Alex?"

"I woke up and my abilities were gone."

"What, all of them?" asked Kenzie.

"All of them," she said.

"Alex's ability—her *real* ability—seems to be the power to absorb another Variant's abilities through touch," said

Declan. He looked pointedly at Grayson. "And I can't help but wonder how she wound up with an ability that only one other person on the planet has ever laid claim to."

Grayson's jaw clenched.

"What? There's someone else out there like me?" she asked. Something akin to hope stirred within her chest. Somewhere out there was someone who could understand what she was going through.

Alex wrung her hands. Declan reached down, first stilling her movements and then reclaiming her hand in his.

Declan's voice was overflowing with accusation. "You going to tell us how Alex wound up with Samuel Masterson's ability, Grayson?"

"Wait... *What?*" Alex yanked her hand from Declan's grasp and climbed unsteadily to her feet. "Masterson? The same Masterson that went crazy and murdered all of our parents? I have *his* ability?"

She spun around to confront Declan. "You've known this since last night... and you didn't *say* anything?"

Even Declan couldn't handle the surge that followed. The lamps on the end tables and the overhead lights blew out simultaneously, leaving the room lit only by the darting flames of the fireplace.

"I didn't want to say anything until I knew for sure," he said in the silence that followed. Even in the dim glow of the fireplace his expression appeared earnest, a silent entreaty for her understanding in his eyes. "I needed to be certain."

Unable to look away from Declan, Alex sank into a seated position on the coffee table.

How cruel the universe could be.

It wasn't enough that her strange gift separated her from her aunt. From Declan, Nathaniel, Kenzie and the others.... But now she knew that the only other person to ever have been like her—and the only one who might ever have been able to *help* her understand what she was—was the same man who had brutally murdered her parents.

A man who had been dead for years.

"But I thought…" She closed her eyes and tried to steady the funny tremor that had worked its way into her voice. "Grayson, I thought you said abilities were *inherited*. Please tell me Samuel Masterson isn't… Tell me that he isn't…"

"No, Alex," said Grayson, with finality. "Samuel Masterson isn't your father."

"Then *how*—" she began.

"Samuel Masterson was not *born* with the ability the two of you possess," said Grayson. "He *made* the both of you what you are today."

"I don't understand," said Cassie. "What do you mean he *made* them like they are?"

Declan frowned at her. His earnest expression had been replaced with annoyance… And what appeared to be righteous indignation.

He was angry that *she* was so angry.

Didn't he get it?

Didn't he realize that he'd crossed a line when he decided to keep the truth from her?

She'd had enough of being lied to. In her mind, Declan was no better than her aunt.

"Is that why he wanted her, Grayson?" asked Declan, his voice low. "Is *that* why our parents died trying to protect Alex?"

"*What*?" Alex choked out.

She flashed back to what Grayson had told her on the first day she'd arrived. *One day, a powerful Variant named Masterson got it in his head that… Well let's just say, he came after one of our own. The team tried to stop him.*

Alex felt sick to her stomach.

It was all her fault.

They were all dead… Had all *died* protecting *her*.

With his back to the fire, Grayson's face rested in the shadows, his words traveling to them through the darkness. "I'm sorry, Alex," he said. "We should have been honest with you from the beginning. *I* should have been honest with *all* of you from the beginning… And it's time you all knew the truth."

A flash of violet light illuminated the large room.

Alex turned to face the new arrivals.

Her aunt had appeared behind her, and stood in the faint light on the other side of the coffee table, leaning heavily against none other than Carson Brandt.

Alex rushed to stand, but misjudged the location of Declan's feet in the darkness and, after a creative two-step, fell into a seated position… in Nathaniel's lap.

Klutziness: 204,231, Alex: Zip.

Declan and Aiden were on their feet in an instant.

"It's alright, everyone," said Grayson. "I told you. Brandt's a… friend. Of sorts. Anyhow, you can relax. He's on our side."

"Harmless as a kitten, me," said Brandt, helping Cil over to the love seat. Aiden stepped aside as Alex's aunt settled onto the ottoman.

"Aunt Cil?" Alex squinted to see her aunt better. "What's happened to your leg?"

"I see you haven't gotten to that part of the story yet, Jonathan," said Brandt. "Why on Earth are you lot sitting around in the dark, anyway? Someone forget to pay the electric bill? Ah, well. No matter."

Brandt drew a small flame away from the fireplace and looked about the room. He found what he was searching for on the mantle and sent the flame sailing toward it.

After the hurricane lamp was lit, Nathaniel floated it from the hearth to the coffee table at the center of the room.

"Thank you, Mr. Palladino," said Brandt, smiling at Nate in a decidedly creepy manner. Then again, everything about this man struck Alex as creepy. He settled onto the ottoman next to her aunt. "My, my. You *do* have your mother's eyes, don't you?"

His arms still around her, Alex could feel Nate's shoulder muscles tense as he scowled at the newcomer.

Alex's attention slid past Brandt and onto Cassie, who was curled up in the love seat, staring nervously at Brandt. Alex wasn't the only one who'd noticed her friend's discomfort. Aiden settled back onto the love seat beside Cassie, surreptitiously taking her hand in his. She relaxed only slightly and inched further back into the cushions, as far from Brandt as she could get.

Despite Grayson's assurances, Declan made no move to sit down. Everyone else remained seated quietly, staring uncertainly at Brandt.

The tension in the room was almost palpable.

"Honestly," Brandt muttered. "D'you see what I mean about the ruination of my good name, Jonathan? *It wasn't me!* It was Samuel Masterson and *only* Samuel Masterson. I had none to do with it, I promise you."

In the silence that followed, you could have heard a pin drop.

"Are you saying Masterson's *alive*?" said Kenzie, finally giving voice to the question Alex had been too stunned to ask.

"Well," Brandt said with a smile. "Now that I've gone and spoiled the ending... Jonathan, I suppose you'd better start at the beginning."

"Yes, I suppose I should," said Grayson, annoyed.

Declan finally turned around, intent on resuming his seat. He paused at the sight of Alex and Nathaniel, arching an eyebrow.

"Are you two comfortable?" he asked quietly. The low

tone stripped his observation of any inflection, but the look in his eye more than made up for it.

Alex slid off of Nate's lap without another word and Grayson began his tale.

TWENTY-TWO

Declan's boots sank into the muddy grounds of the training field. The heavy rains from that afternoon had transformed the darkened clearing into a mire.

She wasn't here, either.

He jumped.

After Brandt had shown up, Grayson had spent the next twenty minutes providing them with a rundown on the history of one Samuel Masterson.

The guy had been something of a whiz-kid. A boy genius that had joined Grayson's unit at the age of 17 with doctorate's in both genetics and biomedical engineering already under his belt.

Grayson hadn't wanted to put him in the field on account of his youth and relative inexperience, so instead, they had created an entire research and development team around him.

Masterson had immediately set to work on the development of gene therapies that specifically targeted Variant DNA. Therapies that, they had hoped, would one day help Variants who possessed some of the more *debilitating* abilities lead normal, productive lives.

It hadn't taken long for Masterson to make a breakthrough.

Declan landed on the cement drive that led up to Alex's home. The lights were out and he couldn't see any signs of movement within the house.

Another dead end.

He jumped again.

While at the Agency, Masterson created two treatments. The first was designed to completely strip a Variant of their ability. The second allowed one Variant to absorb the abilities of another.

It was the second therapy that he'd become obsessed with.

But there was a catch. The second treatment wouldn't work on just anyone. Certain characteristics needed to already be present in the subject's DNA before the treatment would take. As fate would have it, only two people on the team carried those traits.

Masterson... And James Parker, Alex's father.

Within a year, Masterson had developed trial versions of both therapies.

Parker had refused the testing. He was happy with his ability, and had no desire to change himself—even if it would make him more powerful.

Masterson, on the other hand, was desperate to try it.

Grayson had warned Masterson to *wait* until the initial tests had been completed, but he hadn't listened. He'd tried the therapy on himself, the first chance he got.

In the end, Masterson became the Agency's first successful trial... If you called making himself batshit crazy in the process a *success*, anyhow.

Declan reappeared on the dock where they'd met Masterson the day before.

The jetty was empty. Declan wasn't surprised. The place had probably lost most of its charm for her, after all that had happened.

He hesitated before making another jump, taking a moment to think back over the series of events that had led them to this point.

Shortly after Masterson completed his treatments and

knew that the therapy had worked, the contents of his lab had been destroyed in a fire. Grayson claimed ignorance as to how the blaze broke out. But Declan had his theories.

In any case, not long after that, Masterson set his sights on Alex.

Not to kill her, which was what Declan had always believed he'd been trying to do.

No, Masterson had wanted to *take* her. For what purpose was anyone's guess, at the time. Now it seemed fairly obvious.

Alex Parker possessed the same rare trait as her father.

In a last-ditch effort to stop him, Grayson, Alex's Aunt, and Brandt shot Masterson and placed him in a cryogenic suspension—a deep freeze that he'd recently managed to escape from.

Grayson hadn't been too forthcoming on those details, either.

Their efforts to stop Masterson hadn't made a difference, in the end. Somehow, Alex had been given the treatments.

And now they knew the truth.

Well… Grayson's version of it, anyway.

Declan wasn't sure *what* to believe anymore. He simply couldn't trust anyone to give it to him straight these days. In that respect, he could empathize with Alex.

He shoved his hands into the pockets of his coat.

Now if he could just figure out where Alex had disappeared to.

She'd jumped shortly after the meeting ended, stating that she needed to get some air and then teleporting before anyone could stop her.

He racked his memory, trying to think of where else she might have gone.

Jump

Not at Connor's.

Jump

Not on the boardwalk.

Jump

Not on the beach.

Jump

Not on the pier.

He groaned, exhausted from so many jumps. Where had she *gone*?

Didn't she realize how dangerous it was for her to be out on her own like this?

Out of ideas, he readied himself to jump back to the cabin… and then realized that there was still one place he hadn't looked.

Declan landed softly in the grass beside Alex.

She didn't look up, just continued to stare off into the distance, her arms wrapped tightly around her legs and her chin resting atop her knees. Her round face, slender hands and bare feet were as white as snow in the darkness, her alabaster skin shimmering in the light of the full moon.

You know, for someone who lived at the beach year-round, Alex sure was *pale*.

A breeze picked up.

Declan shrugged off his jacket and placed it around her shoulders.

He sank into the grass beside her and they remained there for a long while, two silent and unmoving statues, gazing up at the starry expanse of sky that shrouded the Irish countryside.

"I'm so sorry, Decks," Alex whispered. Silver rivulets of tears glistened on her cheek.

"Sorry for *what*?" he asked. "You don't have anything to be sorry for."

"I do. I have *everything* to be sorry for. If it weren't for me, they'd still be alive. Your parents… Nate's mom… It's my fault, Declan."

Three days ago, he would have agreed with her.

Three days ago, he'd been a benighted, self-absorbed asshole.

But after meeting Alex—after getting to know her and learning the truth about what had happened—Declan had been forced to admit something. Something he'd always known, deep down, but had never wanted to accept.

His parents had made the right choice.

Where the fate of an innocent child was concerned, there wasn't even a choice to be made. It was simply the right thing to do. Protecting Alex had been the right move, no matter the consequence.

And Declan had since realized that, had he been in their place, he would have made the same decision—that he'd *already* made the same decision.

He would protect the girl sitting next to him. Would fight for her until his dying breath.

"No, Lex," he said. "The only person to blame for what happened is Masterson. Don't you *ever* think that it was your fault. You hear me? It wasn't. No one blames you for any of it."

Declan studied her profile and wondered how, in such a short time, she'd managed to leave him so completely undone. How, out of everyone, it had been *Alex* that had somehow managed to sneak past his defenses.

Alex had slipped past the walls he'd spent a lifetime building, and she didn't even realize it.

He'd gotten so good at *not caring*. At distancing himself. But she'd changed everything without even trying.

Declan's world could never go back to the way it was.

And, heaven help him, if it meant losing the reckless, stubborn, *beautiful* girl sitting next to him… then he didn't want it to.

Alex turned her head to face him, resting her cheek against her knee. She wiped the tears away with the sleeve of his jacket. "I just… I don't know what to think anymore,

Decks. Every time I turn around, I find out some new horrible secret. About my family. About myself. About Masterson… It's too much. It's all too much."

He closed the distance between them, hesitantly placing his arm around her shoulders. Declan held very still, afraid she'd pull away.

"I know," he said. "And for what it's worth, I'm sorry. They shouldn't have lied to you. *I* shouldn't have lied to you. I should have told you what I knew about Masterson from the start."

She leaned back into the crook of his arm and rested her head on his shoulder. "Promise me something, Decks?"

"What's that?"

"No more lies?" she said.

"No more lies," he agreed.

They sat there in an amiable silence for another five minutes before Declan grudgingly fished the cell phone he'd been ignoring out of his pocket.

Huh. No messages.

He'd been gone for over an hour, looking for Alex. Surely *someone* should be wondering where they were by now.

"We should get back," he said. "Don't want the others to worry. And your Aunt said she wanted to talk to you about something."

"Great," said Alex, getting to her feet. "*That* conversation ought to be about as much fun as a root canal."

They jumped back to the cabin.

The living room was deserted.

Alex walked to the pass-through and peered into the kitchen. "Where is everyone?" she asked. "Surely they're not all in bed. It's only ten o'clock."

He jumped upstairs.

Up and down the long hall, bedroom doors stood open, the rooms beyond bathed in shadows.

"Kenzie?" he thought, dropping the walls he'd had up. *"Are you there?"*

No answer. Wherever his sister had gone, it must have been a long way from the cabin.

"Declan!"

The strangled cry echoed through the empty house.

Lex.

He jumped back to the living room. Brandt stood in front of the fireplace, gun leveled at Alex.

"Brandt?" Declan had appeared at the foot of the stairs, roughly eight feet behind Alex. He took a few slow steps forward. Brandt cocked the gun. Declan came to a halt. "Brandt, what are you doing?"

"I'm afraid Carson Brandt isn't here at the moment," said the man. Brandt's Scottish brogue had been replaced by posh English accent. "I'm just borrowing his face, you see. I'd intended to... How did he put it? Ah, yes. I wanted to see if I might 'ruin his good name' a bit more. Little did I know, I was late to the party."

"Masterson," said Declan.

"Winner, winner, chicken dinner," he said in a passable southern drawl. Declan couldn't help but wonder what the man's *real* voice sounded like. "But, please... call me Sam."

"Okay, Sam," said Alex, taking a step backward, one hand behind her back. "Where is everyone? What have you done with them?"

Alex wiggled her fingers. Declan got the message: two more feet, and her hand would be within his reach. They'd be able to jump.

The only problem with *that* plan, was that Masterson had already proven himself capable of following them.

"Oh, come now, pet," he said, returning to an English accent. "Such little faith you have in me. *I* wasn't the one that took your friends. They were already gone by the time

I arrived. I'd merely dropped by to return the firearm Jonathan was kind enough to lend me."

What the heck was he talking about?

Declan eyed the pistol in Masterson's hand. It was the same model Ruger that Grayson carried. But if it really was Grayson's gun, then how had Masterson gotten his hands on it?

"If you didn't take them, who did?" asked Alex.

"I have every faith you'll figure that out on your own, pet," he said. "Oh, and I do apologize, but I'm afraid our lessons are going to have to be put on hold for the time being. I've had some matters arise that require my immediate and undivided attention. An unfortunate delay, but a necessary one. And anyhow, you'll have much more free time during your upcoming summer holiday. As it is now, this current break of yours is nearly over and I would so *hate* to distract you from your *other* studies."

How considerate of him.

No doubt about it. The guy was nuts.

"Lessons?" Alex repeated.

"Certainly. Gifts such as ours aren't mastered overnight, you know."

The hand Alex had been holding behind her back dropped to her side.

"How… How did I become like you?" she asked, taking a step toward Masterson, and moving further out of Declan's reach.

Dammit. What did she think she was doing?

"Did you do this to me?" she pressed.

"You're asking the wrong question. The question you should be asking is not *how*, but *why*." He smiled. "And, alas, that is a story for another day… Fare thee well, pet. We'll be together again before you know it."

With that, Masterson set the pistol on the fireplace step and disappeared.

"Time to go," said Declan. He grabbed Alex by the arm and jumped before she could reply.

They tumbled onto hard-packed, rock-covered sand.

Ouch. Okay, so not his best landing. That's what he got for jumping to a place he'd never actually seen in person. All that really mattered right now, is that they were miles away from anything remotely resembling civilization. And from Masterson, or so he hoped.

"Where is this place?" asked Alex, dusting herself off.

The sun had yet to set in this part of the world, but judging from the thin line of yellow on the horizon and the rapidly falling temperature, it wouldn't be up much longer.

A towering rock formation loomed half a mile in the distance, positioned at the center of two long dikes that stretched out in opposite directions like a pair of craggy wings before sinking into the flat plains of the desert.

Shiprock.

He'd seen it on TV once, although he hadn't been paying much attention at the time. All he could really recall was that it was located in the Navajo Nation and that, in their culture, the peak was considered sacred.

"New Mexico," he answered. "I think."

"Why the desert?"

"Because it's isolated," he said. "And because whoever took the others might still be watching the cabin. We couldn't stay there."

"But wouldn't it be a good thing if they *were* watching the house? Maybe we could sneak back and figure out who they are."

Was she serious?

"Alex, there were eight people still at the cabin when I left. Three of whom possess enough destructive power to level that entire house, and six of whom are expertly trained to defend themselves," he said. "Did you see any broken furniture? Chairs knocked over? Shattered glass? Water or fire damage? Did you see *anything* there that was out of place?"

"No." Alex deflated. "No, I didn't."

"Whoever they were, they managed to incapacitate and abduct the others without so much as scuffing the hardwood floor. Now, do you really think we're just going to sneak up on people like that, without them realizing it? We'd just end up getting captured ourselves—or worse—and then who would be left to rescue us?"

"Could they have gotten out?" she asked, still clinging to hope.

"No," he said, checking his phone again. "Someone would have called to let us know what happened by now. And Masterson seemed to think they'd been taken by someone. Not that I particularly trust the word of a murderer, but… I don't know. I think he might be right."

"Alright," said Alex, determined. "Then what do we do now?"

"Now," he said, "I think it's time I paid my friend Oz a visit."

"Oz? As in 'Oz, the Great and Powerful'?"

"I'm sure he'd like you to think so. In reality, it's more like, 'Oz, the Short One from Schenectady.' But I'll tell him you said that. Knowing Ozzie, he'll take it as a compliment."

"You'll tell him? Aren't you taking me with you?"

"You'll be safer here, Lex. I won't be gone long."

"Are you kidding? You're not the only one with family missing, Declan. Besides that," she gestured to their surroundings. "We're in the middle of nowhere, it's freezing cold, and I'm barefoot—*again*, no thanks to you. You know what? No. I am *not* going to just sit here and wait while you run off to play hero. You're taking me with you."

Thrilling heroics hadn't exactly been on his to-do list—he was merely hitting up Ozzie's in search of intel—but Alex's tone brooked no argument.

He sighed and took her by the arm.

Stubborn.

TWENTY-THREE

Alexandra Parker was currently standing smack dab in the middle of a daydream come to life. She'd finally made it to a place she'd wanted to see ever since she caught her first Monty Python's Flying Circus re-run on PBS as a little kid.

Alex was in London.

She shivered.

Okay, so in those daydreams, she wasn't usually standing barefoot on a snowy rooftop in the middle of the night wearing paper-thin yoga pants while a handsome blonde swore angrily at a jammed access door... but she'd take what she could get.

While Declan wrestled with the stuck (or, as was far more likely, *locked*) metal door, Alex crept closer to the rooftop's edge and stared out over the sleeping city. The world below was bathed in the golden glow of street lights and covered by a fraction of an inch of quickly vanishing snow. A sparse amount of foot traffic meandered along the sidewalks below, oblivious to her presence.

The London Eye was lit beautifully by blue and purple lights in the distance, and just to the left of the soaring circular Ferris wheel, and across the River Thames, was the Palace of Westminster and its iconic clock tower, Big Ben, shining like a beacon in the night.

Alex sniffed the air. An enticing aroma was wafting from the direction of a Tandoori restaurant and takeaway up the street. The ensuing growl from her stomach reminded her she hadn't actually eaten anything since the day before.

Declan was still struggling with the door.

"Oh, come *on*." He kicked it in frustration.

"*Use the force, Luke*," she said in her best Obi-Wan impression, smiling at the aggravated look on his face.

"Funny," he said, sizing up the door. "Very funny."

What was it with guys and admitting defeat to inanimate objects?

Sink's broken? Someone get me a wrench. No, no. It's *supposed* to spit water like that. Trust me, I know what I'm doing.

Car making an odd noise? Someone get me a wrench. No, no. That metal bit is *supposed* to fall off every time we take a left turn. Trust me, I know what I'm doing.

Watching Cassie's dad, her older brothers, and Connor over the years had left Alex with an even greater appreciation for her Aunt Cil. At least her aunt was sensible enough to call a repairman when she knew she couldn't fix something.

Declan formed a sphere of electricity and took aim at the door.

"*Declan*," she chided. "What are you—"

"Trust me," he said. "I know what I'm doing."

Alex sighed. "That's exactly what I'm afraid of."

She drew the sphere out his hand and shrank it until the crackling blue light blinked out of existence. Grabbing the sleeve of Declan's hoodie, she dragged him to the back of the building, where it overlooked the alley below.

Empty.

Alex jumped, taking Declan with her. They reappeared in the shadowy passageway.

"It's called a front door, Declan."

Yick. What she wouldn't give for a pair of shoes right

about now. Alex led the way on tiptoe, picking her way carefully across the cobblestones and back toward the main road.

"Which one is it?" she asked when confronted with a long row of identical white doorsteps, each flanked by a pair of white columns and four thin steps leading up to a small stoop and glossy, black lacquered doors.

"You can't guess?" said Declan as they continued on down the street.

A few residences down, one doorstep stood out from the rest.

Attached to the wall, the columns, and even hanging from the ceiling above, were close to a dozen CCTV cameras, each focused on a different area of the doorstep and the street in front of the building.

They climbed the steps and Declan reached forward to press the buzzer on the intercom.

Alex half expected an angry ginger man with a curly mustache to pop out of nowhere and ask who rang that bell. Instead, the cameras mounted above swiveled down to focus in on them.

"Declan!" said a happily surprised—and somewhat nasally—voice though an intercom speaker. The giddy tone was immediately replaced with suspicion. "What are you doing at my *front* door?"

"Need some help, Oz," he said. "And the door on the roof was locked."

"Hm." One of the myriad cameras above twitched to the left, focused on Alex, and zoomed in. Alex pulled Declan's jacket tighter around her. "Who's that with you?"

"She's a friend, Oz," said Declan. "Can you just let us in already? It's freaking freezing out here. And she doesn't have shoes."

The camera panned down. "What are you doing in

London in the middle of the night with a shoeless brunette, Declan?"

"Enough with the shoes already," muttered Alex. She leaned toward the intercom. "Hello, um, Oz, is it? Yeah, hi. We're really sorry to bother you Mr., um... Mr. Oz, but we ah..." A different camera twitched in her direction. "We need help, and Declan said you were the man to see. Can you please just let us in?"

Silence.

"Mr. Oz?" she asked again.

The intercom buzzed and a lock in the door released. Declan pushed the varnished door open and led the way inside.

The front entryway stood bare, bereft of any furnishing, and a staircase disappeared into the darkness at the end of the foyer. Rooms branched off on either side of the long hall. Declan chose one on the left. Alex followed.

Like the entryway, the room was empty, save for a large bank of monitors set against the far wall. Declan came to a stop in front of the display and commenced to wait.

"I don't get it," said Alex. "Where is he?"

"Patience, young Jedi." Declan crossed his arms and stared at the array of monitors. "He doesn't actually live here. This is just someplace people can visit when they want to reach him. Ozzie's a man who values his privacy. Oh, and I should probably warn you, he's a little... *neurotic*. Helpful. But neurotic."

One of the monitors lit up, displaying the grainy image of a bald man in his mid-thirties, wearing square-rimmed glasses and a bow-tie. He looked a little like the rock star, Moby.

Well... Moby, if Moby woke up one morning and decided that being a rock legend wasn't quite cutting it, and decided to change professions to become an account-ant. The man looked as though he were fully prepared to either DJ at an LA club filled with Mathletes… or file someone's taxes. Alex wasn't quite sure which. Nor, for that matter, was she entirely sure what to make of him.

"I'll take that as a compliment, halfwit," said Ozzie. "As a wise man once said, 'Everything great in the world comes from neurotics.'"

Alex recognized the quote.

"'They alone have founded our religions and composed our masterpieces,'" she finished.

"I—What?" Declan asked, looking back and forth between them in confusion. "What are you two talking about?"

"It's Proust, you ignoramus," said the man in the box, first rolling his eyes dramatically and then flashing a wide, gap-toothed smile. "I like this one, Declan. She reads!"

Technically, she'd read it in a coffee-table book of quotes that Cassie had given her Aunt Cil as a Christmas gift two years earlier.

Of course, she wasn't about to admit that *now*.

"Much better than that last floozy you brought with you. Fairly certain that poor girl was destined either for a short-lived foray into the arena of adult entertainment, or for a scintillating career in the fast food industry. Possibly both."

Alex leaned toward Declan and said in a quiet voice, "Floozy?"

"It was for a case," he said, defensive. "Chrissy was a client. I was helping her find her brother."

Chrissy?

Ozzie harrumphed. "Some things that are lost are better left that way," he said cryptically. "Chrissy's brother being a prime example."

"*Focus*, Oz," said Declan. "We need your help."

"Yes, I suppose you do," said Ozzie with a sigh. A second monitor lit up, displaying a four-way split-screen, offering out of focus, black and white video feeds from some sort of surveillance system. "This was taken last night."

Three figures were moving in and out of the frames, making their way through an office of some sort. Alex squinted at the monitor, struggling to make out more detail.

The figures moved closer to one of the cameras and Alex raised an eyebrow. She'd recognized them.

On the screen were Grayson, Carson Brandt and—

"Hang on." Alex stepped closer to the screen. "Is that my *aunt*?"

"Where is this place, Oz?" asked Declan.

"An abandoned underground facility in the mountains of western Virginia. Former headquarters of the Agency and home to Grayson's original unit. They shut it down after the Masterson debacle twelve years ago."

"What were they doing there?" asked Alex.

The four-way split was replaced by a single feed that stretched to fill the large screen, causing the image to blur. Three figures—who Alex assumed to be Grayson, Brandt and Cil—had entered a large room and were approaching a row of towering black objects, but the distortions in the image prevented her from making out any other details.

"They were there to check in on an old friend," said Oz. "Those black masses you see at the center of the frame? They're cryogenic chambers."

"Masterson," said Declan. "They must have gone to check on the unit. Make sure he'd really escaped."

Ozzie snorted. "Yeah? Well they screwed up."

"How so?"

Ozzie didn't have to answer, the video did it for him.

They watched as a fourth figure materialized behind Cil and seized her, prompting Grayson to remove a human body from one of the chambers… And then they watched as Cil was shot in the leg by Grayson's gun.

"So *that's* what happened to her leg," said Alex.

"Who's the other man, Oz?" asked Declan.

Ozzie selected a portion of the image—framing the mystery man—enlarged it, and ran some sort of clean-up application.

The result was a fuzzy but identifiable image of a handsome man in his mid-twenties, with short dark hair and an aquiline nose.

"Impossible," said Declan. "Oz, how—"

"No idea," he said. "I don't have a clue how he pulled it off, either."

"I don't understand," said Alex. "Who is he?"

"That's him, Lex," said Declan. "You're looking at an image of Samuel Masterson."

She studied the image, filing the blurry profile away in her memory. At least she'd know him if she ran into him on the street now. Provided he wasn't wearing someone else's face, that is.

"Well I guess that explains how Masterson ended up with Grayson's Ruger," said Declan. "Alright. We can ask Grayson about all this later. *After* we get them back… Oz, we saw the three of them after this happened. What we need to know now is who took them from the cabin."

"Getting to that," said Ozzie.

Half a dozen screens lit up, a few flashing through digital dossiers of Declan's family while the others offered security camera feeds showing different scenes from the last few days. Alex and Cassie on the boardwalk. Kenzie and Nate wandering through the parking garage looking for Grayson's rental. Traffic camera feeds showing the same black BMW traveling through the streets of DC.

"You've been pretty busy lately. And I think it's safe to

say that the Agency has taken a *very* keen interest in the Grayson family."

One of the screens flipped to a security feed showing two men dressed in plain clothes, kneeling beside a car in a parking garage. A small box sat opened in front of them, a flashing light inside.

One of the men reached into the box and the feed cut out.

The pulse.

"So it *was* Agents that came after us in the parking garage," said Declan.

"Yep," said Ozzie. "And I happen to have read a fascinating report about two Agents who pursued a 6 Series Beamer off the edge of an uncompleted bridge… A Beamer that then proceeded to *vanish* into thin air. No video on *that*, sadly. You're quite the show off, Mr. O'Connell. I know jumpers much more experienced than you, who never could have managed such a feat."

"What does the Agency want with Grayson's family?" asked Alex.

"Oh, it's not Grayson's family they're after, my shoeless minx," said Ozzie.

The screens went black. Two monitors lit up to replace them. On the first was a scrolling profile detailing the vital statistics of one Alexandra Catherine Parker. On the second, the scanned images of her Bay View High School ID card and her driver's license stared back at her.

"The person they want," he continued. "Is *you*."

"*Me?*" Alex repeated dumbly. "What could they possibly want with *me*?"

"Honestly? I haven't the faintest," said Ozzie. "They've got most of the files pertaining to you classified and encrypted at a level even *I* haven't been able to crack. And that's saying something."

"They took the others to get to Alex," Declan surmised.

"They wanted to bait us into coming after them, so that they could get their hands on her."

"I think that's part of it," said Oz. "The directives pertaining to Alex are coming down from the top—and I mean the *very* top—and they're all saying the same thing: approach with extreme caution and detain, but under no circumstances are they to harm her."

Well, at least their orders weren't to exterminate her with extreme prejudice. That was something, right?

"I guess that explains why the Agents in the parking garage were such lousy shots," said Declan.

Ozzie nodded. "And the good news is that they're *also* under orders not to hurt your family. They're detaining them, but they weren't harmed when they brought them in."

Relief washed over her. Aunt Cil, Cassie and the others were okay. Beside her, Alex sensed Declan relax, his rigid posture loosening with a slow exhalation of breath.

"Not all that surprising, if you think about it," said Ozzie. "Can you imagine the political shitstorm they'd rain down on themselves if the Agency was ever implicated in bringing harm to John Grayson or his family? The man's considered a saint in most Variant households. The Agency would lose what little credibility it has left."

"Something's bugging me, Oz," said Declan. "Why didn't the Agency just raid the cabin while Alex was *there*? Surely that would have been one of their options."

"That's the thing," said Ozzie. "They're dying to get their hands on her, but for whatever reason, they're also terrified of her. Taking your family was probably their round-about way of drawing her to *them*, while still maintaining some sort of leverage over her."

The idea that a shadowy government organization was scared of a 16-year-old seemed laughable to Alex.

But it also meant that, somehow, they must know about

her ability. And they seemed to believe that she could be as powerful as Masterson.

Someone should have told them not to worry.

Even if she *could* amass his supposedly endless array of powers, she wouldn't be able to hang on to them for long.

Alex tried to focus on her jumping ability. Now that she knew what to look for, she could tell that the powers she'd borrowed from Declan were, very slowly, starting to fade. At this rate, she had maybe six hours before she couldn't sense the currents at all and would once again lose her ability to jump.

"So where are they keeping them, Oz?" asked Declan.

"They're in a military facility near Saranac Lake," said Ozzie. "Closest thing to the cabin they could find. They must not have wanted to take them far."

"I didn't know there *were* any military sites in Saranac Lake," said Declan.

"And that's the way the government would like to keep it, I'm sure." He smiled.

An aerial image of a large metal roofed building surrounded by forested land appeared on the screen.

"Thought you might want to see it," said Ozzie.

"Thanks, Ozzie," said Declan, taking Alex by the arm. "I owe you one."

"Nah," said Ozzie, smiling. "Just go and give the Agency what-for, and we'll call it even."

Twenty-Four

Alex and Declan reappeared in Alex's empty bedroom.

"The cabin?" said Alex, looking around. "What are we doing back here?"

"Had to risk it," said Declan. "There's a couple of things I wanted to pick up before we left. Besides. You kept complaining about your stupid feet. Thought if I brought you back here to grab a pair of shoes, you might actually be able to *focus* when we go after Grayson and the others."

"Really?" she said, surprised.

"Well, that. And I thought it might make you a little easier to put up with."

She rolled her eyes. "What I *meant*, was are you really taking me with you?"

"Could I actually stop you at this point?"

"Not a chance," she said, smiling. "But it's nice to see you finally owning up to it."

Declan left the room, promising to return in a few minutes once he'd found what he was looking for.

Alex seized the opportunity to change into something other than her pajamas. She settled on a pair of jeans and a lightweight, long-sleeved tee. She was working her feet into her trusty Chuck Taylor's when Declan materialized in the doorway with a gun in each hand.

She gave him a skeptical once-over as she tied her shoelaces. "Easy there, Rambo. You know, when you said you wanted to *pick up* a couple of things, I didn't realize that *that* was what you had in mind."

He deposited the Beretta in the pocket of his hoodie and then held up the Ruger.

"Ever used a gun before?" he asked.

"My Aunt's a card-carrying member of PETA and—up until this week, anyway—I haven't been in too many situations requiring the use of heavy artillery." She stared at the gun. "Unless you count paintball. But I wouldn't, because I lasted about two minutes and the only thing I managed to take out was a tree."

"Right," he said, offering her the gun. "I should probably give you some pointers, then."

It was heavy. Far heavier than she had expected.

They always made them look so *light* on TV.

After receiving a quick run-down on what-not-to-do with the gun, a lesson on how to remove the safety, and a few tips on firing and how to hold the pistol—and after promising Declan repeatedly that she would *only* use it if she had no other option—Alex tucked the Ruger into the back of her jeans, and then slipped Declan's jacket back on in an attempt to conceal it.

He stood slouched against a bedpost, watching her as she rolled up the too-long sleeves of her borrowed coat.

The chill of the metal was seeping through the flimsy material that covered the small of her back.

Alex took a few steps to make sure the gun was secure and wouldn't be falling out by accident. The weight of it resting against her back was heavy and awkward, and altogether alien. But she had to admit, she definitely felt a little safer for having it there.

When she could get past the growing fear that the gun might accidentally fire while still in her pants, that is. She'd seen it a thousand times in the movies. Some dummy with no experience with firearms shoves the gun into the front of their jeans and *bang!* No more pinky toe... Or worse.

And she was pretty attached to her left butt-cheek. She'd rather not part with any of it.

"You look nervous," said Declan. "Maybe giving you a gun isn't such a good idea."

"Are you kidding?" she said. "It's a *terrible* idea. But I'm fine. Honest."

"Just, *please*," he said. "Remember what I've told you. And *don't* take off that safety until you're ready to use it."

Alex created a small sphere of electricity in her hand, just to test her strength, and then dispersed it. "Hopefully I won't *need* to use it—I think I've still got a few hours before I'll lose my jumping ability. Besides. I have a much more powerful weapon at my disposal."

"The spheres?"

"My brain."

"Oh," he said, cracking a smile. "I'll be sure to add that to our list of assets for next time."

"Smartass."

"Always."

"You should be more careful what you say to me, Decks. I *am* armed, you know. And it's never wise to piss off a girl capable of first electrocuting you, and then shooting you, and then dropping you in a lake. It's only asking for trouble."

"Yeah, well," he said. "I trust you not to kill, maim, or drown me without just provocation. Now c'mere."

"Why?"

"We need to do one last thing before we go."

"Oh?" said Alex, taking a step closer. "What's that?"

Declan reached out, took both of her hands in his, and drew her toward him. The current flowing between them grew stronger.

"Figured you could use the pick-me-up," he said softly, a roguish grin on his face.

The long list of reasons Alex had conjured to ensure that she stayed away from the caustic, self-assured and insufferable blonde that now held her captive by his gaze, had been utterly forgotten. All the arguments she'd had with herself over the course of the last three days had faded to nothing under the weight of those hazel eyes.

The lamp on the bedside table flickered.

Declan's gaze slid down to focus on her mouth and Alex's heart started beating double-time.

She took another step closer... Just as the sound of a creaking floorboard reached them from the hallway.

Declan's attention shifted to the open bedroom door—and they jumped.

They landed in a wooded area in the dark of night.

He dropped her hands.

Whatever moment they'd been heading toward back at the cabin, they'd left behind them when they jumped. Declan glanced around, finally fixing his attention on a glaring white light that was shining from the other side of a nearby hill. He started toward it.

Alex followed, tripping clumsily over fallen branches and pitfalls in the darkened forest.

"Saranac Lake," said Declan, over his shoulder.

"What?"

"It's where we jumped to. I figured you were about to ask where we were," he said. "You usually do."

She didn't say anything, just kept following him through the black.

When they reached the crest of the hill he pulled her down beside him. They knelt there in the underbrush, taking in the scene below.

The compound was surrounded on all sides by a ten-foot-high fence topped with razor wire, with only a small yard standing between the fence and the metal-sided building. A single watchtower loomed by the front gate. From this height and vantage point, Declan and Alex could see down into the darkened tower. A single guard sat in the enclosure, his feet propped up in a square cutout window, watching something on a mini-television.

In the yard below, a second guard appeared to be walking in a perpetual circle that took him through the yard and around the exterior of the metal building.

Most interesting to Alex, however, was the sight of her aunt and her friends all seated in the yard at the front of the building. All eight of them appeared unharmed.

"Something's not right," said Declan after the guard finished another lap around the complex. "There are only two guards watching them. Even if they had used a pulse to knock out your Aunt's ability to jump *before*... there's power in the facility. All she would have to do is take some from those floodlights, grab the others, and *jump*. So *why hasn't she*? What's stopping her?"

"Maybe they did something else to her," said Alex, suddenly frightened for her aunt. "Something that took her power away."

Declan shook his head. "I don't think so. They have plenty of methods for disabling other types of Variants, but for Jumpers, they only ever use a pulse. I don't know what else they could have used on her."

Alex examined the group more closely. They didn't *look* afraid. Some of them, like Brandt and Aiden, simply looked bored. Others, like Grayson and Nate, looked decidedly *pissed* about something.

"Well standing here hypothesizing isn't going to help them," said Alex. "I say we jump over there, grab the others, and jump back to the cabin."

"It's too easy," said Declan. "This whole thing feels *wrong*."

"Do you have any other ideas?"

Declan frowned. "We'll need to take out the guard in the tower."

Alex stared down at her hands in the black. She had an idea, but she was frightened that it might not work the way she wanted it to.

"I think I should go," she said. "I have something I want to try."

"No way, Lex. I can handle it."

Maybe he was right. Alex wasn't really sure her plan would work, anyway... And Declan *was* trained for this sort of thing.

In the yard below, Kenzie and Brian were sitting off to one side. She couldn't quite see Kenzie's face, but she could see Brian's clearly. He was crying, although he seemed to be trying his best to hide it from the others. He wasn't doing a very good job of it, though, because his sister had taken notice.

After watching Kenzie reach over and hug the boy tightly, Alex got to her feet.

"Alex?" said Declan. "What are you doing?"

Alex materialized in the cramped watch tower behind the guard. He whipped around to face her, reaching for his holster. Alex was faster. She placed her hand on his chest—and sent a surge of electricity cascading through her palm.

The man fell from his chair and lay sprawled on the ground.

Cassie had only been half right, earlier, when she'd said that Alex had no backbone.

When it came to defending *herself*? To fighting for what *she* deserved?

Alex was a coward. Every time.

But when it came to defending her family and friends? To fighting for the people she cared about?

Well, in those all-important moments Alex was a true force to be reckoned with.

She knelt beside the fallen guard, checking for a pulse. Strong and steady. He was merely out cold.

Alex smiled and jumped back to Declan's side in the forest.

"What did you just do?" he hissed. "I told you not to—"

"It's *okay*, Declan. Calm down! I just knocked him out."

"How? Those spheres would have blown him to bits!"

She wiggled her fingers in the dim light. "I electrocuted him. Knocked the poor guy out like a light."

"You... We can *do* that?" he asked, a hint of awe in his tone.

She smiled. "So, what now, Decks? He won't be out for long."

Declan shook his head slowly in amusement, then returned his attention to the compound below.

The guard's circuitous pacing had led him around the side of the building. They had maybe thirty seconds before he reappeared.

"Alright," he said, taking her hand. "Let's go."

They jumped, but as they started to reappear an unyielding pressure pushed against them, forcing them to materialize a few feet from where Declan had intended.

"Decks! Alex!" Kenzie said, jumping to her feet.

Declan glanced at the empty space behind him where he'd intended to reappear. "Well, that was weird."

"What just happened?" asked Alex

"It's like something was there," said Declan. "We'll figure it out later, right now it's time we got you guys out of here. Come on. Before that guard comes back."

No one moved to get up.

"We can't, Decks," said Brian.

"What?" said Declan. "Why not?"

A tremor rippled through the air, encircling their group. The sight reminded Alex of the rippling waves of heat that hover above scorching blacktops during the middle of summer. The mirage shuddered violently, and in the next instant, fourteen Agents armed with assault rifles shimmered into view.

They were surrounded.

"*That's* why not," said Aiden. He nodded toward the massive man that had his rifle trained on Declan. The Agent had a shaved head and every patch of skin visible below his chin was covered in tattoos. Alex was fairly certain he'd be able to bench-press half of Bay View High's varsity football team with each massive arm, if put to the test. "His name's Dimitri. He's from Vladivostok. Two guesses what *he* can do."

Declan, impudent to the last, grinned up at the giant Russian. "Playing hide and go seek with you as a kid must have been a real bitch."

Dimitri only smiled.

"Miss Parker and Mr. O'Connell," said a woman's voice. "Welcome."

The wall of Agents parted, allowing a petite woman with short gray hair, dressed smartly in a gray pantsuit and pumps, to enter the circle.

Grayson and the others finally stood.

"I believe I made you a promise, Jonathan," she said. "Cil? You can take Brian, Cassandra and Mackenzie home now. You can go too, Carson. You'll see no more trouble from the Agency. We thank you for your cooperation."

"*Cooperation*," said Brandt. "That's a laugh."

"I'm not leaving without my niece," said Cil angrily.

"Cil, it's alright," said Grayson. "I'll take care of her. You have my word. Please, take the children back to the cabin and wait for us. We'll be there soon."

Cil looked to Alex.

"It's alright, Aunt Cil," she said. "Please… Just get them out of here."

After a long moment, her aunt took hold of the others and jumped, but she was definitely *not* happy to do it.

"Why don't you let the others go, too?" asked Alex.

"Leverage," said Aiden. "That's right, isn't it? Alex jumps and you shoot the rest of us? Isn't that how it works?"

An almost paralyzing fear gripped her.

They were well, and truly, *stuck*.

Realizing that there was no possible way of escaping this place that didn't involve someone ending up in a body bag, Alex decided to do the only thing she could do: offer herself in trade for the others.

"It's me you want, right?" she said slowly. "I'll stay— *willingly*—just so long as you let them go."

The offer hadn't worked on Masterson, but she prayed that the Agency would be more inclined to negotiate. She simply hoped that Ozzie had been right about Grayson and his family being untouchable.

"Alex, wait," said Grayson. "Just give me a moment to talk to Director Carter before you agree to anything. She's a reasonable woman." His words carried a bitter edge. "I'm sure we can figure something out."

Director Carter? So this was the woman behind the Agency?

Alex had been expecting someone… taller.

"I really don't think so, Jonathan," said the Director. "You know her best option is to come with us willingly. The Agency can protect her. We aren't the bad guys, no matter how hard you try to make us out to be. What I'm offering Alexandra is a chance at a *better* life."

"What?" Alex asked, confused. "What do you mean, you want to give me a 'better life?' Are you arresting me?"

"No, child." The Director laughed. "We're not *arresting* you. You'll simply become a… a ward of the state, in a manner of speaking. You'll come to live and work at the Agency. We'll be your new home."

Grayson scowled. "For heaven's sake, Dana. You can't just *take* her."

"We can," she said sternly. "And we will. The blood running in that girl's veins is the last *undamaged* resource of VX-2 in existence. That makes her Agency property, Jonathan, whether you like it or not. Now, we're not heartless. We could put her down and eliminate the threat, but we *won't*. We have every intention of training her as an operative and teaching her to control her gifts. We'll be giving her a better life."

There was that phrase again.

"Will you listen to yourself?" said Grayson. "How could that *possibly* be a better life than the one she's got? You'll be taking away her freedom, not to mention her future. And for what? For the chance of training her as a *weapon* to be used at your disposal?"

"We can protect the girl, Jonathan. It's what Nora and James would have wanted—for her to be *safe*. Not just from Masterson… She also needs to be protected from the world. Do you know what the extremists would do to her if they knew what she was and what she was capable of? If they *knew* there was another like Samuel? *We* can keep her safe. The Agency is the best choice she has."

"That's not a choice that's a jail sentence. Cil and I can keep her safer than you lot could ever hope to. Alex has the right to be with the people she cares about. To take her away from the life she's built in Florida is tantamount to—"

"It's not that simple, Grayson, and you know it. Alex isn't the only one who needs protection. We also need to protect the *world* from *Alex*. You know she's far too powerful to be allowed to live amongst the norms while she's still learning what she can do... She might hurt someone. *She's only a child*."

Alex bristled at that. She'd be seventeen next month and was more responsible than a lot of the adults she knew. The events of her life had forced her to grow up faster than most.

To be labeled a child felt like an insult.

Grayson was furious. "Now listen here, Dana, you're talking about a human being, not a weapon. And I hardly see how the Agency can help her any better than I can..."

Their argument continued, but Alex was no longer paying attention.

Why was it that, every time something major happened in her life, Alex always found herself standing on the sidelines while other people fought her battles for her?

As a child, her parents and six others had sacrificed their lives in order to protect her from Masterson.

Every time someone had picked on her at school—every time Jessica, Connor, or anyone else had done anything to hurt her—it had been Cassie to the rescue.

And now, for the last three days, Declan, Nate, Grayson and the others had done everything in their power to keep her safe and out of danger, ending up bruised, battered and then *abducted* by their own government in the process.

But it was all to no avail, because here she was.

In trouble, yet again.

Only this time it was her future in the cross-hairs.

Was she really going to stand idly by while these people decided her fate? Was she really going to let the Agency take her away from everything she'd ever known and everyone she'd ever loved without at lest *trying* to put up a fight?

No.

Alex pulled the gun from her waistband. Raising it toward the sky, she released the safety, pulled the trigger and fired off a round.

Fourteen rifles were aimed in her direction.

The arguing stopped.

She had their attention.

"That is *it*!" Alex hissed, lowering the gun. "I'm no one's *asset* and I'm sure as hell not the Agency's *property*. I'm a living, breathing, *thinking* teenage girl who can speak for herself!"

Declan and the others gaped at her. The Director folded her arms across her chest and fixed Alex with a steely glare.

"I know you think you own me, Director, but you don't. Grayson's right. I'm a human being, not a weapon for the Agency. Legally you have no claim to me. And if word got out about what you were trying to do here, I'm pretty sure you wouldn't like the results. I have a life, I have a family and I have friends that mean everything to me and I am not *about* to stand by and watch you take all that away. I have no intention of going anywhere with you. I trust Grayson and his family more than I will *ever* trust you *or* your organization. If they're willing to help me— to keep me safe—then *they* are the ones in whom I will place my trust. Not you.

"And you're not getting my blood. That one's non-negotiable. The last thing this world needs is an army of freaks like me. There's no telling what they might do. Look at the trouble *one* Masterson has caused. Are you really willing to risk the creation of another?

"What I'm saying, Director, is that I will obey your laws and I will follow your rules, but I will *never* be your asset. I have no desire to be turned into a weapon. All I want is to be left in peace."

Her words were met with a stony silence.

The Director's eyes had narrowed to slits. "Very well,

Ms. Parker," she said curtly. "We'll do this on your terms... for now."

Alex let out a slow breath.

"However," she continued. "If your burgeoning powers should prove dangerous to the public—or if the Agency should find any reason to doubt Mr. Grayson's ability to handle your care—then there will be no more room for negotiation. The Agency will at that point become responsible for your... *maintenance*. You will be taken into custody and dealt with accordingly. Have I made myself clear?"

"Crystal," said said, handing the gun to Grayson. "Now if you'll excuse us, Director. I'm taking my friends and we're going *home*."

With that, Alex and the others vanished from the yard.

TWENTY-FIVE

"**O**h, that poor, poor girl." Cassie lowered her aviator sunglasses and peered over the top of the frames. "What did she do? Go to the spray-on tanning place and request the Oompa Loompa treatment?"

Alex glanced up from the pages of her novel to see who it was that had so captured her friend's attention.

Miranda Pierce—a sophomore Alex and Cassie had hung out with occasionally before the "incident" in the computer lab—was standing at the edge of a makeshift beach volleyball court in a barely-there, lime-green bikini, flirting shamelessly with Connor and half a dozen guys from the varsity soccer team.

It was the same barely-there, lime-green bikini that Alex had been eyeing in a boardwalk shop earlier on in the week.

It felt like a hundred years ago.

Alex tugged at the hem of her tank top, trying to keep the material from riding up high enough for her scar to be visible. While Cassie had been lying stretched-out, working on her tan beside her, Alex had been sitting cross-legged with her back to the water, trying to ignore the rowdy gathering of her former friends partying a short way down the beach.

Now that she'd started watching them, however, she couldn't seem to look away.

It didn't help that Miranda's skin was like some strange orange beacon, mesmerizing in its unnatural brightness.

Poor girl. Alex could sympathize. They both had the sort of fair skin that made sunburns inevitable and a healthy tan almost impossible to achieve. Sometimes, even neon was preferable to pasty. And Alex had seen worse fake tans.

None that immediately sprang to mind.

But, you know.

She was sure they were out there.

Not that Miranda *needed* her sympathy. With that figure, her skin could have been bright purple and she'd still be holding Connor's attention.

"I don't know," said Alex. "It's not *that* bad. She looks tan... -ish."

"There is a fine line between *tan*, and looking like you just rolled around in a giant bag of Doritos. And Miranda seems to prefer the nacho cheese variety."

Alex smiled as she watched their erstwhile friends horsing around and playing volleyball near the pier. They were just close enough that she could hear the sound of their laughter over the crash of waves breaking against the shore.

She sighed, remembering a time, not so very long ago, when it had been *her* standing at the edge of that court where Miranda now stood, surrounded by friends, without a care in the world.

Miranda, she now realized, had become her replacement.

"Do you ever miss them, Cass?"

"Who? Those rejects?" she asked, pushing the aviators back up the bridge of her nose. "No. And after the way they treated you, you shouldn't either."

Alex stared down at her hands, wiggling her fingers experimentally, attempting to form a sphere.

Nothing.

Not a single watt.

It was Tuesday—their last day of spring break before school was back in.

Alex had spent every waking moment since Saturday morning avoiding any sort of physical contact with her aunt. After the events leading up to the weekend, she wanted nothing more than to be ability-free for as long as she could make it last. She wanted to feel normal. Even if the sensation could only ever be temporary.

The past few days had been relatively quiet. No contact from the Agency. No unexpected visits from Masterson. And she hadn't been back to the cabin since she left on Saturday morning.

If anything, her life had taken a turn for the boring.

And Alex couldn't be happier about it.

"So tell me, G.I. Jane—did you *really* shoot that gun into the air before going all women's lib on the Director?" asked Cassie, breaking into her thoughts. "Or was that just Aiden trying to liven up the story?"

"I wouldn't exactly consider standing up for myself an act of female empowerment," said Alex. "But I'll admit. Telling her off felt pretty good."

"That wasn't my question."

Alex grinned. "I *might* have shot a gun in the air."

"Like a boss, I'm sure."

"Naturally," she said. "But I still hate the things."

Actually, she'd be *quite* happy to never see another firearm in person ever—*ever*—again.

"Damn. And here I'd planned to sign you up for an NRA membership as a gift for your birthday next month." She settled back onto the red blanket, her bronzed skin glistening with sunscreen. "Speaking of which. You still haven't said how you want to celebrate. I'm thinking we need to go shopping on the Champs Élysées and find you a hot Frenchman. Or maybe we should hit up Hollywood Boulevard, looking for celebrities. Oh, I know! London!

You've always wanted to go there, right?... What's with the face? Come on, Lex. My best friend can zap me anywhere on the planet in the blink of an eye. You *know* I'm going to find every way I can to con you into abusing this new power of yours."

"Mm-hmm."

Jessica Huffman had joined the group by the pier. Her first act upon arrival had been to pull Connor off to one side. They were currently arguing about something amidst the pylons.

Her aunt wasn't the only one Alex had been avoiding since her return. She hadn't spoken to Connor since that late night phone call after Declan took him home.

After two days of Alex refusing to take his calls, he'd resorted to hitting up Cassie for information.

Vee had been declared missing over the weekend. According to Connor, Jessica hadn't told anyone about what had happened that day on the dock. Probably a wise decision on Jessica's part.

Who would have believed her?

Alex had gone by the dock only once since returning home—and had been surprised to discover that Vee's remains had disappeared. Alex suspected that the Agency had probably had something to do with it.

She wondered what, if anything, they would tell her poor family...

Her stomach twisted. Connor had left the group of cheerleaders and varsity athletes and was walking resolutely in their direction.

What did he think he was doing?

Surely he wasn't coming to talk to her. Here. On the beach. In full view of the who's-who of Bay View High.

It would be social suicide.

Alex's phone rang.

She reached into the large straw bag sitting in the sand

beside their blanket and fished out her new phone, answering it distractedly.

"Hey, Kenzie," she said.

"It's Kenzie?" Cassie leaned toward the phone. "HI KENZIE!"

"Christ," said a masculine voice on the other end of the line.

"Declan?" asked Alex.

"I think I'm deaf," he said.

"Yeah, well," said another voice in the background— Kenzie's. A scuffling sound traveled over the line and her voice developed an echo. They'd put her on speakerphone. "Serves you right for grabbing the phone, butthead... Just set the phone on the console, Nate."

"What's up, guys?" she asked.

Connor had covered half the distance between them and showed no signs of stopping.

"Declan wants to know where you're at," said Kenzie.

"Thank you, Kenzie," said Declan. "I *can* speak for myself, you know."

"Fine. Then speak."

"Where are you, Lex?" he repeated.

"Um. I'm at the—"

"What does that moron think he's doing?" Cassie asked. She'd noticed Connor's trajectory and now sat propped up on her elbows, watching his progress.

"Dammit, Decks!" Kenzie yelled into the phone. "*Slow down*! And watch the road!"

"Beach," Alex finished. "I'm at the beach."

"What does *what* moron think he's doing?" asked a third voice. It was Aiden's. "The *road*, Declan! Christ. If I die in this car and you miraculously survive, I'm coming back to haunt your ass."

"Hey, I was all for letting Nate drive," said Declan. "Kenzie's the one who nixed it."

"Never again," said Kenzie. "Ever. You should *see* some of the nightmares I've been having."

"Again," said Nate. "*My driving was excellent.* Us driving off the bridge was *Declan's* fault. Not mine. He's the one who dragged his feet with the jump."

"Same spot as last time?" asked Declan, ignoring his brother.

Last time? The only time Declan had been here with them was the first day they'd met. And she'd only ever noticed him on the boardwalk and the pier. Not on the beach.

And *certainly* not on the supposedly *isolated* strip of beach where Alex had stupidly decided to remove her tank top, thus revealing her scar and leaving her clad in only a string bikini, so that she could work on those stubborn tan lines.

"Wait. You were *there*?" She cringed. "Never mind. Of course you were… No, Declan, we're closer to the pier this time. Why do you want to know?"

Connor had dropped to one knee in the sand beside their blanket and was grinning at her.

Caught off guard and distracted by the phone conversation, she smiled back at him before she could stop herself.

Cassie sent her a look.

Oops.

"Hey, Alex, Cassie," he said. "How's it going?"

"Don't go anywhere," Nate was saying. "We'll be there in a few minutes."

"But—" she protested.

Too late. The line was dead.

"Did you take a volleyball to the head?" asked Cassie.

"No," he said, confused. "Why do you ask?"

Cassie sighed. "What do you want, Connor?"

"Just wanted to see how you guys were, is all. After

what happened last week... I don't know." He looked sadly at Alex, puppy-dog eyes in full effect. "I was worried about you. Wanted to make sure you were doing okay."

"*We're* fine." Cassie leaned to one side in order to look past Connor's broad shoulders. "But judging from the attention *you're* getting right now, your social life is about to flat-line."

Down by the pier, the others had halted their game and were now watching them with interest. Jessica, meanwhile, had her arms crossed angrily over her chest, apoplectic with rage. Alex had started to wonder if the girl's face was even capable of showing an emotion other than annoyance, or if it had become permanently stuck like that.

Connor shrugged. "If they've got a problem with it, screw 'em."

Cassie appeared mildly impressed by his indifference.

"Lexie," he said. "I know you're still angry with me. And you've got every right to be... All I'm asking is that you give me one more shot."

This was exactly why she hadn't answered the phone.

"I'm sorry, Connor. I just... I need some time."

"It's alright." He stood and began moving slowly backward down the beach. He flashed her a confident smile. "You're worth the wait."

As soon as he was out of earshot, Cassie chimed, "Just say, 'no,' Alex, dear."

"You make him sound like a drug."

"That's exactly what the guy is, for you. He's your addiction," she said. "Trust me. Just say no to crack, spray-on tans, and *Connor*. All three have the potential to end badly. Especially where you're concerned."

"*Ladies*," Aiden said in a slow, goofy drawl from behind Cassie. "Mind if we join you?"

Aiden, Nate and Declan were approaching from the direction of the boardwalk. Somehow, the trio had done the impossible and grown even *more* attractive in the four days since she'd last seen them.

Then again, maybe it was simply the fact that this marked the first time she'd been able to observe the guys without the threat of impending doom hanging over their heads. Frown lines weren't good for anyone's features.

And relaxed and happy seemed to be a *really* good look for them.

Alex glanced back in the direction of the pier.

Most of the girls were blatantly staring.

She smiled.

Miranda Pierce, eat your heart out.

"Where's Kenzie?" asked Alex. "Wasn't she with you?"

Aiden dropped down on the other side of Cassie.

"Red left us in search of coffee." Nate settled in next to Alex, taking the last open spot on the blanket and forcing Declan to find a seat in the sand. "Said she needed a caffeine fix."

"At six p.m.?" said Cassie. "Won't that keep her awake all night?"

"I asked her the same question," said Aiden. "She just marched off down the boardwalk shouting, '*Death before decaf!*'"

"Someone should put that on a t-shirt," said Declan.

Alex smiled.

Declan smiled back, bumping her shoulder with his. "Hey, you," he said softly, below the level of Nate and Cassie's conversation.

"Hey, yourself."

"You haven't been by the cabin," he said, fiddling with his car keys. "Everything alright?"

"Fine," she said. "Just needed a break, you know?"

"Yeah," he said. "I figured."

Kenzie was walking toward them with a massive iced coffee in one hand.

"Death before decaf!" Cassie shouted with a smile, raising a fist in the air.

"Death before decaf!" Kenzie echoed. "Nice to see a little caffeine-lover solidarity. So few people out there *understand*."

She plopped down in the sand beside Declan.

"So have they told you yet? Or do I get to be the one to break the happy news?" asked Kenzie between sips.

"Told us what?" asked Alex.

"That Bay View High has two new transfers," she said, breaking into a brilliant smile.

"What?" said Cassie, sitting up a little straighter. "Who?"

"Mackenzie and Declan *O'Neill*, at your service, miss!" she said with a mock salute. "That's O'Neill with *two* L's, by the way."

"Hey, that's great!" Cassie smiled wide.

"Man, I love getting to use a fake name," said Kenzie. "I'll be incognito! At school! How awesome is that?"

Cassie's expression became a guise of mock severity. "I do hate to be the one to tell you this, Kenzie… But you see, you've made a *major* tactical error by being seen with us in public. We're not exactly on speaking terms with the *cool kids* these days."

"Damn," said Kenzie. "There goes my lifelong dream of being made Prom Queen. And I look so *cute* in a tiara… Tragic."

"Not that I don't think it's great, cause I do…" said Alex. "But why in the world are you two transferring to our high school?"

"It's to make the Agency happy," said Nate. "They wanted us to be able to watch you more closely, so… we've temporarily relocated to Florida."

"Hooray for sunshine and sandy beaches," said Aiden.

"What?" said Cassie. "You're moving too?"

"Yeah, well. My last place is now in ruins, I lost my job at the docks when I went MIA over the weekend... and Grayson owes me one. Least he can do is rent me a room for a while. And anyway, I've been living in the cold and dreary Pacific Northwest for too long. Time for a fresh start in the sunshine state."

That revelation had Cassie as happy as a lark. Alex *really* needed to find out what was going on with those two.

"Declan, I thought you'd already graduated," said Alex.

"I did," he huffed. "Trust me. I'm not looking forward to going back, but it was either me or Nate—and I'm still 18 for another month, so I'm the youngest. Agency thought I might still be able to pass as a high school junior."

"Having you guys around ought to make things a little more interesting," said Cassie. "I'm all for making things more interesting."

"Just... maybe not *quite* as interesting as last week," Alex amended.

"No. Definitely not *that* interesting," Cassie agreed.

"What? Not a fan of living in an action flick?" asked Aiden.

"You know, it's funny," said Cassie. "Getting kidnapped twice in one week really ain't all it's cracked up to be."

"Is it still considered kidnapping when it's a government agency doing the abducting?" asked Kenzie.

"Semantics."

Kenzie leaned toward Cassie and whispered something in her ear. They both smiled wide.

"I happen to think that's an *excellent* idea," Cassie replied.

"Alright! All you hooligans off the blanket. Now. Up. Move it or lose it!" Kenzie jumped up, set her coffee in the sand, and began shooing the others off of the bright red stretch of fabric. Everyone scrambled to get up, voicing their protests.

Kenzie and Cassie grabbed either end of the large red blanket and held it up in between them, standing apart, as if they were about to fold it—which conveniently blocked the group from any potential prying eyes in the direction of the pier.

Suddenly, Alex knew what they were up to.

Down the shore, in the opposite direction, a solitary couple lay basking in the sun, the man sound asleep and the woman too engrossed in her paperback to pay them any mind.

Declan stood staring at them, arms crossed over his white t-shirt, the bottoms of his jeans and his black boots half buried in the sand. He was dressed almost the same as he had been on the first day they met. The only thing missing was the gray military jacket.

If they were going to do this, the time was now.

She sighed. So much for boring.

"What? Are we leaving already?" asked Declan, misinterpreting their movements.

Alex got to her feet and shimmied out of her jean shorts, leaving on the tank top. No *way* she was taking that off in front of him again. She turned around, leaned in close to Declan and took him by the hand.

"You know what, Decks?" she said in a soft voice. A slight tingle shivered through her palm. Just a few more seconds… "I'm really glad you came by. There's actually something I've been wanting to do since that first day we met."

Declan smiled lazily down at her.

Poor guy didn't have a clue.

"You remember?" she purred. "That day you dropped me in a lake? Twice?"

Alex released Declan's hand, took three steps backward and nodded to Nate and Aiden. They closed in on him, grinning.

"What are you doing?" Declan asked warily. Realizing too late that he was their intended target, he tried to turn and make a break down the shore.

Nate and Aiden were too fast.

Declan soon stood hostage, only a few feet away, Nate gripping one arm, Aiden the other.

"What the heck are you guys—" He finally noticed Alex, standing by the blanket, a wicked grin on her face. "Oh, no. No, no, n—"

His last word of protest was clipped short by Alex's tackle. As they fell toward the sand, Nate and Aiden released their hold… and Alex jumped.

They splashed down in the salty water after having reappeared, tangled together in the air, thirty feet from the shore, and too close to the surface for Declan to even *think* about teleporting himself anywhere dry.

Back on the beach, the others were cheering.

Declan surfaced and slicked his hair back.

Alex smiled at the sight of a very angry, very *wet*, Declan O'Connell.

Oh, yeah. Revenge was *sweet*.

"I suppose this makes us even?" Declan looked back at her from under an arched eyebrow, his ire slowly fading.

"Not by a long shot." She smiled and started back for the shore.

A strong current of cooler water surrounded her. She swam with the flow, the water providing little resistance as she sailed onward toward the coast.

"Oh, come *on*," Declan groused from behind her as he struggled against a sudden onslaught of unusually large waves. "Cut it out, Aiden!"

"What's that, cousin?" Aiden called back. "Can't hear you!"

Alex laughed as the helpful tide sent her coasting back toward the beach.

Maybe she *wouldn't* ever be normal again. But in moments like this one, Alex was willing to concede—normal was terribly overrated.

15991813R00163

Made in the USA
Charleston, SC
30 November 2012